Death of a Russian Doll

Also available by Barbara Early

Vintage Toyshop Mysteries

Murder on the Toy Town Express

Death of a Toy Soldier

Bridal Bouquet Shop Mysteries
(writing as Beverly Allen)

Floral Depravity

For Whom the Bluebell Tolls

Bloom and Doom

Death of a Russian Doll

A Vintage Toyshop Mystery

Barbara Early

CROOKED
LANE

NEW YORK

Copyright © 2018 by Barbara Early

Published in the United States by Crooked Lane Books, an imprint of The Quick Brown Fox & Company LLC.

Crooked Lane Books and its logo are trademarks of The Quick Brown Fox & Company LLC.

Library of Congress Catalog-in-Publication data available upon request.

ISBN (hardcover): 978-1-68331-702-9
ISBN (ePub): 978-1-68331-703-6
ISBN (ePDF): 978-1-68331-704-3

Cover illustration by Hiro Kimura
Book design by Jennifer Canzone

Printed in the United States.

www.crookedlanebooks.com

Crooked Lane Books
34 West 27th St., 10th Floor
New York, NY 10001

First Edition: October 2018

10 9 8 7 6 5 4 3 2 1

To my granddaughter, Abbie, wishing you a lifetime of giggles, hugs, and books. And to Elizabeth and Andrew for making me a happy grandmother.

Chapter 1

I never should have opened the box.

My heart now racing, I flipped the lid shut, then grabbed for the nearest folding chair and sank into it. Our vintage toyshop had become a swirling kaleidoscope of colors and shapes, so I closed my eyes until the vertigo passed. I finally forced them open to distract myself from the memory: dismembered body parts, matted hair, and worst of all, those cold, lifeless eyes staring up at me.

"Cathy?" I said, my voice hoarse and soft. "I found another box of doll parts."

"Sorry!" My sister-in-law looked up from the baby swing, where she had just placed Drew in an attempt to keep him entertained while we finished setting up for her meeting. Cathy and Parker had chosen the name Andrew—and the nickname "Drew"—to thwart Dad's desire to see all his progeny named after toys in some way. Of course, Dad had immediately begun to call "Drew" by the name of "Andy" and informed my brother that the first girl would be "Ann." What Parker told Dad in response isn't to be repeated, but he didn't seem to object to Dad supplying a rag doll costume for Drew's first Halloween.

I jumped as a hand grasped my shoulder.

"Easy there," Dad said. "You okay? You look pretty pale."

I nodded but didn't reply.

"This is your fault, you know." Cathy wagged a finger at my father.

"Mine?" Dad flashed back his most innocent look, his eyes shining and cherubic under his wavy salt-and-pepper hair. Maybe a little more salt than pepper these days.

Cathy put her hands on her hips and continued her lecture. "Letting her watch that silly *Trilogy of Terror* on television when she was only . . ." She turned to me. "How old were you?"

"Nine."

"Nine years old," Cathy scolded, her broad sleeves flying. Her wardrobe choices, as usual, were bold and eclectic as she decided best fit her artistic temperament—today it was bright coral leggings and a draped, oversized tunic ranging in colors from coral to turquoise—but her tone and expression were becoming more maternal by the day. "Voodoo dolls coming to life. Back to back with that 'Talking Tina' episode of *Twilight Zone*!"

"You can't pin that all on me," Dad said. "I wasn't even there. Your husband turned it on."

Cathy folded her arms. "Parker wouldn't do that."

"Actually," I said, "he did. He was seven at the time, but I forgave him long ago." But the damage had been done. Dad had been working, investigating some important case, as usual. And Mom was sleeping one off. That day sparked my long-lived fear of dolls—something that had become more problematic since I began managing Well Played, the vintage toyshop my father opened when he retired as East Aurora's chief of police. Now I worked every day adjacent to a whole room full of the demonic porcelain, rag, and plastic creatures. When the shop was especially quiet, you could almost hear them plot world domination.

"But you'd been doing so much better," Cathy said, pressing my cheeks with her cool fingers.

I took a fortifying breath. "I'm good. And I want to help. I love your whole idea of refurbishing old, donated dolls. Well, maybe not *that* part, but getting them into the hands of needy girls who would appreciate them. That's such a worthwhile cause, especially for the holidays."

"Starting so late," Cathy said, "we'll be lucky to finish a dozen by Christmas. But I'm hoping it's enough to get folks excited." She looked at me. "But not terrified."

"I should be fine once everybody gets here. I'll just make sure I stick with the less hands-on—and eyes-on—parts of the process."

"Don't worry," Cathy said, "there's plenty of that. Ordering materials. Working with the groups from the sewing center who are making new clothes for the dolls. Fund-raising." She ticked off the items on her glittery turquoise-tipped fingernails.

"Coordinating with the nonprofits to make sure the repaired dolls get into the hands of the neediest children," I added. "Working with the folks at the art center who'll be repainting features. Getting the dimensions to the knitting and crocheting clubs."

"I think it's fun that they want to make little coats and sweaters for the dolls," Cathy said.

"They could make Santa hats, too. Cover some of that hair." I shuddered. "Or what would you think of mini ski masks? Cover the whole face?"

I expected maybe a polite laugh at my suggestion. Instead Cathy sucked in a breath and looked at Dad, who seemed to be studying the floor tiles.

"It's true, I'm not that good at hair," Cathy said, then winced. "But it wouldn't be right just to cover it."

"No. Not if we figured out a way to fix it," Dad said, still not meeting my eyes.

"Or found some*one* who could fix it." Cathy also failed at the whole eye-contact thing.

"Someone?" I repeated. Then it hit. "Some*one*? As in some new stylist who recently moved to town?" I could hear my voice grow shrill.

"Not quite recently. Almost a year ago, as I recall." Cathy swallowed. "And Marya can do doll hair. Said she's been doing it all her life. And she *wants* to volunteer. How could I turn her away?"

"I can think of about fifty ways to do that," I said.

"I can understand how you feel," Dad said.

"Oh, can you?" My words came out a little more bitter than I'd intended. I took a moment to compose myself. I looked up at Othello, our tuxedo cat, as he inched toward his favorite spot on the train tracks that circled the shop, just below the ceiling. Another cat was in his favorite perch, however, her black tail twitching. He sniffed her, then turned and took up his second favorite spot. If he could do it . . . "Sorry, I didn't mean to jump at you."

"It's all right," Dad said, massaging my shoulder. "I do bear some of the blame. I practically tried to throw you and Ken together. I had no idea."

"That he was married?" I finished with a sigh. Ken Young— or maybe I should say Chief Young—and I had been dating casually, and nonexclusively, for a year when I'd put aside my reservations about dating a cop to see where our relationship might take us. Where it took us was the front steps of the toyshop when his *wife* showed up out of the blue and glommed onto him.

"I still say I should've taken a swing at him," Dad said.

"And that would have accomplished what, exactly?" I said. "You all over the local news and possibly in the clink? After all, physical violence against the chief of the police department is frowned upon." I sighed. "For what it's worth, I believe what he said about thinking things were over between them when he moved up here."

Cathy huffed. "Then why not say, 'By the way, Liz, I just want you to know that I'm still married, but in the process of divorcing my wife'? At any time he could have mentioned that little fact."

"You're preaching to the choir," I said, my hands up. "Things were just heating up between the two of us, and he *had* alluded to something he said I needed to know. I think he would have told me, even if Marya hadn't . . ."

"Waltzed into town intent on picking up where they'd left off?" Cathy said with false sweetness. "Or was that more of a tango?"

I bit a chapped spot on my lower lip, and then reached into my cardigan pocket for my lip balm. "I'd like to believe she was being honest, too."

"That she'd just come to town to make amends?" Cathy said. "I don't care what twelve-step program you're on. That shouldn't take a whole year." She did a double take at the shelf behind me. "Very funny, Liz."

"What?"

5

She reached up and pointed to a Russian nesting doll, properly called a matryoshka, that had been turned so her back was on display.

I raised my hands. "I didn't touch it."

Cathy eyed me doubtfully but tempered her tone. "She's no good for him. Everyone thinks so. I can't believe he was blind to her manipulation."

"Not blind." Dad said, turning the doll around. "I'll bet he saw it twenty-twenty but just thought it was something he could fix. It's not uncommon in cops, really. We're attracted to the broken ones, the victims. Then it comes back to bite us in the . . ."

I looked up.

"End," he finished as the bell over the door rang.

The first volunteer in the door was Glenda, the owner of the local yarn shop, followed by Lori Briggs, the mayor's wife. I'd never known Lori to pass up a committee—although her specialty was making elaborate plans and then not following through with any of the work. They had just pounded the snow from their boots and removed their heavy coats when Diana Oliveri poked her face inside. "Right place?" Diana was a self-described "old Italian broad" with a thick accent and round, ruddy face.

"Come on in," Cathy said, greeting her at the door and offering to take her coat. It was Cathy's show, after all.

Diana craned her neck, looking around the shop. There was a lot to take in, everything from Fisher-Price pull toys to action figures to vintage board games. Even a whole wall of lunch boxes spanning decades of cultural icons from the Three Stooges to the Fonz was on display. And now, for the holidays, Dad had pulled out all the stops. Glittery snowflakes dangled from the ceiling. Ribbons and bows placed on toys and games throughout the store served as a not-so-subtle reminder that vintage toys also made great gifts. And our sound system had been extolling the virtues of walking in a Winter Wonderland even before our Thanksgiving turkey defrosted.

"You know," Diana said, "I don't think I've ever been inside your shop."

"I'm glad you could join us now," Cathy said.

"I wouldn't miss it." Diana shrugged off her coat and hung it from the back of a chair. "There's no way you could know this, but my family arrived in this country just a few months before Christmas when I was seven years old. We had nothing, and my father was too proud to ask for help. I knew not to ask for anything. But Christmas Eve, we went to church, and someone had put a gift on our pew with a big tag with my name on it. It was a doll." She sniffed. "It wasn't new, but I didn't care. I loved her and taught myself to sew making her clothes.

"I'm not sure why I never thought of giving back. But when I heard about this . . ."

While Cathy hugged her, I ran to get refreshments for our visitors. I was rounding the corner with a tray of hot chocolate, when the door pulled open and Marya walked in.

We shared one of those slo-mo moments where everyone else seemed to freeze. I don't say this about many people, but even if she and Ken had never had a relationship, I'm not sure I would have liked her. Maybe that was petty jealousy on my part. She had all those impossible anatomical features idealized in the fashion dolls. As everyone unfroze, Marya flipped back her blonde locks and curled those perfectly proportioned lips, just a little, before erupting into a plastic smile. "Hello!"

she said, with just a trace of her native Russian accent. She slipped off her coat and dragged it over her shoulder like a fashion model prancing on the runway, that analogy reinforced by the four-inch heels on her boots. Perhaps not the most practical volunteer committee attire.

It would be technically correct to say that both she and I wore jeans and sweaters. That's where the comparison ended. Her jeans could have been painted on, and her fitted sweater bore numerous flirty cutouts. Not sure if it kept her warm. The only hole in my sweater, incidentally, was on the left elbow, and I kind of hoped that nobody would notice.

What a night. Creepy dolls and Marya Young.

Dad put his hand on my arm and leaned to my ear. "Remember, it's for the children."

# # #

Cathy did a great job of presenting her project to the group. She'd already collected quite a few donated dolls, and more were arriving daily—many in gory pieces. Her plans to repair them, dress them, and get them in the hands of needy children, especially those in shelters and in the foster system—and just in time for the holidays—were met with enthusiasm by the capable workforce she had recruited.

Unfortunately, the project also hinged on someone—namely me—finding additional funding. More donated dolls would arrive as soon as we could pay for the shipping and for the fabric yarn, buttons, zippers, and spare eyeballs (shudder) that were needed to keep the volunteers busy.

"Try the Browning Foundation," Diana had said, rubbing her fingers together. "I hear they have deep pockets."

Cathy's head snapped up. "We have some donated materials. Do we need that much extra cash?"

"The more that's available, the more the volunteers will have to work with," Glenda said.

"Any relation to Browning Construction?" Dad asked. We had consulted them for an estimate for our shop expansion, but apparently our project was a little small for them.

Glenda nodded. "And Browning Properties Management. And a small list of other highly profitable offshoots that put Marvin Browning on Millionaire Acres."

Cathy looked at me. "Worth checking out."

I dutifully wrote it on my burgeoning to-do list.

After the meeting, attendees lingered and chatted. Awash in good feelings, I resisted the urge to run upstairs to my room.

That proved to be a mistake.

Marya sidled up to me when I stood at the coffeepot with Lori Briggs. "Liz?" She held out her hand. "I want to say that I'm happy that we can work together on this project. Considering . . ."

"Marya," I said. "You do understand that nothing happened between your husband and me."

"Oh, I know that!" She waved me off, then looked me over from head to toe using her x-ray vision. Maybe that part was my imagination, but I shuddered and pulled my sweater tighter.

"Kenny explained it to me," she continued. "Many women are attracted to the office and the uniform."

My jaw might have dropped, but I was too busy gritting my teeth.

"That may be so," Lori said, beginning to pace in a circle around Marya. Sharks suddenly came to mind. "Especially when that man in the uniform is apparently un . . . encumbered."

"Encumbered?" Marya said, arching an eyebrow.

"Married," Lori explained with a smirk of her own. I felt like a flyweight watching the heavyweight match from the stands. She squinted. "How are things going, anyway?"

Marya eyed her coolly. "Very well."

Lori shrugged. "I only ask because Ken always looks so tired and worn down. He hasn't seemed himself lately."

"Maybe he is not getting as much sleep as he is used to." Now it was their turn to share a moment. Cue the *Jaws* soundtrack. These were dangerous waters.

But before any blood was shed, Marya shot Lori a half smile, threw her coat over her shoulder, and said, "Speaking of which, my ride is here."

I followed her gaze to the door, where Ken was standing just outside. He shrank back when multiple eyes turned to him. Lori was right when she said he hadn't seemed himself. He was still serious about his job, of course. He was a dedicated cop, and that much hadn't changed. But where he once could be cajoled into a smile or laugh, now the corners of his mouth turned down in a perpetual frown. Laugh lines were becoming wrinkles. And his eyes, which used to light up when he saw me, now quickly diverted from mine, looking to rest anywhere else. He shifted his focus to Marya, and his jaw tightened even more.

See you all next week!" Marya called out to the room, seemingly oblivious to her husband's body language.

All eyes watched her prance out and take a possessive hold on Ken's arm. As soon as the two had disappeared from view, Diana called her an impolite name.

She turned to me. "Don't *you* be jealous. Watch out for the *Malocchio*."

I must have looked confused.

"The evil eye, a curse," Diana explained, then vehemently wagged a warning finger at me. "She's not worth it."

As Diana turned to leave, I wondered if she was putting me on. But Val, one of the two cats who now occupied our toyshop and our apartment above it, chose that moment to hop down from her perch on the model train tracks near the ceiling and strut along the aisle. Diana crossed herself at the sight of the black cat in her path and gave Val a wide berth, shimmying against the wall to get to the door before she gave us a wave.

Lori started laughing and put a hand on my arm. "Diana's a bit over the top, but she might be right about that whole evil-eye thing. Oh, the look on your face when I started messing with Marya!"

"I'm apparently out of my depth," I said.

"And stay that way," she said. "It suits you. I wouldn't have taken her on at all except what I said was true. Ken hasn't seemed himself, not since that witch arrived. She's killing him."

My head jerked up.

"I'm not saying she's putting arsenic in his tea, but he hasn't been himself, and that's such a shame. Not that I was ever really interested in him, you understand. Just fun to flirt and watch him blush. But you." She softened her tone. "I thought you and he might have something."

"Yeah, well." I sighed. "I guess it wasn't meant to be."

Chapter 2

It was a pleasant winter day in East Aurora, which, for me, meant that prevailing weather patterns weren't attempting to dump the whole contents of Lake Erie onto our heads in the form of snow. The air, though crisp, wasn't threatening to launch pedestrians to Oz, and the sun made an occasional appearance, clearing ice from the sidewalks and putting a crust on the accumulated snow plowed from the streets. Othello—our tuxedo cat, named for the board game and not the Shakespearean play—had taken up residence in the sunniest part of the display window next to his favorite Scotty pull toy. Today he even shared the space with Val.

It had taken us months to name the naughty black cat who'd come to us last November. She'd gone through a dozen or so names that didn't stick, some that seemed too sweet and others she just ignored. Finally, Dad started calling her "the cat that could not be named." It was a short leap from there to Voldemort, which we eventually shortened and feminized to Val, although Voldemort better described the clawed creature that terrorized our shop and apartment. For now she was looking all innocent, just enjoying the sunshine.

This was the kind of day that lured shoppers out of their houses onto Main Street, and we'd seen a few of them already at Well Played. One woman was Christmas shopping from a list she'd stolen from her husband—a BOLO list of 1950s American Flyer train engines and cars—and she was surreptitiously trying to help expand his collection. These were rarer S-scale models—although the purists will say only S-*gauge* models—and we didn't have any currently in stock. I'd photocopied the list and her contact info for when Dad was around. If he didn't have what she needed, he could probably find it.

A little after eleven o'clock I went to fetch another cup of coffee but stopped to turn around the Russian doll, which once again faced the wrong way. I wasn't sure who the joker was, but I figured I'd get the blame. I'd just set her right again when the bell over the door rang, and I glanced up to see Irene and Lenora, two elderly sisters I'd met a couple of years earlier. A less-welcoming era would have labeled them as spinsters, but these two enjoyed life too much to be worthy of that sad title.

They did not remove the colorful scarves tied to their heads even as they loosened their coats and greeted Cathy and me with hugs all around. They were drawn like magnets to Cathy's baby and left a few lipstick kisses on Drew's cheeks, which suited him just fine. He cooed and sang and looked happy to see them.

"May I?" Lenora asked, holding arms out to Drew.

"Of course!" Cathy carefully handed him over.

Lenora bobbed him against her hip while Irene rubbed his head, sweaty from a recent nap.

"Soon," Lenora said, "he's going to be too heavy for me to hold."

"When that happens, we'll get you a chair," I said. "What brings you ladies to Main Street this fine morning?"

"We were next door getting our hair done while the weather held up," Irene said. The neighboring barber shop had recently gone unisex, since the aged barber decided to take more time off. Instead of closing, he rented his chairs to several local stylists. Including She-Who-Must-Not-Be-Named—and no, not referring to the cat this time.

"Let's see!" Cathy said.

Irene removed her scarf to show off her new hairdo, which looked remarkably the same as it always had. As did Lenora's after she'd handed Drew back and removed her scarf.

"Were you expecting blue streaks or something?" Lenora laughed. "At our age, we know what works. Marya keeps it that way for us, which is just fine."

"She does good work," Cathy said, glancing in my direction. "You ladies look lovely."

"And it's so pleasant to be away from all that banging at home," Irene said. "Jackhammers. Power tools."

"I heard Jack started remodeling Sy's old place," I said. Jack Wallace had been my on-again, off-again childhood sweetheart, right up until we permanently offed our troubled relationship so we could remain friends. After a brief property dispute, Jack had bought out the rest of the heirs to his uncle Sy's estate, leaving him the proud owner of a dilapidated and possibly haunted Victorian.

"Hired some fancy-schmancy outfit," Lenora said. "Browning Restoration," she added in a posh transatlantic accent. "They have signs up all over the yard. Right next to the bright green porta-potty."

"Better than the workmen peeing in the bushes," Irene added, "which is what they were doing before the porta-potty arrived."

"Did someone complain?" Cathy asked.

"No," Irene said. "They just caught *someone* watching them pee in the bushes." She glared at her sister who blushed.

"Anyway, all kinds of heavy equipment. Never a moment's rest. Sy never made that much noise," Lenora said. "It was his best quality."

"You're forgetting the eighties, my dear," said Irene. "The Madonna years."

"That's right," Lenora said. "Foolish old man, blasting 'Like a Virgin' as loud as his boom box could manage, not caring a lick what the neighbors might think."

"Incidentally, we thought it was some kind of midlife crisis," Irene said. "Although in Sy's case, his midlife crisis lasted about thirty years." She stopped herself. "May he rest in peace."

"Jack's a good neighbor, mind you," Lenora said. "And we like his new girlfriend, too. And the boy."

"Yes, Amanda's sweet," I said, referring to our most recent part-time employee. She and her autistic son had moved to East Aurora last December. "She'll be here this afternoon, in fact. School conferences this morning. She found a great private school that works with Kohl's special needs."

"Although we are still a little sorry that things didn't work out between you and Jack," Irene said.

I waved her off. "No worries. Jack and I have been friends for years, and I couldn't be happier that he found someone. They seem good together."

Irene looked unconvinced.

"Trust me," I said. "I'm fine with it. Jack and I were a mistake we kept making and kept regretting. We're better off as friends."

"And your police friend?" Lenora said.

I sighed. "I'll admit that's a little harder to take."

"Now I feel like a rat for going on about that haircut," Lenora said.

"Now look," I said. "It's no secret I'm not exactly fond of Marya Young, but we all live in the same town. I guess it's time to learn to get along."

"Does that mean you *don't* want this nice juicy bit of gossip we just picked up?" Irene said coyly.

"And maybe lunch on us?" Lenora added, pulling a handful of Wallace's gift certificates from her pocket and waving them in front of my face. "Jack gave them to us when we complained to him about the noise."

Cathy started laughing but nudged me. "I'll watch the shop. You go, but bring me back the dirt. And maybe a doggie bag."

# # #

I removed my foggy glasses after entering Wallace's. The place hadn't changed much since Jack had assumed control from his mother. Just after Thanksgiving, he'd hung up the same dated Christmas decorations—faux wreaths with their crushed velvet bows—in exactly the same places. The same silk poinsettias sat atop every table. And mistletoe dangled from the rafters above the bar. In past years, when I was dating Jack, I might have sought it out. Today I avoided it like a tofu burger at a rodeo.

One recent change was that a few sports jerseys now hung in glass cases near the bar. Jack's brother Terry's influence, perhaps? I'd also heard that the kitchen had been totally over-hauled, of course. Jack had always thought of the place as more of a family restaurant than a tavern, as the sign had always advertised. He clearly placed his emphasis on the food; the bar took a backseat, and nobody I knew seemed to have a problem with that. Today, the familiar spicy tang of chicken wings lay heavy in the air, mingling with the aromas of various sauces and gravies. Instead of competing with each other, they some-how created the counterpoint for a symphony of scents that made my stomach rumble.

A patient hostess wearing reindeer antlers led us halfway around the restaurant before finding an empty table that suited Lenora.

"I don't care for the booths anymore," she explained. "I think my ability to scoot has scooted."

Once our orders had been taken and our soft drinks had arrived, Irene leaned in, looking ready to spill. "You know, of course, that Marya is from Russia."

"That I gathered," I said.

"Now, you young people," Irene went on. "To you, the Cold War is nothing but spy stories and a footnote in your his-tory books. But it was real. Much of the world, after World War II ended, stood holding their breath. Nuclear weapons. Air raid drills. Bomb shelters."

"Fear and distrust and balance of power," Lenora said.

"But Marya," I started, trying to remember when the wall went down and the USSR disintegrated. "She'd be too young to be involved in any of that, so if you're suggesting she's some kind of communist spy . . ."

Lenora put her hands up. "No, not at all. But when did she leave Russia?"

Irene leaned forward. "Her English is very good. Just a faint accent. We figured she's been here a long time."

"I'll buy that," I said.

"We got to talking about that today," Irene said. "Well, I did, anyway. Lenora was still under the dryer."

"I can't hear anything from under the dryer," Lenora said.

"And I asked her about Russia," Irene said. "She didn't remember it at all, so she couldn't have been more than two or three when she came over."

"We think," Lenora said, "she might be one of those illegal aliens. And I bet that's why she was so keen on marrying that policeman friend of yours."

"I suppose it's possible," I said. "I'm not sure Ken would marry her just to help her."

"Oh, I'm sure he *thought* he was in love," Lenora said. "There are lots of ways a cunning young woman can convince a man of that."

"It would explain why she's so determined to make it work," Irene added. "Or at least make it look like it's working. Being married to an American can be a big determining factor in granting citizenship. And once she's gotten it . . ." Irene drummed her fingers on the table.

"You think she's going to leave him," I said.

"Which would open the door for Chief Young to pursue *other* interests," Irene said.

My cheeks flushed, but our food arrived before I could respond, so our conversation hushed while the waitress laid plates in front of us, refilled drinks, and scrounged up a bottle of ketchup. I'd opted for a Buffalo chicken sub, which arrived with enough curly fries to feed twelve.

We were several bites in when Irene said, "So, what do you think?"

"Well, the sub is amazing," I said.

"I mean about getting back together with your old boy-friend," Lenora said.

I took another bite and considered what they had said. Was theirs a marriage of convenience? Or was the pair once genuinely in love?

Jack picked this time to visit our table. His face was flushed from working in the warm kitchen, and his white apron sported a few food stains. "Hi, Liz. Ladies," he added with a flirty tone. "I hope you're enjoying your lunch."

Lenora patted her lips with her napkin. "It's very good." Then she sent him a dentured smile. "Thanks for paying for it."

"Least I could do," Jack said. "Look, I know it must be really loud over there. If it's any consolation, they're doing a great job, and that's gonna help property values in the long run."

The sisters shared a glance.

"Probably," Lenora said. "But we'd never sell, you know."

"Then I'm going to be blessed with the best neighbors for many years to come," Jack said.

Lenora laughed. "You are full of something, Jack Wallace, but I'm too much of a lady to say what."

I laughed at their conversation, then the thought hit. "Jack, did I hear right that Browning Restoration is doing the work on your place?"

"That's right," Jack said. "Not the lowest estimate, but you can't argue with the quality of their work."

"Any way that you could wrangle an introduction to Marvin Browning? Cathy's starting up this doll project . . ."

"Amanda told me all about it," Jack said. "I think it's great. I'd be willing to make a donation, especially if you have any sponsorship opportunities."

"There's an idea," I said.

"But if you're interested in applying for a grant from the Browning Foundation, you don't want Marvin. Ian Browning handles that end. He also manages Browning Restoration. And you're in luck, because I know him quite well."

I squinted at him. "You've been hiding your wealthy friends from me?"

Jack laughed. "Guilty. He's still a bit of a playboy, and back when you and I were dating, I guess I worried that the temptation of old money might lure you away from me."

"And now that we're not?"

"I'll be happy to introduce you." Jack's face grew serious. "Look. Ian and I go way back. Believe it or not, we were altar boys together. But still, he's from a whole different world. He's used to having his own way."

"We used to say someone like that was born with a silver spoon in his mouth," Lenora said.

"Platinum," Jack said. "Adjusted for inflation."

"Well, if I do get to meet him, I'll be careful not to flash him too many of my feminine wiles," I teased.

Jack opened his mouth to answer but then jerked his head toward Terry, who stood by the kitchen door waving to him. "Gotta go. I'll let you know what I can work out."

When he'd cleared earshot, Irene said, "Another young man. And rich, too. Does that mean you're not interested in rekindling what you had with Ken?"

"No one has ever called me a gold digger," I said. "And I

understand what you're trying to say. But with Ken? I don't know."

"But if he married Marya just to keep her from being deported . . ." Irene said.

"It could explain a few things," I said, "because I've never sensed a lot of warmth or chemistry between them."

"If Marya does skedaddle," Irene said, "maybe a little forgiveness and understanding might patch things up between the two of you."

Lenora placed a wrinkled hand on her sister's forearm. "That's something that Liz will have to decide. Don't go all matchmaker on me now." She turned to me. "You see, my sister and I have seen a lot of years go by. We've watched a lot of relationships come and go, and it is nice when two young people get together."

"That's what I'm saying," Irene said.

"But it's also a nightmare when the two wrong people get together," Lenora said.

Irene let out a long breath.

I wasn't sure if she meant Ken and me, or Ken and Marya.

Chapter 3

Darth Vader made me do it.

No, not the mind-bending, evil Sith overlord. It was a missing action figure that lured me to the dark side. The "dark side" in this case was Dad's latest pet project, the hotly debated comic book room, still under construction.

Kohl favored the space. Amanda suggested that perhaps her teenage son found the dimly lit area calming, that it gave him a retreat from the sound and lights and commotion of the shop that his autism sometimes rendered over-stimulating. The electrician, due next week, had canceled twice, and none of us had the heart to hurry up the process.

I found Vader on the table, next to a few sketches of the figure. Kohl's colors were vibrant but well balanced and his lines bold and confident. The private art classes Amanda had found were doing wonders to hone his natural ability.

His timing, however, was all wrong.

In just a few days, the walls would have been more sound-proof. As they were now, only drywall on one side of the new wall separated the comic book room from the old barber shop. After a savvy business deal—at least on the part of the barber—Dad had acquired their underutilized storage room and added three hundred square feet to our floor space.

"Got a great deal," Dad had bragged around town, but our bank account balances still kept me up at night.

And as I picked up the stray Darth action figure, the voice I heard through the wall made my skin crawl more than James Earl Jones's ever had.

It was Marya.

I wasn't exactly *trying* to overhear, at least not at first. "Were you checking up on me?" she screeched.

A male voice rumbled, but I couldn't quite make it out. I stayed stock-still and closed my eyes. When that proved inadequate—not that I'm proud of it—I found the largest gap in the drywall and put my ear up against it.

"I wasn't checking up on you," Ken said, the frustration in his voice mounting. "All I did was poke my head in the library when you said you'd be there—"

"Did you look in the *whole* library? How do you know I wasn't in one of the study areas? Or back in the stacks somewhere? Did you check everywhere?"

"Trust me, I looked."

"A-ha! Then you *were* checking up on me."

"This isn't about me," Ken countered. "This is about you. About you not being where you told me you would be."

"Okay, Mister High-and-Mighty, this has nothing to do with whether I was at the library or not. This is about control and why you feel you have to check up on me. I'm not a criminal. I'm not on probation."

"You very well could be."

"What's that supposed to mean?" she demanded.

"Don't play games. You know exactly what I'm talking

about." Ken said. "And if you think I'm going to allow you to start pulling the same . . ."

Right about the time the expletives started flying on the other side of the wall, a hand grasped my upper arm. I whirled around to see Cathy. Somehow I managed to stifle a gasp.

She brushed her index finger in the universal sign of "shame on you," but I let out a quiet breath of relief that Cathy—and not Dad—had caught me eavesdropping.

I followed her back to the main part of the shop. "What in the world?" she said.

I put my hands up, still holding the action figure. "Not something I'd intended to do. I went to get Darth and I heard them arguing."

"Who?" This is why I was glad Cathy had caught me. Any scorn she might have felt for my nosiness would soon be buried under her own curiosity.

"Ken and Marya."

Cathy worried her lip but didn't reply.

"I thought you'd be curious," I said.

Her brow crinkled. "A little curious, but mostly concerned."

"Yeah, they were really going at it."

"No, hun." She took a step closer. "Concerned about you."

"This has nothing to do with me."

"I know that. Just not sure that you know that. Do you think you can be an adult and work with Marya?"

"I can be an adult," I said, but I practically had to push my lower lip back into alignment.

"Liz, it's not healthy for you to keep pining over what might have been."

"You think I'm pining?" I repeated. "That ship has sailed."

"Glad to hear it. But maybe it's time to put the binoculars

away and leave the docks." Her eyes widened, as if she surprised herself. "That's a good metaphor. I need to write that down. Someone in my writing group said I was getting too literal. Let's see them try to write anything figurative on three hours of sleep. I'm lucky I remember my alphabet." She sighed. "Then again, I now sing it about twenty times a day."

"I thought Drew was sleeping better." I mentally crossed my fingers, hoping she wouldn't notice the subject change.

"Oh, he does good most nights," she said. "But he's been fussing a little. The pediatrician thinks he might be teething."

"Already?"

"It's a little early but not unheard of at four months."

With that topic off the table, we finished out the rest of the day easy enough. It wasn't until I'd made my way upstairs and weaved around the boxes of comic books stacked in our apartment that I thought again about what I had overheard.

Cathy had been right to caution me. Ken was no longer my boyfriend. But from what I'd just heard, his marriage with Marya wasn't likely to survive much longer. Had it been a sham from the beginning? And if they did break up, would I want him back?

I pushed the thought from my mind. It was way too early to consider that question. And, truly, whatever they were arguing about was none of my business.

With Dad spending the evening with Parker and Cathy, I had the apartment to myself, which meant grabbing a bowl of cereal for dinner, turning on a Hallmark Christmas movie, and herding literal cats, who seemed to think having boxes of comic books stacked from floor to ceiling in the apartment was incredible fun. They treated it as their own private jungle gym.

I put Ken and Marya out of my mind until about eleven at night when the colored flashes from the police lights started reflecting against the glittered popcorn on my bedroom ceiling. I rushed to the window and peered outside to see a couple of patrol cars, an ambulance, and just about all of East Aurora's finest in front of the barber shop. And I'd bet two bits they weren't there for a shave and a haircut.

Chapter 4

Dad beat me to the stairs, but only by a couple of steps. He'd already dressed, although I suspected he'd just climbed out of bed and thrown on the closest thing. He was unshaven and wrinkled, and I stopped him long enough to spit-tame an errant lock of his hair that made him resemble Alfalfa from the old *Our Gang* shorts.

I didn't want to know what I looked like. I'd thrown a robe over my Scooby-Doo pajamas and slipped on my Tribble slippers, a birthday gift from Parker.

We cut through the shop and went out the front door to the sidewalk. Lights flashed and reflected from storefront windows, ice, and slushy puddles, creating a light show of red, amber, and blue. A barrier of crime scene tape was being erected around the barber shop, and Ken and his chief detective, Howard Reynolds, were having a healthy debate as Reynolds escorted Ken to the outside of the barrier.

And by escort, I don't mean he held up a suave arm like a nervous prom date escorting his girlfriend to the dance floor. A lot more physicality was involved as Reynolds first guided, then pulled Ken toward the barrier.

"I should be in there!" Ken said, once he was able to summon words of more than four letters.

"There's nothing you can do in there that I or my men can't." Reynolds grasped Ken by the shoulders.

Ken looked pale, even in the dim light of the street. He opened his mouth as if to argue, but then looked to the edge of the barrier where a few more people had arrived, some spilling out of local bars and some, as indicated by their rumpled sleep-wear, out of their beds. He raked a hand through his hair and turned back to Reynolds. "What am I supposed to do?"

"Let's get you off the street at least." Reynolds beckoned my father over.

Ken cast a final glance toward the barber shop, as if he might dart inside as soon as Reynolds let go of his arm.

"Can you get him out of here for a little while?" Reynolds asked my dad. "Let him warm up, but keep him away from the barber shop and reporters."

"Sounds like a good idea," Dad said, then grabbed Ken's arm. "Let's go."

Only then did Reynolds let go.

I sprinted over to Detective Reynolds—if one could truly sprint while clutching a bathrobe and wearing Tribble slippers. "What happened?"

He looked at me for a moment and I pulled my robe tighter, maybe because of the cold or perhaps to shield Scooby from news I suspected would be catastrophic.

"It's Marya Young," Reynolds finally said. "She was found dead in the barber shop."

"Dead? Marya?" She'd been the picture of health just the other night. What could have happened? The truth hit like a punch in the gut. "Murdered?" The word caught in my throat.

Reynolds gritted his teeth and gave a curt nod.

# # #

There was no sign of Dad or of Ken in our shop. Dad had probably hustled him upstairs. I locked the front door and then glanced over to the comic book area where I'd overheard that argument through the shared wall just hours earlier.

Murdered. The word seemed to echo through the empty shop.

Marya Young.

No, I hadn't liked her much, and that might be an understatement. But that had more to do with the fact that a Mrs. Young existed and Ken had neglected to tell me about her.

I mentally recounted everything I knew about her. She had come from Russia when she was very young. She never talked about her childhood. And thanks to my own petty resentfulness, I'd never asked.

I suspected that was the case with much of the town. I'd found out later that not only Dad but also half of East Aurora had been hoping Ken and I would end up doing the whole orange blossoms and picket fence thing. I think someone in the chamber of commerce even set up a secret pool as to when he'd pop the question.

Marya's existence had sent a shockwave through the gossip network, and every old biddy in town sent me consoling looks whenever I walked down the street for about a month after her arrival. Her continued presence was met with a cold ambivalence that I'd taken some guilty pleasure in.

My face grew warm at the memory. It was horribly unfair to her.

And now she was dead. Not only dead, but someone had killed her.

A lump grew in my throat and I struggled to swallow. I'd heard Ken argue with Marya just that afternoon. That news would come out at some point. Ken would be a suspect, and there was no getting around that.

I returned to the new comic area, cursing Darth Vader for making me a witness to something that could cast more suspicion on Ken. I sat down at the table where Kohl had been drawing and pressed cool fingers against my warm face and eyes.

Ken would be a suspect even if I said nothing of what I'd overheard. As the husband of the victim, he'd be the first suspect the police considered. One didn't have to be the daughter of a cop to know that.

That their relationship was strained was public knowledge.

The fact that Reynolds had removed him from the scene was also telling. It had been good police work, of course. Even if the man is your boss, you can't give the prime suspect in a murder investigation more access to the crime scene.

He was innocent, of course. Although I rolled my shoulder as I thought it.

Did I know for sure he was innocent? How?

Marya was a newcomer. Small towns are like that—it takes years to lose that title, even if the deck *isn't* stacked against you. She didn't have close friends here or strong ties. One would think she hadn't made too many enemies, at least not that I'd heard of. And I probably would have heard if she had.

Who else would have motive to kill her?

I drew closer to the wall to see if I could overhear anything taking place in the shop, but except for the indistinguishable low rumbles of voices, I gathered nothing.

I shivered and considered going upstairs. Upstairs to where my former boyfriend was now grieving the loss of his wife.

I closed my eyes. Why did she ever have to come here? Life would be so different, so much easier if she'd never shown up. Or never existed.

My eyes flew open. Who else had motive to kill her? *I did.*

Nobody had said anything yet, but if this stretched out, no way would the investigation conclude without me being considered a suspect. From all outward appearances, she'd destroyed my budding relationship with Ken. They'd consider that as motive.

And whose shop stood just next door to the crime scene? I'd been home alone most of the evening; not even Dad could provide an alibi for me. They'd look on that as opportunity.

As to means? I couldn't answer that yet, since I had no idea how she had died. But perhaps those answers were sitting upstairs.

# # #

The smell of fresh coffee greeted me when I reached the landing. Ken was already seated at the kitchen table warning his hands around an oversized mug of Dad's high-test. If they'd been talking, they stopped when I came in, but I'm not sure I missed anything. An experienced interrogator, Dad would take his time to make sure Ken felt comfortable and at ease. Well, as "at ease" as one could be in this situation.

I poured myself a cup, added sugar and a healthy dose of milk, and joined them at the table. "I locked up."

Dad nodded but never looked up. As he sipped his coffee,

his gaze swept over Ken's face, and mine followed it. Ken stared, unblinking, at our kitchen clock. I wasn't sure if he was replaying something in his mind or was in some kind of shock.

I glanced back up at Dad, who took my hand and squeezed it.

Ken seemed to come to. He blinked hard then scrubbed his face with his hands.

"What exactly happened, son?" Dad said, before Ken could get lost staring into his coffee.

"I don't know."

"Who found her?" Dad asked.

Ken startled and looked up. "I did. She hadn't come home. She didn't answer her cell. I figured she was just mad at me." He glanced over at me. "We'd argued earlier. But it was getting late, so I went looking for her in just about every bar in town. The barber shop was the last place I thought to try. She must have never left work."

"Was she alive when you found her?" Dad asked.

"I . . . I don't think so." He swallowed hard then drained the last of his coffee. "She was slumped in one of the styling chairs with her back to the door. The lights were on. The door was unlocked. I thought maybe she had passed out in the chair. Only when I rounded the corner, she had a hair dryer cord wrapped around her neck."

I fought to keep that mental picture out of my head. So much for not having the means. Everyone did. The weapon was already there.

"What did you do then?" Dad said.

Ken rose to refill his cup. When he'd returned to the table, he looked a little more awake and aware. "I acted like a complete idiot. I thought maybe she could still be alive, so I unwrapped the cord from her neck, laid her on the floor, and tried to resuscitate her." He mouthed a few more words, but I could tell he was quietly cursing his own stupidity. "It was pointless. She was cold. I should have known that. Instead, I contaminated all the evidence."

He looked up at Dad. "Who? Who would do this?"

Chapter 5

Dad left Ken's question unanswered, but after maybe ten minutes of silence, he leaned his forearms on the table and reflected it back at him. "Who do *you* think might have killed her?"

Ken scratched his cheek. "She didn't have a whole lot of friends in town, but she had been going out more lately." He drummed his fingers on the table. "It's going to come out. I thought there may have been someone else. Or that maybe she was back to her old—"

A loud banging downstairs interrupted him.

"Liz, could you?" Dad said.

I nodded and went to see what the commotion was. With the shop lights on, I could see someone pounding on our front door, but I couldn't identify the two figures, lit only by the streetlights and flashing of the emergency response vehicles. As I drew closer, their faces came into dim focus. Reynolds paused to tent his eyes and peer inside the shop. The mayor stood next to him.

"Good evening, Miss McCall," Mayor Briggs said as I cracked opened the door. Then he glanced at his watch. "Or rather morning. May we come in?"

I pulled the door open a little wider.

Reynolds looked around. "Is Ken still here?"

"He's upstairs with Dad."

"Can we see him, please?" Reynolds said.

"Sure. Right this way." I couldn't recall if Mayor Briggs had set foot in our store. At least not since the grand opening where he'd wished Dad and me the best of luck in all our endeavors. It struck me as a cold and rather generic speech, considering how long and hard Dad had served "at the pleasure of the mayor."

The balding, slightly portly man was considerably older than Lori, or at least appeared to be. He had only three years on her, but without the benefit of Lori's spa maintenance and pricy makeup, his age was much more apparent in the deep lines around his eyes and the wattle of his neck.

I cleared my throat when I reached the top of the stairs, lest the mayor and the department's senior detective catch Ken saying something incriminating. Not that I thought he was guilty.

The coffeepot gurgled again and Dad was poised to get the first cup when I pulled open the door. He glanced up at me, then at Reynolds and the mayor as they cleared the threshold.

"Howard. Mayor," Dad said as he nodded to them.

"Hank." Mayor Briggs surveyed our small apartment, made even smaller by the piles of cardboard boxes.

Of course the day the mayor comes to call is when we look ready to appear on an episode of *Hoarders*. I straightened the chairs at the table, as if that made a difference. "Would you care to sit? Coffee?"

Mayor Briggs waved me off. "We won't be but a moment," he said, his attention on Dad. "I suppose you heard what happened."

"I got the gist of it," Dad said.

"We just learned the news crews are on their way. We're going to have to make a statement."

Ken pushed himself out of his chair. "Give me a moment to clean up."

But the mayor shook his head vehemently. "I don't want you anywhere near a camera. In fact . . ." He paused and drew a long breath.

"You're firing me?" Ken said.

The mayor laid a calming hand on Ken's arm. "Let's call it a temporary paid suspension, pending the results of a thorough, impartial investigation."

Ken's jaw tightened, but he didn't raise an argument. Finally, he clapped Reynolds on the shoulder. "Howard's a good man. He'll get the job done."

"Not me." Reynolds put up his hands. "They don't pay me enough to touch this one. I'm not going to lead an investigation that could end up . . ."

Ken quirked an eyebrow.

"Sorry, boss," Reynolds said.

"Don't apologize for loyalty, son," Dad said before turning back to the mayor. "So, what are you going to do?"

The mayor grinned at Dad, the first smile since the men had entered the room. "Hank?"

The meaning of that smile washed over me instantaneously. "No!" I said.

The mayor ignored me and kept his gaze on Dad. My stomach was performing rhythmic gymnastics in anticipation of the words I knew would follow.

"Would you consider serving as interim chief of police? Just until we can clear this mess up?"

Dad didn't respond immediately. He studied the mayor's pudgy face before redirecting his gaze toward Reynolds. Then he looked at Ken's blank expression. Finally, Dad sent a brief apologetic glance to me. "My daughter may kill me." He shook the mayor's hand. "Yes, I'll serve as interim."

"You can be impartial?" the mayor asked.

Dad took a long breath. "Always."

# # #

While Dad, Reynolds, and Mayor Briggs turned our kitchen into a war room, strategizing how best to confront the media, I was elected to drive Ken home.

"My truck is here," Ken said, pulling out his keys.

Dad made a grab for them. "You're in no condition. I'll get someone to drive it home for you. Uh, permission to search the vehicle?"

Ken had stared, or perhaps glared, for a moment. I held my breath wondering if he'd make Dad try for a search warrant. He'd probably not get one. What might he be looking for in the truck? If Marya was strangled with an object close to hand, there would be no missing weapon, no gun, smoking or otherwise. But there might be evidence of the couple's recent marital disputes.

Ken threw up his hands. "Have at it."

He pushed himself out of his chair and out the door so fast, I rushed to gather my purse and follow him. Fortunately my Civic was parked in the alley behind the store, so at least I didn't need to face the responders, the bystanders, and the media in my Scooby-Doo pajamas.

I drove a couple of blocks out of the way to avoid doubling back down Main Street, not that it was open to traffic yet.

"You know where?" Ken said.

"Yeah," I said.

When Marya had moved to town, Ken had given up his rented bachelor digs and had purchased a smallish house just a few blocks off Main. I might have driven past it once or twice, especially early on. It was probably the petty part of me that inspected Marya's attempts at landscaping and choice of drapery colors and found them wanting.

Jealous? You betcha, not that I admitted that to anyone.

But this time I pulled in the drive noting that Marya would never return to her little starter home, and it just made me sad. Sad for her. Sad for Ken.

I shifted the car into park, turned off the headlights, and silenced the engine. Ken made no motion to get out.

"You okay?" I asked.

He sniffed and stared down at the dashboard. "Can you come in for a minute?"

"I'm not quite sure I should."

"Liz," he said, gripping my hand. "I didn't kill her."

I gave it a squeeze. "I know that. But you know what this town is like. If some neighbor sees me going into your house right after your wife . . ."

He flung his head backward into the headrest. "I'm beginning to hate small towns. As soon as this whole thing is over, I'm packing up and moving to the biggest city that'll hire me. That is, of course, if your father doesn't lock me up and throw away the key out of spite."

"He wouldn't do that. If you're innocent, he'll clear you and find the killer."

"If?"

"A logical argument. Of course I think you're innocent.

38

The argument I heard could have occurred between any married couple."

"What argument?"

"The fight you had in the barber shop yesterday afternoon."

"You could hear that through the wall? Did your father hear?"

"He wasn't in the shop," I said, not volunteering that I'd had my ear to the drywall. Before Ken could look too relieved, I added, "Besides, you admitted as much to him in conversation sitting at our kitchen table. Also that you suspected there was someone else."

Ken's eyelids popped as if this was news to him. "That's not something I know for sure. Just that she'd been secretive lately, going out more. I'd caught her lying to me, and I was trying to get to the bottom of it." He turned to look out the passenger window. "They're going to crucify me."

"Not legal in this state," I quipped.

"Liz, I need your help." He paused to take a long, deep breath. "Keep me apprised of the investigation?"

"I'll do what I can to help, but I'm not sure my father's going to tell me much. He'll try to keep me out of it. Maybe you should step back, too."

"What am I supposed to do? Sit on my hands?"

A nearby porch light flickered on, and I pulled back my hand, which he'd been clutching until this point. "Did Marya have any family to notify?"

"None that she kept in touch with," he said. "Long story." He rubbed his hands down his thighs. "But I suppose I should call my sisters. They kept in contact even when I thought our marriage was over. I honestly think they liked her better than they like me sometimes." He stared at his house through the windshield, making no move to go. "They had a lot to do with Marya coming here. I don't think they wanted to lose her as a sister-in-law." He glanced up at me. "You'd like them, I think. But they're a force to be reckoned with."

If they were responsible for sending Marya, I doubted we'd get along all that well, but I just nodded.

"So one phone call," he said, "and then I don't know what I'll do. I've never been that good at thumb-twiddling. Any pointers?"

"Frankly," I said, "my technique is a little rusty, too. But try to get some sleep. Take a shower. Eat a good breakfast. And put all those little gray cells of yours, as Hercule Poirot might say, into coming up with a list of anyone you think had a motive to kill your wife."

"Other than me, you mean." He reached for the door handle.

"Other than you." I turned the engine back on and watched as he made his way, shoulders hunched, into his dark, silent home.

Chapter 6

Sleep or no sleep, with Dad out once again managing the police force, I went back to managing the toyshop. Or trying to, anyway. Business was brisk with half the town beating a path to the door to make nominal purchases—and then to casually ask me what I knew about what happened next door. Oh, the joys of small town life.

I smiled and feigned ignorance. When pressed, I remarked that yes, it was scary happening so close. And I took their cash, checks, and credit cards.

Not that I could brag. Cathy did the same thing all morning, only she did it with a baby balanced on her hip.

During a brief lull, she managed to get Drew down for a nap. Seeing his peaceful form snoozing in the small playpen made me seriously jealous for my own bed. I yawned.

"Don't get me started," she said. "I'm running on fumes myself. If you wanted to put up the closed sign and dim the lights, I'd happily catch some Zs on the floor like we did back in kindergarten."

I shook my head. "We're doing too much business to close now."

"You'd think folks would have learned that we don't know anything."

"But until they do . . ." I rubbed my fingers together. Not that I was greedy or trying to capitalize on what happened. But like so many other small businesses, we had our struggles, and I'd take customers in any legal way possible. "Besides," I told Cathy, "we actually do know a few things. Not that I want to share them with customers."

Cathy put down the doll she was preening and drew closer. "What do we know?"

"We know that Ken had an argument with Marya yesterday afternoon," I said.

Cathy winced. "That makes him a suspect, right?"

"Gives him motive that can be corroborated by at least one witness." I pointed to myself. "Did *you* hear any of the conversation through the wall?"

"*I* didn't have my ear to it. Oh, Liz, that's going to be rather awkward if they call you to testify."

"Tell me about it," I said. "They'd only call me if a case against Ken went to trial. Hopefully it won't come to that."

When I glanced up, she was focused on the shelf behind me again. "Liz, considering what happened, that might not be in the best of taste."

I felt my shoulders tighten. "Is that doll turned around again?"

"You telling me you didn't do it?"

I shook my head. "But I found it that way yesterday, too. Seems we have a practical joker."

"Or maybe a poltergeist." Her face grew more animated. "Maybe trying to tell us something about the murder!"

"Cathy"—I closed my eyes—"I've gotten better with the

dolls around, but I'm going nowhere near a haunted one. Can you take it away?"

"Okay, I believe you."

I kept my eyes closed while I heard movement around me. "Is it gone?"

"She's in the doll room. Sorry, I really thought you were joking around. You sure you didn't touch her?"

I mustered my courage and opened my eyes. The shelf where the matryoshka had stood was now empty. I rearranged merchandise to fill in the space.

"Who do you think did it?" she asked.

"Moved the doll?"

"No, killed Marya Young."

That stopped me short. "No idea," I said after a long gap.

"Maybe someone she met at work?" Cathy said. "A client, perhaps?"

"A customer irate over a bad haircut?" I suggested, but it sounded absurd even to my ears.

Cathy frowned. "There's too much we don't know. We all thought we knew Ken, but he had secrets. Like the fact that he had a wife. And neither of us went out of our way to get to know her."

"I feel bad enough about that already."

"Oh, Liz." Cathy gave me a warm hug. "Nobody expected you to be on the welcome wagon. Nothing for you to feel guilty about." She pulled back and lifted my chin so that I was staring into her eyes. "We'll have none of that. I'm sure Dad has the case half-solved by now."

"I feel helpless here," I said.

"Someone has to mind the shop," she said. "Speaking of which, there's a bunch of cardboard boxes in the back ready to be broken down and put into the recycling bin. Would you rather do it while I mind the shop and Drew, or—"

"Let me do the boxes," I said. "The fresh air might do me some good."

# # #

As soon as I opened the alley door, I knew I'd made the right decision. The sun shone against a clear blue sky, and I leaned back against the brick building and paused to watch a drop of melted snow from the awning glisten as it tried to race down the already forming icicle before refreezing. It failed. A lungful of stale, hot air condensed in front of me, and I enjoyed the cool crispness that replaced it.

The faint scent of ammonia tickled my nose. I glanced around to see if I could spot the source, maybe a feral cat. Only I kept the door open too wide for too long. Nearby, a bird fluttered its wings and took off. When I turned my head, there was Val, who had taken the opportunity to escape. She'd missed the bird, but stopped to lick her paw nonchalantly, as if to say, "I meant to do that."

"Here, kitty?" I tried sweetly, letting her know just who was boss in our relationship. (She was.)

She ignored me, but at least didn't run away. Instead, she froze, craned her neck, and then went into full-on stalker mode, sniffing around the dumpster before creeping toward a narrow walkway between two buildings. With my luck, she'd find that alley cat and pick a fight.

I trailed after her, speaking loudly enough to chase away stray cats from three counties. But when I rounded the corner, I found her sniffing the shoelaces of Lionel Kelley. Or maybe I should say, Lionel Kelley, private investigator, as his cards and ads all over town read.

Kelley shot me a frozen smile. "Hi, Liz. Is the cat friendly?" Instead of waiting for an answer, he reached down to pet her, and she took a nip at his hand.

"Sorry!" I scooped her up, gripping her front legs so she couldn't claw me. "She's not friendly at all, but we're working on it." Which was true, but it had become clear in the past year that Val was never going to change.

"Then maybe you should keep her inside. Shouldn't she have a collar?"

"We try to keep her inside. She has other plans." And she'd pulled a Houdini with her collar, slipping out of it repeatedly until finally she'd ditched it. "She has all her shots up to date," I added, as he inspected his hand.

While I struggled with the squirming cat, Kelley made no move to leave. I found this peculiar until I noticed a chair and a small cooler in the little walkway.

"Are you watching something here?" I asked. I tried to consider the vantage point, and the only things he'd be able to see from this particular spot were the backs of the toyshop and the barber shop.

Kelley bristled. "I can't divulge the details of a particular investigation. Client confidentiality and all that."

"Which means yes," I said. "But are you watching our place or the barber shop?"

He didn't answer, only stared back at me with the condescending look that tended to dominate his face.

I squinted at him. "My guess would be the barber shop if it has anything to do with the murder."

His eyes widened. "Murder?"

"You didn't hear?" I tipped my head toward the barber shop. Although our comic book area now took up most of the back portion of the building, they'd retained a narrow passage to the back door for safety reasons. "Right in there."

"Who? Who was killed?"

I paused for a second, tempted to reply that I couldn't divulge the details of an ongoing investigation, but I wanted to see his reaction to my answer. "Marya Young."

The young man paled and wobbled on his feet, failing to keep a poker face.

"Was *she* your client?" I asked. Perhaps Marya had been aware of a threat and had hired him to protect her.

He licked his lips then shook himself out of his surprise. "I've said too much already." He glanced up at the building and then massaged the back of his neck. "Who killed her?"

"Police don't know that yet."

"Chief Young . . ."

"Has been relieved, mainly because he's too close. The mayor made my dad interim police chief, and he's heading up the investigation."

Kelley set his jaw. "I see." Kelley and Dad had a history. Kelley had served his rookie years under my father. Well, part of a year, but the young man's overexuberance—the term my dad used when trying to be nice about it—had led to his dismissal after numerous complaints.

By this point, the demon-cat grew more verbal in her complaints, trying to squirm out of my grasp.

"Lionel," I said, "maybe we could help each other."

He stared at me skeptically, as if to suggest that I couldn't even control a cat. Then again, he didn't know this cat. "I don't think so." He struggled to cram his folding chair into the flexible fabric case then carried it, a duffel bag, and his cooler back down the passageway.

I watched him leave, but only for a few seconds, because Val was close to extricating herself from my grip. I wrestled her back into the shop, where she practically launched herself out of my arms and took off running. I closed the door and waited for my eyes to adjust to the relative dimness of our back room, then examined my hands and arms to see if Val had drawn blood.

Had Marya hired Lionel Kelley? Or was he watching her for someone else? And if so, for whom?

# # #

A little after two in the afternoon I felt practically comatose and was trying to wake myself up with a lethal combination of Coca Cola and Pixy Stix when Jack Wallace poked his head in the door.

"If you're looking for Amanda," I said, "it's her day off."

"This time, Liz, I'm here to see you."

"Sure. What's up?" I smiled at him. Often when former couples decide to "just be friends," those friendships fall apart. Ours, however managed to survive. Cathy had asked me once if I felt jealous at all, considering our long history. If I did, it was only of the way Jack and Amanda's relationship seemed to progress so naturally and seamlessly, as if they were always destined to be together.

"If it's about what happened last night," I added, "there's not much I can tell you."

"I'm not here for gossip." He paused and studied my face. "Are you all right?"

"Nothing that a few hours drooling into my pillow won't cure." I tried to wave it off, but my fingers started shaking.

He gave me a curious look then took in the Coke cans and candy wrappers. "Liz, seriously. Are you twelve? No wonder you're shaking. As soon as I'm done here, I'm going to get you some real food to balance all that sugar and caffeine."

I put up my hands. "You won't hear any complaints from me if you do."

"All right, then." He shoved his hands into his pockets. "Sorry."

"You're acting awfully paternal lately. Any reason behind that?" I added coyly.

"Well, if you're not sharing *your* news . . ."

"So there's news, is there?"

"There might be. Any day now." He pinched his eyes shut. "Man, Liz. I never could keep a secret from you." He wagged a finger at me. "No coaching Amanda."

"Why not? You planning on keeping secrets from her?"

"Only good ones," he said. "You got me so twisted around, I almost forgot what I came in here for. Cathy will want to hear this, too." He waved her over. "Did you two still want to meet Ian Browning?"

"Can you fix it?" Cathy asked.

"I learned this morning that he's going to be at the grand opening gala for new riding stables tonight."

Cathy's shoulders sank. "That leaves us out. No invite."

"Someone's not been reading their *Advertiser* faithfully," Jack said. He pulled a folded copy out of his coat pocket and smoothed it on the counter. There, circled in red was an advertisement for the public event and the admission fee.

"A bag of feed?" I read.

Jack tapped the fine print. "It's a fundraiser for the new hippotherapy program they're starting at the stables."

"Disabled hippos?" I said. "At the stables?"

Jack chuckled. "I think *hippo* is Greek for horse or something. I guess it's a special riding program for kids with physical disabilities or emotional problems. The specialist they're bringing in will draw a salary from the Browning Foundation, but the horses still need to be cared for and fed."

Cathy clapped my arm. "Liz, we should go. What a great time to meet Ian Browning when he already has charity on his mind."

"Cathy." I pointed to my drooping eyelids. "Dead on my feet. Do we have to do this tonight?"

Her jaw dropped. "We don't run in the same circles. Who knows when our paths will cross again? Besides . . ."

"If you say it's for the children one more time, I may grow violent."

She took one giant step backward and sent me a toothy grin.

I knew when I was licked. "What time?"

"Says here eight," Jack said.

"It *starts* at eight?" I said. "How late will this thing run?"

Cathy put her hands up. "We can leave as soon as we accomplish our mission. We 'accidentally'"—she added air quotes to the word—"run into Ian Browning, casually mention the doll rehab program, and ask if we can pitch it to him formally. Why, we could be out of there by eight fifteen if everything goes well."

I eyed her skeptically.

"We are talking about the upper crust here. It depends on how fashionably late everybody arrives."

49

I winced.

"And remember, we both have tomorrow off," she said. "Miles and Amanda are opening so we all can celebrate Parker's birthday. The games won't begin until after lunch. Even if tonight's festivities do go late, you can always sleep in."

My shoulders slumped, whether in fatigue or defeat, I wasn't sure.

"And look," she continued. "How about I cover for you here? You can go out and get the horse feed, and there's probably enough time to catch a nap before you have to dress for the gala."

"A nap?" I'd found the one bright spot in her plan. "I just have to get horse feed and then I can take a nap?" It sounded heavenly. I gathered my coat and purse and made it halfway to the door murmuring "horse feed and then nap" almost as a mantra, when I turned around and tilted my head. "What do horses eat, anyway?"

# # #

What does one wear to a fundraising gala held in a drafty barn in the middle of winter? I decided on a sparkly red tunic with a festive Christmas scarf over heavy wool pants and my best boots.

When Cathy arrived to pick me up, she stepped back, eyed me head to toe, raised one eyebrow, and headed straight to my closet.

"*Gala*, Liz," she said, working her way through my wardrobe. Occasionally she pulled out a garment, eyed it, and tossed it on one of two piles on the bed. Othello rose from sleeping on my pillow, stretched, and watched her lazily. "What were you thinking?" she asked.

"I was thinking cold barn in the middle of winter."

She squinted at an asymmetrical blouse, adjusted it on the hanger, then frowned and tossed it onto the larger of the two piles.

"That looks quite nice on," I said.

She shook her head and juggled three garments, holding them up against me. She threw the other two down and handed me the black cocktail dress she'd bought me last Christmas. It still had the tags on.

"It's too short and a little snug."

"It's supposed to fit like that."

"And it doesn't go with my boots."

She rolled her eyes. "You're wearing heels."

I pointed down to her sparkly flats.

"I'm an old married lady."

"But we're just going there to try to meet Ian Browning."

She held the dress up to me and focused my attention to the mirror. "And with you in this dress," she said, "I'd say our odds of meeting Ian Browning go up about eighty percent." She winked.

# # #

The most difficult part of the evening proved to be walking from the car to the barn. The rough stone drive wasn't very friendly to heels, especially while I clutched the thin wrap that Cathy had allowed me to take. A brisk December gust seemed determined to steal it away from me, and I struggled to keep the wind from whipping up the skirt and exposing my other assets.

I was grateful when we made it inside. Not only was the barn warmer, but some brilliant event planner had installed a portable dance floor in the whole structure. They'd pulled out all the stops. Glittering chandeliers hung from rough beams, and twinkle lights illuminated humongous festive flower arrangements and dazzling ice sculptures.

Dad had once asked why I let Cathy dress me for special occasions, as if I were one of her fashion dolls. Truth was, while her own wardrobe choices tended to be somewhat Bohemian, she could pull together a nice ensemble, even from the meager offerings of my closet. Much better than I could, at least. My choice would have left me seriously underdressed.

I leaned toward her. "Thanks for the wardrobe consult. You were right."

"I don't mind. It's fun."

"Like dressing a Barbie?" I teased.

"Better," she said, leaning into me for a hug. "Your elbows bend and all."

"And my hips and knees work, too," I said, doing a little shimmy to illustrate.

Cathy laughed and swatted me on the arm. "Then again, I can't pop your head off if the neck opening is too small."

A very masculine throat-clearing sounded behind me. "I hope there's a band so I can see that move again."

I whipped around to spot Mark Baker, and my face erupted into what I suspected was a fierce blush. I'd met Mark Baker, forensic accountant with the FBI, the previous year, when an investigation he was working on intersected with a train and toy show—and the unfortunate demise of a drugged-out comic book dealer who thought the cape he wore meant he could fly. Since then I'd run into Mark occasionally at community events, and he'd come to a few game nights recently at the shop.

"Don't stop on my account," he said. "Frankly, you might be the only one here having fun."

"Really?" I survey the room. The crowd was decidedly older, well-dressed, and rather staid, and many happened to be surveying me at the very same moment. Some quickly turned their heads in a failed attempt to hide furtive smiles.

Cathy rolled her eyes. "I can dress her up, but . . ."

I covered my face with my hands and peeked out through my fingers. "How badly did I embarrass myself?"

Cathy pulled my hands down and whispered. "I'll let you know when you stop."

Mark laughed, a full baritone laugh that filled the room and diverted attention. "You girls are the bright spot of the whole evening. I, for one, am glad you came."

"What brings you here, Mark?" I asked. "Not working, I hope."

He gave no direct answer but a slight twitch of the shoulder.

My skin tingled. "Something's happening here? Tonight?"

He ushered Cathy and me over to the wall where he'd be less likely to be overheard. "Nothing serious or definite," he said. "And nothing dangerous. There are just a few people here that I'd like to keep an eye on."

"Criminals?" Cathy asked, her eyes dancing at the prospect. "How exciting!"

Mark shrugged. "Most of what I deal with is white-collar stuff. Businessmen who lack a certain ethical balance. This is the kind of event where some of those things come to light, when they're relaxed and a little happy."

"Meaning there's a bar," Cathy said.

Mark dipped his head. "And that makes them a little less careful. I just came to be the fly on the wall."

"These are stables, so you might not be the only fly," I said, gesturing to the elaborately decorated barn. In doing so I managed to jostle the tray of a server who juggled it deftly and kept it from the floor.

"Bravo!" Mark said to the black-tied server. "You passed the test with flying colors. If I have anything to say about it, you might see a little extra in your check. Good work." Mark rescued two crushed hors d'oeuvres with a napkin and popped one into his mouth.

The server sent him a sideways glance and moved on with his tray.

"Is this a private tête-à-tête?" Lori Briggs sidled into our group, then gave Mark a once-over—an embarrassingly long once-over—before she sent him that flirty smile of hers. "Hi, I'm Lori." She shuffled her drink and appetizer into one hand and held the other out to him.

"Lori, this is Mark Baker," I said. "Mark's an accountant," I added, not so sure he wanted it to get out that he worked for the FBI. "And Mark, this is Lori Briggs, our mayor's wife."

I could have sworn she flashed me a dirty look, even without letting that smile dim.

"How exciting," she said. Now I knew she was up to something. Not many people in this world find accounting very exciting, and that includes most accountants that I've met.

"Is your husband here, Lori?" Cathy asked.

"Yes," she waved her hand toward the center of the room. "He's over there talking with the Brownings."

I turned and searched for the mayor's portly figure. "Ian Browning?" I asked.

"Don't I wish," Lori said. "*That* would make it a party." She put her hand on my arm. "Have you met him? He is"—she looked around, then leaned closer—"*hot*. But no, last I saw, hubby was glad-handing the senior set." She let out an exaggerated sigh then adopted a dour expression. "Very important people."

Cathy laughed and tapped the rim of Lori's glass. "How many of these have you had?"

"Almost enough to get through this stuffy party," she said, taking another swig. "Why, you want one?" She turned to look for a server.

"None for me," Cathy said. "Nursing mother."

"Liz, Liz, Lizzie, try one," Lori said, then snatched one off a nearby tray and stuck it into my hand before I could respond.

"Thanks," I said with a practiced smile. Had Lori been sober, she'd have remembered that I'm an ardent teetotaler. Not quite ready to march for prohibition, and not that I wanted to rain on anybody else's parade (an expression I preferred to "pooping" at their parties), but being brought up in a home with one alcoholic parent had influenced my feelings toward drinking. During my few experiments in college, I didn't find the loss of self-control and good judgment fun, nor did I find the slurred speech or slow wit of my less sober classmates charming, which made keeping up a cheerful countenance at this kind of party even harder. Maybe I *was* the proverbial pooper.

I stared down at the drink in my hand. "If you'll excuse me for a moment, I'd like to check out the buffet."

As soon as I was out of their sight, I deserted the drink on a side table and headed toward the food. Now I was in more familiar territory, and they'd laid out quite a spread. I picked up a plate and started loading it with fruit, cheese, and a couple of meatballs. Okay, six meatballs. But there were three kinds, so just a couple of each. And I was only halfway through the line.

I licked a bit of sauce from my thumb and turned to the gentleman behind me in line. "Open bar and this kind of buffet? How are they going to raise any kind of money with people just bringing one bag of feed?"

He chuckled at my remark and pointed at the door prize table. "Did you put your name in for a prize?"

"Not yet," I said.

"If you do, they hit you up for another donation. And, of course, the speeches are designed to pull at the heartstrings and open the wallets, too."

"Speeches?" I yawned just at the prospect. "I don't know if I can stay awake for any long-winded speeches."

Then I turned and truly took in my new companion for the first time. The first word that sprang to mind was dapper, but then again, I watch a lot of old movies. He wore a tux, and it wasn't one of those rental numbers, either, where they *mostly* fit. This had been tailored to his trim figure. I wouldn't call his face handsome—he was no Cary Grant—but his features were pleasing enough. His hair was a bit on the disheveled, sandy side, and his nose a tad crooked, but he carried both with that self-assured way that said he was comfortable with himself, and that made him attractive.

"I'll see what I can do about that," he said.

Seconds later, the lights flickered, and a few ting-a-lings on glasses focused all attention on a small podium. I took my plate and ducked through the gathering crowd to find Cathy and wait out the speeches. She sidled up to me and snagged one of my meatballs.

After a brief comment—okay, ten minutes, but for our mayor, that's brief—he introduced Ian Browning, chairman of the Browning Foundation.

And yes, it was my tuxedoed friend from the buffet. I tried to replay our conversation in my head to see how badly I'd embarrassed myself.

He took the mic and opened with, "I've been encouraged to keep the speeches short tonight." He winked at me and I could feel my cheeks flare. "But I do want to say a few words."

He went on to talk about the kinds of kids the stables would serve, offering therapy to the disabled and mentally challenged, and how horses help some kids open up and deal with ugly realities. I'm not sure if it was his personal charisma, the artfulness of the speech, or the worthiness of the cause, but you could almost hear purse strings loosen by the time he wrapped up only five minutes later.

"And I've been told that no, we can't be making any money holding this kind of party for only horse feed."

He paused while a few people chuckled.

"So, my friends, tonight eat, drink, and be merry, but please consider what you can do for this place"—he gestured around the barn—"but especially those kids. Thank you."

Speech done, he made his way directly toward me. "I clocked it at five minutes. Short enough?" But he said it with a wink.

"I'm so sorry." I closed my eyes. "I didn't realize." I squinted one eye open. "I feel like an idiot."

He laughed. "I appreciate your candor. I don't get enough of it." He held out his hand. "As you may have guessed, I'm Ian Browning. Call me Ian."

I shook his offered hand. "Liz. Liz McCall." Then I somehow had the presence of mind to introduce Cathy and Mark.

Ian pumped Mark's hand. "You look familiar."

"I get out to a few of these things," Mark said.

"What do you do?" Ian asked him.

"I'm an accountant," Mark said vaguely.

"Ah," Ian said, "good place to drum up business." He leaned closer. "Lots of these folks are loaded."

"You don't say," Mark said, as if the thought had never occurred to him.

"You two don't mind if I steal Liz for a moment, do you?" Without waiting for an answer, Ian took my arm and started leading me across the room.

"What's this about?" I asked.

He put a hand up, then opened a door that led outside to a dressage area. "Private tour."

We strolled a path to a nearby corral where the horses were apparently waiting to be allowed to return to their borrowed digs. He leaned against the fence. "Aren't they something?"

I looked at the horses. Their sleek hair caught reflections from the moon, even as their breath frosted in the chill night air. "You sold me. It sounds like such a great program. There's something calming, just being out here with them." I unconsciously rubbed my bare arms against the cold.

Moments later, Ian tucked his tuxedo jacket around my shoulders. "Sorry. I thought you might enjoy a little equine therapy of your own. I didn't notice that you weren't dressed for the cold."

"If it had been up to me, I'd be wearing boots and a heavy sweater. Fortunately, Cathy set me straight."

"If Cathy put you in that dress, I'll have to thank her. So what brings you to our stuffy little party?"

"I didn't call it stuffy."

"But you thought it, and you're not alone. And you're a first-timer. I thought I'd met most of the girls in town. Have you lived here long?"

"Most of my life," I said. "Although I did move away briefly after college, but I came back when my father retired."

"McCall." He snapped his fingers. "With the police?"

"He was. I guess now he is again, but temporarily."

"And don't think I didn't notice that you never answered my question."

"What question?"

"What brought you to our stuffy little party?"

"I never called it—"

He shot me a warning look that broke into a throaty chuckle.

"Fine, since you like candor, I'll tell you. Cathy and I mainly came here to try to meet you."

"Hmm." He leaned against the fence. "To meet me as the suave, man-about-town bachelor that I am? Or as head of the Browning Foundation?"

I winced. "As head of the Browning Foundation, if you want me to be completely honest."

"I take it you have some charitable cause that needs funding."

I opened my mouth to start the pitch Cathy made me memorize, but Ian put a silencing finger on my lips.

"Please," he said, "not in front of the horses. It would be a terrible waste of moonlight. And if you'll allow me to borrow a corny line from the old crooners, moonlight becomes you."

My earlier chill subsided, but I wasn't sure if I was blushing from the compliment or from some developing attraction to Ian. Or perhaps it was merely his physical closeness that caused the apparent spike in the mercury level. "Now, Mr. Browning," I pushed him back. "I've been warned that you have a certain reputation as a playboy."

"Totally undeserved." He drew back and put up his hands. "It's true that I've dated a lot, but it's because I haven't found the right woman yet. It seems my family's money, if you want *me* to be completely honest, has made me a magnet for that species known as the *aurum fossarious domesticus*, otherwise known as the common gold digger. Came *this close* to marrying one once." He shuddered. "We let her keep the china she'd picked out. Some of the species are particularly good at camouflage." He squinted at me. "It's why I prize candor."

"I don't know what to say."

"Say you'll go out with me."

"What?"

"Go out with me. On a date. It can't be an uncommon request. You're not married or engaged or something."

"No."

"Then go out with me. No strings. If we hit it off, we'll call it a date. If we don't, you can pitch your charitable idea, and I promise I'll listen without prejudice. Deal?" He held out his hand, and I stared at it for a moment.

Ian Browning wasn't like any of the men I'd ever been attracted to. To put it bluntly, he was way out of my league, and I suspected he'd realize that soon enough. But then I'd get to pitch our idea to him, anyway. And Cathy would kill me if I'd turned down such an opportunity.

I pumped his hand once. "Deal."

Chapter 7

When I finally dragged myself out of bed the next morning, Dad was already gone. He'd left half a pot of coffee and a plate of cold bacon on the counter covered with a paper towel. Or at least, that's what I think he'd been going for. In reality, I found a shredded paper towel on the floor and some ragged looking partial strips of bacon still on the plate, mingled with a few telltale black cat hairs.

"Val?" I called out. Not that I expected her to come. I found her sitting impudently on top of the refrigerator, licking her paws.

"I should take you to the vet just for spite."

She paused for a moment as if considering my words, then went right on licking while I tossed the rest of the bacon into the trash and dug out my phone to look up whether bacon was safe for cats.

That's when I saw the texts. Three from Ian. I'd half expected them to say, "Never mind. Just fooling with you." But instead, he seemed more determined than ever to have this date. I left his texts for later, once the caffeine hit.

I clicked on the text from Mark.

Bachelor and the Bobby Soxer *is playing at the Aurora Monday night. I know you're a Cary Grant fan. Care to go?*

I slid my phone away and buried my heavy head on the table.

Ian *and* Mark. Great. Not only was the universe stingy when it threw men in my direction, but when it finally did, they came two at a time. Kind of like that phenomenon where you can only find a job when you already have one.

I drummed my fingers on the table. What *did* I want?

The answer came like a shot: more coffee.

# # #

I was still drying my hair after a leisurely morning and a late shower when Dad returned. He poked his head in the bathroom door.

I must have jumped half a foot. I bobbled the hair dryer and managed to catch it before it hit the floor. I turned it off. "Don't you have a murder investigation?"

"Yeah, but it's Parker's birthday."

A wad of unresolved hurt feelings welled to the surface and lodged in my throat. "You've missed plenty of birthdays."

He shoved his hands into his pockets and paused before answering. "Very true. And no, this is not favoritism. You know I've missed plenty of Parker's important moments, too."

"Then what gives?"

"Maybe Mars and Jupiter have aligned. Or maybe my

priorities have. The older and hopefully the wiser I get, the more I value family over work."

"But this investigation . . ."

"Is important," he said. "But it's not going anywhere, and I have a capable department working on it. So when do you want to head over to Parker and Cathy's?"

I unplugged the hair dryer and wrapped the cord around the handle. "We have some time yet. Cathy said sometime in the afternoon."

"Good. I brought home lunch. I thought you and I could have a talk."

"I'll be right out." I shooed him away, stalling. "And if lunch is in the kitchen, you'd better keep an eye on it. Val's up to her old tricks."

Dad turned toward the kitchen, and then started yelling. "Val, get down!" As if she would listen.

I closed the door and took a deep breath. Not sure what Dad wanted to talk about, but since East Aurora is a small town, he'd probably already heard about last night's adventures. While I stalled, I scrunched up my curls with some goopy gel. I simplified my makeup routine, going instead for light powder, mainly on the nose, and a tiny bit of blush that played well with the magenta tunic I'd put on. Comfy jeans. Funky Christmas socks. Sneakers.

This was me.

I was no dewy-eyed eighteen-year-old in a mad rush to get to the altar, nor was I an old maid, destined to live a solitary, lonely existence. I had much to fill my life, to fulfill my life. And if any man was going to enter this equation and upset the fragile balance, he'd better be worth it.

Yes, it took a while, but I was comfortable in my own skin. I smiled in the mirror. And the mirror smiled back.

Maybe just a touch more blush.

# # #

For lunch, Dad had gone all out. Beef on weck from Wallace's. He'd even put the sandwiches on real plates, instead of just unfolding the paper wrappers. He poured two glasses of Pepsi over ice. For Dad, this was fine dining.

"Do I need reservations?"

He smirked at me then pulled out my chair. "I'm afraid all the reservations are mine today."

I took a fortifying breath and sat. This free lunch would cost me. "How's the investigation going?"

He cocked his head but didn't answer, code for either "I'm not allowed to talk about it," or "I'm not going to talk about it." So lunch started with a deafening silence. He waited until I was two bites in before he broached another subject. "A little bird said you met Ian Browning last night."

"Did Cathy have much else to say about it?"

"Cathy didn't tell me," he said, shaking his head. "First thing this morning, I hadn't had a chance to meet with the men yet, and the mayor shows up at my desk. Does he want to know how the case is going? How his police chief is holding up? No. He wants to know if it's serious between my daughter and Ian Browning. And there I am with egg on my face, perhaps literally because he caught me in the middle of eating my breakfast sandwich, and I had to tell him I knew nothing about you and Ian."

"The mayor?" I leaned my elbows on the table. "What business is it of his who I date?"

"So you are dating him?"

"He may have asked me out." I tried to take a casual bite, but Jack's sandwiches were so generous that I found this nearly impossible.

Dad wiped his fingers and took a long drink before responding. "I think we need to have a talk."

"About boys?" I quipped. "We had that talk years ago. It was confusing then."

"About the Brownings."

"I know we don't exactly move in the same social circles," I said.

"That's not what bothers me." He bit his lower lip before continuing. "Without getting into too many details, the mayor is concerned about a Browning dating the daughter of the current chief of police. That's all. But I admit, I have my own concerns."

"I know Ian has a bit of a reputation as a playboy."

"I wish it were only *his* reputation I was concerned about."

My head jerked up. "Meaning?"

Dad rubbed his hands together, as if he were kneading out his next words. "The Browning family is one of the oldest and wealthiest in our community. And the most generous to local charities."

"So the mayor is afraid of ruffling feathers."

Dad closed his eyes. "Without going into too many details, the Browning family has also been the target of recent allegations, and may or may not be currently under investigation."

"Under investigation for . . ."

"I'm not at liberty to say." He drummed the table. "But one could *imagine* with a family that rich and powerful, allegations might be made if certain bids get accepted over others, or if

65

zoning restrictions are lifted, or if red tape seems to disappear when they approach the right people."

I quirked an eyebrow. "So fraud, racketeering, and bribery?"

"Wow, you have a good imagination." His face had remained grim, but a slight twinkle of pride in his eyes betrayed him.

"And this investigation includes the whole family?"

"I never said there was an investigation," he hedged.

"Could one *imagine* this investigation includes the whole family?"

Dad shrugged. "Mainly Ian's father. I imagine. Remember, no charges have been filed, and nothing has been proven. Nor did I confirm that there was an investigation."

"Is that who Mark Baker was watching at the party?"

"Mark was there?"

I nodded once.

"Possibly. I'm not privy to any FBI involvement."

I traced the rim of my glass with my finger. I found it disturbingly coincidental that Mark's sudden interest in me came so quickly on the heels of my meeting with Ian Browning. Was Mark interested in me? Or just what info I could get about Ian's family?

I pushed away the half-eaten sandwich, my appetite gone. "Seems a whole lot of people in this town are more interested in me dating Ian than I am. Should I just cancel?"

"That's up to you. I just didn't want you to be swept off your feet before you knew the score."

"Or before I could *imagine* the score."

"And if you do see him, I'd appreciate it if he didn't know of this conversation."

"What conversation?"

He patted my hand. "Good girl."

"And now that you know I can be discreet, perhaps you could give me a little hint as to how the murder investigation is going?"

His shoulders stiffened. "I'm afraid that wouldn't be appropriate, other than to say it's a huge can of worms." He let his hand rest on mine. "Life sure has gotten a whole lot more complicated since I used to bounce you on my knee." His eyes glistened ever so slightly. "Even though you'll always be my little girl, I want you to know I'm proud of the woman you've become."

"But you're still not going to tell me anything."

He tapped my chin. "Not on your life."

# # #

After lunch, Dad returned to the station for a "few hours," but had promised to meet me at Parker's later. Before picking up his birthday cake at a local bakery, I wanted to check in at the shop. Not that I didn't trust Amanda and Miles, but as official manager, I thought I should at least poke my head in and make sure the place wasn't burning down or anything.

"No, no, no!" Amanda tried to shoo me out of the shop. "A day off is a day off!"

I put my hands up. "I'm not working. How's everything going?"

Miles looked up from his laptop at the counter. "We've had a few people in. In fact, we finally sold that old *Bonanza* action figure."

"Hoss is gone?" I felt a tinge of sadness. TV westerns were a favorite of my father's and something I'd grown up with, and Hoss had been my favorite Cartwright brother. Well, at least after Little Joe, he was cute. And Adam was smart. But

Hoss? Hoss was kind, and that put him right up there in my book.

The next thing I knew, Amanda waved a hand in front of my face. "Earth to Liz."

"Sorry." I startled out of my daydream. "A little short on sleep lately."

"I heard you had another late night last night," she said airily.

I laid a hand on her arm. "What did *you* hear?"

"Just that you hit it off with the town's most eligible bachelor."

"Where did you hear this?"

"Jack."

"Where did Jack hear?"

"From said bachelor. Apparently Ian came to the job site this morning and they had a nice little chat. Really, Liz, I know you and Jack are history—and for that I'm personally grateful—but you could have given the man a heads up that you were seeing one of his oldest friends."

"I'm not seeing him. Well, I guess we have one date coming up, and not really a *date* date. Well, it might be a *date* date, but it's certainly not fodder for the town's gossip network."

Amanda blushed.

"How many people?"

"A few may have stopped in to ask about it. Or casually mention it, to see if we might supply a few details. Which, of course, we couldn't, because we had to tell them that we didn't know anything about it."

"I still say we should have made up something juicy," Miles said. "I wanted to tell them that you had eloped to Peru and were having his love child. Or better yet, twins."

"Why Peru?" I asked. "Twins, *what*?"

"The more details you add, the more people tend to believe you. Up to a point, that is," he said.

"I appreciate that you didn't add to the nonstory. If anyone else hints around, just tell them there's nothing to it."

Amanda saluted. "Any other orders?"

"Just keep doing what you're doing." I looked over at Miles, still behind his computer. "Unless you're playing Words with Friends or something on the company dime," I teased.

He turned around his computer to show me an online auction page of doll heads. "Just trying to source some parts for Cathy's new pet project."

I averted my gaze. "Better you than me. Carry on, then. Dad and I will be at Parker and Cathy's. If you need us, call." And then I considered Miles's prowess at online research.

"Miles?" I asked. "Do you think you could look up something for me?"

"My Google-fu is at your disposal. Want me to search for hidden skeletons in your new boyfriend's closet?"

"Not exactly." I leaned in closer. "Marya Young. I want to know what you can find out about her life before she moved here. There's a rumor that she was an illegal alien. And I'm curious if there's any truth to that and when she came to this country. Has she been in any trouble? Anything you can dig up."

"Liz." Miles looked uncomfortable with my request. "You know I like helping, but is this a secret from your father? Because I think that man can read minds."

"I wouldn't mention it unless he asks," I said, "but if he does, you can say I twisted your arm."

He held out his arm, and I gave it a slight pivot.

"Gotcha."

# # #

It was Parker's first birthday as a father, and he held Drew in his lap while we sang to him, but Dad took the boy before Parker leaned in to blow out the candles. Cathy snapped pictures of the whole thing on her cell phone and paused to wipe an errant tear from her eyes. It was hard to imagine that just a year ago she'd been nervous to tell him they were expecting, and now Parker and Drew were best buds.

Dad had arrived half an hour after he'd promised and seemed distracted. We played a newer game that Parker had unwrapped for his birthday, Lost Cities. The premise was that we each had a team of explorers looking for artifacts and the game had a nice blend of chance and strategy. Once we worked through a practice round, we were all hooked. Or "digging it" as Dad deadpanned.

But around seven, his phone started going off, and his eyebrows furrowed at the most recent text.

"It's okay, Dad," Parker said. "I know that face. You're needed."

"You sure?" he asked, already out of his chair.

Parker laid a hand on Dad's arm, then hugged him. "I'm so glad you came."

Dad paused only long enough to rub Drew's head before waving goodbye to Cathy and me and heading out.

I crossed my arms. "There's a familiar sight."

"Now, Liz," Parker admonished as we heard Dad's engine start. "He stayed longer than I thought he would, considering."

"Has he mentioned the case to you at all?" Cathy asked.

"No, he's left me completely out of the loop."

Cathy slid back into her chair at the table. "You can see

why, can't you? After all, he's leading the investigation, and you and Ken were once . . . intimate."

I laughed. "Ken and I were never intimate. At least in the sense I think you mean. Look, I understand why Dad's not talking to me. He really shouldn't be."

She leaned her chin on her fist. "But that bothers you?"

"Absolutely."

She raised her eyes. "Why?"

"Okay, Sigmund. What are you after? Yes, I'm upset that Dad is back working. I almost lost him once. When he retired, I thought everything would be different."

"Liz." Parker slid back into his chair. "This is how it's always been."

"But this isn't how he promised it would be."

"He's worked other cases since he retired," Cathy said.

"Unofficially," I added. "Temporarily."

"This is supposed to be temporary," Cathy said. "Just until they figure out if—"

"If Ken killed his wife?" I asked. I could feel the emotion welling up again.

"Are you concerned about Dad or Ken?" Parker asked.

I stared down at my fingers and picked at a cuticle. "I've worked hard to get over Ken. And I think I succeeded, mostly. Only now I can't help feeling sorry for him." I raised my face, even as I felt hot tears in the corners of my eyes. "You didn't see him go into that empty house."

"It's sympathy?" Cathy asked.

I inhaled deeply. "I hope so. All my emotions are just so jumbled. I keep thinking that if I could help, I'd feel better."

"Help Dad or help Ken?" Cathy asked, her voice trembling as she bounced Drew on her lap.

"If Ken's innocent, that's the same thing, right?"

Cathy didn't answer but sent a questioning look in Parker's direction.

It had to be the same thing.

# # #

Dad hadn't returned home by ten, but I was determined to try once more to pry info out of him. So I stole a page from his playbook, from back when I was a teenager. A chair against the door—with some tin cans and metal pie plates balance precariously on the edge—alerted me to his homecoming just before three in the morning.

I staggered down the hall in my pajamas.

Dad was picking up the cans when I hit the kitchen. "What was that for?"

I crossed my arms. "What time was curfew, mister?"

"Liz," he collapsed into the chair and untied his shoes. His shoulders were hunched, his hair mussed, and his face pasty with dark circles growing under his eyes. "I don't have time for whatever this is. I'm so tired, and I only have a few hours before I have to be back."

"Have you eaten?"

"Yeah." He leaned his elbows on the table. "Look, I know you're curious."

"Dad, not just curious. I want to help. I can't sit home doing nothing when you're out killing yourself."

"Not killing myself."

"Look in a mirror on the way to bed and try saying that. Look, I know this is what it takes to solve a case, and I know this is how you're used to working, but you're not as young as you once were."

Dad made a shocked sound, as if this was news to him.

I slapped his arm. "Don't make light of this."

He yawned. "And you want to help me *how*?"

"If you haven't eaten, there's a plate in the fridge that just needs microwaving. I have a fresh uniform pressed and hanging on your bedroom door. And a lunch and some healthy snacks packed and ready to go."

"And?"

"And . . ." I swallowed hard to get up the courage to say what I hoped to get out. "I have helped you in the past. You've told me as much. Said I had a good mind for detection."

He began dramatically wagging his head.

I put a finger up. "Use me as a sounding board. A sanity check. I won't say anything, and you don't have to tell anyone that you've shared anything with me."

"If it got out . . ."

"It would be using all of your resources to get at the truth while making sure Ken gets a fair shake. Unpaid consultant?"

He stared at me under drooping eyelids then reached into his bag, pulled out a couple of file folders, and slid them on the table. "I brought these home to look through. Under no circumstances are you to touch them."

I leaned forward. "Pottergate?"

He closed his eyes. "I'm going to bed."

Chapter 8

Pottergate, for those unfamiliar with the term, which is just about everybody outside our immediate family circle, refers to the controversy surrounding me bringing in the first Harry Potter book that ever entered the McCall family dwelling.

Mom had just finished up another rehab, this time a religious-based program that seemed to last longer than a few of the others. The only problem was that now she was not only against the devil of drink, but a host of other gateway things that could "open up our home to evil." She burned Dad's collectible Ouija board with some ceremony. Out went the Magic 8-Ball, since apparently it had roots in fortune telling. Also out went playing cards, her favorite soap operas, and all our videos except those with a G-rating. Cabbage Patch Kids could reportedly be possessed, at least according to her counselor (might be some root to my doll phobia right there), so they were bagged up and trucked off. *Scooby-Doo* had ghosts and was therefore not suitable entertainment, nor was *I Dream of Jeannie* or especially *Bewitched,* since apparently all witches should be burned.

Into this mix, I'd brought home a boy wizard named Harry. Mom had gone nearly apoplectic. I'd argued that I had to write a book report. Mom had been adamant. Dad had stood between us like Moses holding back the raging waters of the Red Sea.

"Here's what we're going to do," he said. "I'll read the book and decide if it's appropriate."

Before Mom could say a word, he shot her a warning look. Since Pastor Bob down at the church also encouraged her to be a submissive wife, she'd pinned her lips together so tight they turned white.

Dad had wagged a finger at me. "And you are not to touch the book until I do. Hear?"

"Yes, sir," I'd said, wondering when exactly he'd get around to it and how flexible my teacher would be about the due date.

On my bed that night I found a brown paper bag containing the book, a pair of evidence gloves and two knitting needles. At first it was awkward turning pages with the limited dexterity of the gloves, but it didn't take long to figure out that was what the knitting needles were for. And, happy to say, I received an A on my report.

Of course Mom didn't learn about Pottergate until she was well off the wagon several months later, "resting her eyes" while she caught up on *Days of Our Lives*.

So, in that spirit, I hadn't "touched" Dad's files he'd left on the table. Instead, lacking evidence gloves, I'd shoved my hands into plastic sandwich bags and used my cell phone to take pictures of all the pages. There were reports and witness statements that I'd need to be more fully awake to digest, and copies of crime scene photos that were frankly difficult to look at.

Marya had been so beautiful. I'd not given her enough credit. Not only were her features naturally attractive, but always well made up and her clothing fashionably put together.

She would have been appalled by these photos of her sprawled on the floor in the shop surrounded by cut hair.

Cut hair? Didn't stylists generally sweep up after each haircut? Perhaps the hair on the floor could belong to the killer. Had the police considered that? But even squinting at the photograph, I couldn't make out the color of the hair.

I made one mental note to mention that idea to Dad and then finished taking pictures, leaving the file exactly as it had been lying on the table. Untouched. Well, at least by human hands. Othello decided the manila folder looked like a great place for a snooze, and before I left the room, he started curling up on it.

I set my alarm for seven. The shop was closed on Sunday, but my recollection of Pottergate had me thinking about heading to church. Although that church-based rehab program didn't work for Mom, it was still highly popular among those recovering from addiction. And since I recalled all the talk about Marya and her twelve-step program, I wondered if she might have ended up there, too.

Time to pay a visit to Pastor Bob.

# # #

Dad was out of the house before I woke up, and he'd whisked away his precious notes. I found evidence that he'd fed the cats, though Val circled my ankles trying to convince me she hadn't eaten in days. I stroked her sleek fur. "You little liar, you!"

Halfway through my coffee—the caffeine must have pried my eyes open, because I realized I'd never answered Mark about the movies—I texted a noncommittal, "Sounds good." I still doubted his motives, but I was curious if he might be investigating the Brownings. And if he'd let anything slip.

Othello jumped up on the table and nudged my arm, and I scratched his chin. "Yes, because the FBI are known for being loose-lipped."

Othello meowed his assent.

The sun streamed through the apartment windows that morning, so instead of hopping into my car, I put on my boots and decided to hoof it to church.

Main Street was quiet but not deserted. When I passed Lionel Kelley's PI office, the miniblinds were rocking ever so slightly, but there were no sounds or other signs of movement. Perhaps a heating vent by the window?

I pulled my coat tighter, and quickened my pace. The sunlight deceived me. It was *cold*.

Pastor Bob's historic little white church was a block off Main. Its once-grand stained glass had dimmed and showed signs of poor repair, and its siding needed a fresh coat of paint. It had changed names and denominations several times in my lifetime. Now it simply bore the name of Lighthouse Nondenominational Church, and a small lighthouse stood, half buried in snow, in the front lawn next to the peeling, almost unreadable sign.

I was greeted warmly at the door, given a visitor's card and a handful of cheery pamphlets featuring the flames of hell on the cover, and ushered to a pew containing a friendly elderly woman determined to carry on a conversation with me, despite the fact that she couldn't hear anything I said. I was glad when the singing started.

The service proved better than I had anticipated. The congregation sang enthusiastically about the love of God, and when the pastor rose to speak, it wasn't Pastor Bob. The burly gentleman in the pulpit asking people to turn to Colossians— and maybe this was power of suggestion from my conversation with Miles at the store a day earlier—resembled a young Hoss Cartwright. I leafed through the bulletin I'd been handed at the door. Pastor Pete.

And Pastor Pete was rather good. He held my attention, anyway.

After the service, I stood at the tail end of the line to shake his hand. "I wanted to tell you how much I enjoyed your sermon. I didn't realize when I walked in this morning that Pastor Bob wasn't here anymore."

"Ah," he said. "Pastor Bob left maybe six months ago. Is there anything I can help you with?"

"Just something I'd like to ask."

He looked around, but most folks had departed, and nobody competed for his attention. He pointed to a pew in the very back. "Care to sit?"

He folded his long legs under the pew. "What can I help you with, Miss . . ."

"Liz," I said. "Liz McCall. I wanted to ask if you still had the addictions program here at the church."

His smile dimmed a little and I could see his Adam's apple dip as he swallowed hard. "We do. Can I ask what you're having an issue with?"

I closed my eyes. "That came out wrong. I'm not having any issue. See, my mother was with the program a number of years ago."

"And she's relapsed?"

"She did, but she's no longer with us."

"I'm sorry. Was her passing recent?" Confusion washed over his face and I couldn't help but chuckle.

"Maybe I ought to start over," I said. "I was interested in someone I thought might be coming to the program now. Did you know Marya Young?"

"I'm not at liberty to discuss . . ." Then he squinted. "*Did* I? Past tense? Has something happened to Marya?"

"I'm afraid she passed away. You didn't know?"

"Nobody said anything to me. I guess nobody had to. She's not a member here or anything. She just came to the program."

"I'm sorry to break it to you this way. But can you tell me anything about Marya? Was she having any special problems lately?"

He inhaled deeply before answering. "Marya . . . I don't know what to tell you. She came to meetings, but she never said much. It's hard as a pastor to step into someone else's shoes. Some folks were happy I wasn't Pastor Bob; the others seemed to be trying to turn me into him. I gather she opened up more with him. I hoped things would improve over time." Then he sat up straighter. "Before I say anything else, can I ask what your interest is?"

"She was killed next door to our toyshop."

"As in *murdered*?" Pastor Pete sat frozen for a moment, staring into empty space, his face stoic and unreadable. Finally, he licked his lower lip and turned back to me. "I take it you're not part of the investigation."

"Not the official one," I said. "I served with Marya on a charitable committee and knew both her and her husband." Probably overstating my relationship. "Now I'm afraid they're going to suspect Ken."

"Her husband?"

I tapped my fingers on the back of the pew. "I grew up in a cop's house. I know that the victim's significant other is often the first suspect."

"And you don't think he did it."

I let out a frustrated breath. "I thought maybe someone

who knew her well might be able to cast a little light on who else had motive."

Pastor Pete scratched his chin. "Since confidentiality ends at the grave, I will say that Marya's relationship with her husband was a bit turbulent. Marya was terribly jealous of another woman."

"Ken was seeing someone else?"

Pastor Pete gave a brief shrug. "That I couldn't tell you. But dealing with those feelings was crucial. A lot of addicts try to bury their pain in drugs or alcohol."

"What was Marya addicted to?"

"That never came up. I gathered she'd been clean a long time. Said she came to meetings to remind her she needed help to stay that way."

"And do you have any idea who this other woman might be?"

"Marya never mentioned her name, just someone that her husband had begun seeing before she moved here. Marya used to call her 'the brazen hussy,' and only because we told her she couldn't use her original term in church." Pastor Pete chuckled. "Not sure that helps."

Hopefully he didn't notice my cheeks flaring pink. "I think it might." At least that line of questioning was a dead end.

"Other than that, she talked a little about work."

"Problems there?"

"Not that she mentioned. I think she was actually trying to drum up a little business from the women in the group. Handed out coupons. Look, if you're trying to find someone with a reason to kill her, I'm afraid I can't help you much."

As I headed home, I felt a little disappointed with the information.

Yes, the conversation pointed to another person, but since

that brazen hussy was me, I sure hoped that the official investigation wouldn't run along those same lines.

When I passed Kelley's PI office, once again the shades were
swinging. I went to the door and tried the handle but found it
locked tight. I knocked, then strained to hear anything inside
but could make out nothing over the traffic. I tented my eyes to
look inside but could see little through the tinted glass and
lowered shades.

I mentally noted the office hours posted on his door. Lionel
Kelley had been watching someone from that alley behind our
shop. Sooner or later, he and I were going to have a nice little
chat.

# # #

I stayed home just long enough to bake a batch of peanut butter cookies. The apartment felt too quiet with Dad off working
himself to death. Any other time I might have enjoyed the
homey solitude. Instead I felt myself being pulled into action,
as if somewhere a clock was ticking. Or more like a giant hand
winding a jack-in-the-box, and when I least expected it, Detective Reynolds was going to jump out of a closet and arrest me
on charges of being a brazen hussy.

I piled the still-warm cookies onto two plates and loosely
covered both with clean towels, then headed out to my car. I
quickly brushed off a thin layer of snow and headed first to
Ken Young's house.

The brazen hussy comment aside, I hadn't liked the way
he'd sleepwalked into that cold, dark house, and I was concerned for my friend. Minutes later, I pulled into his driveway
behind a red Toyota with North Carolina plates.

The recent snow hadn't been shoveled, but a path had been

worn to his front porch steps. I barely rang the bell before a blonde swung open the door. "I got it," she called in a thick Southern accent to someone else behind her. When she turned back to me, her voice was saccharine: sweet as honey but not quite genuine. "Can I help you?"

I lifted my plate of cookies. "I'm a friend of Ken."

"Aren't you sweet." She pushed open the storm door just wide enough for the plate to pass through.

"And I hoped I might see him," I added.

"What did you say your name was?"

"I'm sorry. I didn't." I tried to laugh off my poor manners. "Liz McCall."

"I don't think so."

"Pardon?" Even as she started to close the door, I wasn't quite sure I heard her right.

"Nancy, for Pete's sake," Ken said from somewhere behind her. "She's a friend of mine. Let her in."

Ken pushed past her and swung the door fully open. "Come on in, Liz."

I stepped into the living room and took a good look around. I'd seen Ken's old apartment, but I'd never been in his house before—and this wasn't exactly Ken's house. This was clearly Ken's and Marya's house, and the couple never had time to marry their styles in a way that worked. His big, chunky granite sectional took up most of the room, and his hunting trophies—always gave me the willies—hung over the fireplace. But lighter touches mingled in, here and there. And a lot of delicate gold and crystal accents—apparently Marya had been a fan of bling—that just looked out of place amid the otherwise woodsy style. As did the glittery aluminum pencil tree in the corner.

When my survey of the room ended, my eyes took in the two

dark-rooted blondes who'd taken positions on either side of Ken, like Secret Service agents, sans the dark glasses. Instead were heavily made up eyes, overplucked eyebrows, and demure expressions as fake as that Nigerian prince who keeps emailing me.

"Liz," Ken said, "I'd like you to meet my sisters, Nancy and Grace."

"Oh, you must get teased a little about that."

"Why?" Nancy said.

"Nancy. Grace. Nancy Grace."

Nancy flashed a cold smile, reminding me more of a dog baring its teeth, while Ken turned back to his sisters. "Liz is a friend of mine."

"So you've said." Nancy eyed me up and down. She handed the plate of cookies to Grace who set them on the coffee table.

"Come, sit," Ken said, waving us all to the sectional, where his sisters took the same positions on either side of him, leaving me the small accent chair halfway across the room.

I turned to Nancy, who seemed to be the spokesperson. "I saw the North Carolina plates. You made good time getting here."

"We couldn't leave Kenny to deal with this all by himself," she said.

Ken pitched forward in his seat. "Have you heard anything about the investigation?"

"Bits and pieces," I said. "Not enough to be of any help. I hoped you might have news."

He shook his head. "I've been going over everything backwards and forwards, a million different ways 'til Sunday, and I'm coming up blank. I have no idea who might have wanted her dead."

"I'm assuming they've interviewed you," I said.

"If you ask me, they could have been a little nicer about it," Nancy said.

Grace seconded.

"They grilled him for hours. Hours! And with him in such grief. That temporary police chief should be ashamed of himself." She scrunched up her face.

Grace gave a decided nod.

"That police chief is Liz's father," Ken said, "so . . ."

Nancy waved it off. "That explains that, bless her heart."

"I'm sorry?" I said. I could tell she was miffed, so I assumed it wasn't the good "bless her heart," but I wasn't quite sure what "that" explained.

"He didn't squeeze enough blood from the turnip so he sends you over here to finish the job."

"My dad didn't send me," I said.

"Did you call me a turnip?" Ken said.

Grace just nodded.

"Look, I'm just trying to—" Nancy started, but Ken silenced her like a conductor ending a symphony.

"I know what you're trying to do," Ken said, "but I don't need you two protecting me. I'm a big boy and can take care of myself."

Nancy sank back in her seat, silent but looking unconvinced.

Grace continued to nod as if on autopilot.

I stood up. "If I'm intruding, perhaps I should go."

Ken stood up too, but nobody said the obligatory, "Oh, you're not intruding." I'd never even removed my coat.

"I'll walk you out," Ken said, shooting a warning look at his sisters.

I waited by the door while he shoved his bare feet into slippers.

"A bit stuffy in there," Ken said, pulling the door shut behind us. "Sorry about that. I'm afraid they're not going to be very pleasant to you. They know I was seeing you before Marya came. To them . . ."

"I was a potential home wrecker."

"I told them that you didn't even know about her, but I'm not sure they believe me. I'm afraid Marya had them bamboozled into thinking she was the love of my life. I never saw the need to enlighten them into the reasons for our separation. Maybe that was my mistake, one of them, anyhow. I'm sure they were just trying to help."

"I'll do my best to stay out of their way. I was worried about how you were doing, and I baked cookies."

"Appreciated." He took my hand and held it. "Thanks so much. And if you do hear anything about the investigation that might help, will you tell me? I'm being smothered alive here."

"How about I text you?" I pulled my hand back. "They still allow you to use the telephone and all, right?"

"As long as it's before nine." He rolled his eyes.

"You poor thing. But at least you have someone to look after you."

He glanced back at the house, where Nancy had pulled back the drapes and was watching us. "If I survive it."

Chapter 9

When I climbed out of bed Monday morning, I found Dad's damp towel in the hamper and his empty coffee cup in the sink. They were the only evidence that he had been there at all, and I doubted it would hold up in court.

So when it was time to open up the shop, I headed down to make sure Cathy had arrived and could handle everything.

She came out of the doll room with wide eyes and a scary, plastic smile.

"If the next words out of your mouth," I said, "have anything to do with that creepy Russian doll turning around on her own again, please don't say them."

She ran an imaginary zipper across her lips, and a chill shot up my back. Toys were supposed to be fun, cute, innocuous. Somehow our shop had become a magnet for the spooky ones.

I did my best to shrug it off then went back to the apartment to bake orange-cranberry muffins. I had two goals for this baking spree. First, Dad needed to eat, and second, it gave me an excuse to go to the station to see what I could pick up from the investigation.

But the walk to the station took me past Lionel Kelley's office, and when his pulled shades fluttered again, I went straight to the front door.

Not sure what I expected to see inside. An office perhaps? But only if that office belonged to Q, James Bond's gadget man, not the omniscient alien from *Star Trek: The Next Generation*. While I took in the scenery, Lionel made a valiant effort to conceal something behind his back.

"Who are you watching, Lionel?" My words were more demanding than usual, but they seemed to do the trick.

"Not you, if that's what you mean."

"That's not what I asked," I said.

"I'm afraid I'm not at liberty—"

"Don't play that card with me," I said. "Marya Young is dead, and if your surveillance has anything to do with—"

"It doesn't." He sucked in his upper lip. "At least, I don't think it does."

I inched forward, until I could partially see what he had behind his back—a video camera.

"What have you got there?" I then went to his window to see where that camera might have been focused, and found myself looking at the toyshop and barber shop.

"How long have you been recording?"

"Off and on, about a week."

"A week? Lionel! You could have something on there that might help the police. You need to tell them."

"They'd take it from me." He sat back on the corner of his desk. "It's hard enough to make a go of it in this town without the police confiscating all your work. Liz, if I lose this client . . ."

"It looks like you're doing okay." I gestured around the

office. "Look at all this cool gadgetry." I picked up a small camera with a flexible tube. "Do it yourself colonoscopy?"

"That's great for seeing into small spaces and going around corners and stuff." His trademark smirk faded. "I haven't actually used it yet. Mom thought . . ." He hung his head. "Go ahead. Laugh at me. My mother bought it. She bought most of this stuff."

"I'm not going to laugh at you," I said.

"But please don't tell your father about the footage."

"Look, I think you should take it to him and let him worry about whether it contains any useful evidence."

He opened his mouth to protest, but I silenced him. "If you're worried about losing it, make a copy first."

"If I need it for a trial, not sure they're going to accept a copy."

"Trial? What *are* you working on?"

Kelley ran an imaginary zipper across his lips.

I paced his office then spun back to face him. "Would you make *me* a copy? Because, you know, I *could* tell my father you have it, and he *could* get a search warrant and take it."

Kelley crossed his arms in front of him. "Not sure he'd have the grounds."

I wetted my lips. "And then there's the matter of that 2007 Pinkie Pie I found for you."

I let that sink in. Few people outside the shop knew that Kelley was a closeted brony, an adult male fan of *My Little Pony*. There was nothing wrong with this, of course, but since he'd gone to great lengths to keep it hidden thus far, it was leverage.

"You wouldn't."

I quirked an eyebrow. "A copy?"

He stared down at the stylish blue-and-gray carpet tiles that I suspected his mother also had picked out, then looked up. "Do something for me first? A trade?"

"What is it?"

"I need someone to do a little undercover work. Just one assignment."

"Me? Work for you? Is it dangerous? Dark alleys, shady characters?"

He laughed off my question. "Not. At. All. But it will take you into no-man's-land."

I squinted at him. "Tell me about this undercover assignment."

# # #

Dad wasn't in the station when I dropped off the muffins. And his men were noticeably tight-lipped during my brief visit. Did they not want to involve me because Ken was a suspect? Or because *I* was?

I was almost out the door when Howard Reynolds rounded the corner. "Good morning, Miss McCall. You have a minute?"

"What's up?"

"How about we go someplace quiet?" He gestured toward the conference/interrogation room.

"Am I a suspect?" I asked, as soon as he closed the door. If the location was meant to intimidate me, Reynolds failed. Dad used to send me into the empty room to do my homework ever since grade school, so I was in familiar territory. "Does my father know you're talking to me?"

"He's the one who suggested it." Instead of taking the seat opposite of me, Reynolds perched on the corner of the table. I suspect the move was meant to come across as casual, friendly even, while giving him a height advantage. Interrogation feng shui. "You must have figured out that we'd need a statement from you."

"I thought my father might . . ."

He shook his head. "Not appropriate considering your relationship. And please understand I'm probably as uncomfortable with this as you are." I could see the investigation was already taking a toll on him. His smile, when he remembered to don it, was practiced and didn't quite reach his eyes, which were glassy and heavy-lidded from lack of sleep.

"Fine," I said. "I'd be glad to answer any questions you have." I looked at his empty hands. "Do you need to take notes?"

"Nah," he said, gesturing toward the corner of the room. "We have the video camera."

There were no surprise questions. Did I have an alibi? No. What was my relationship to Marya, and to Ken? That was fun to answer, but it was nothing the whole town didn't already know. Did I have any conflict with Marya? I could truthfully answer no.

And did I know if Ken had any conflict with Marya? That's where I was compelled to relate the argument that I'd overheard through the walls. Could I think of anyone else who might have had motive to kill Marya?

"Sorry, I've been racking my brain trying to come up with something. I don't think I knew her well enough to answer that."

"That seems to be everyone's answer to that question," he said. "Thanks for coming. Just be available if we have any more questions."

I assured him I would, and as I shrugged on my coat, I let that sink in. That last question was designed to generate more leads, more suspects than Ken—or me. And right now they had none.

When I stepped out of the station, I filled my lungs with invigorating, frigid air. The stakes were never higher and I needed to focus. After all, I had a new mission of my own. I was going undercover.

A couple of hours later I felt substantially less James Bond-ish as I mounted the library steps.

By no-man's-land, Kelley had meant that no *men* attended this particular event, so he needed a woman. What he'd failed to tell me, and what became painfully obvious as I poked my head into the small meeting room just off the lobby, was that no woman under the age of sixty attended this event, either.

The room was full of elderly women. Blue-hairs, some folks call them. A few were already seated at tables around the room, others still standing, some with the help of canes and walkers. Usually this was an age group I got along with pretty well. But these women started whispering amongst themselves the moment they saw me.

"What's she doing here?"

"She can't stay, can she?"

"What do the rules say?"

When the hard-of-hearing start whispering, what they're talking about seldom remains a secret for long.

I stood up straighter. Lionel Kelley had said he didn't exactly know what this group did, only that they met here at this particular time every Monday morning at ten. Might be one of the least friendly book clubs around.

"Am I welcome?" I finally asked, flashing my best innocu-ous smile.

A woman who'd been paging through a folder flipped it

shut and tossed it on a table. "Nothing in the rules against it."
But she sounded as if the rules committee would be holding an
emergency meeting PDQ.

"It's not fair," another woman complained. "Hard enough
as it is without someone sending in a ringer."

I wondered about the frigid response when the folder lady
told everyone to take their places. I got stuck behind a woman
with a walker, but within moments all the women staked out
their spots, each at a separate small table. With some misgiv-
ings, I did the same.

When everyone was seated, Folder Lady went to the corner
of the room and unlatched a dividing wall. The motorized wall
retracted to reveal maybe a dozen or so geriatric men standing
on the opposite side.

"Good morning," Folder Lady said. "And welcome to
senior speed dating!"

She hadn't finished her sentence when a round man with
two tufts of dark hair over each ear—separated by a dome so
shiny I could do my makeup in it—pulled out the other chair
at my table, then leaned in so close I could smell the Bengay.
"Hi, cookie. I'm Lance."

I plastered on a grin. "Hi, Lance."

I managed to maintain that smile until refreshment time.
And Lionel would be pleased. Not only did I discover the mysterious purpose of this meeting, but I could deliver the names
and phone numbers of every single man present in the room.

But I barely had time to swallow my snickerdoodle when
Lance and a few others headed in my direction. I managed to
elude them—mainly because I might have been the only attendee
without arthritis or gout—and ducked into the ladies room.

Two of the senior ladies followed me in.

"I have to apologize," I said. "I didn't know what that meeting was all about. I thought it might be some kind of book club."

"Book club meets on Thursday," one of them said. I'd heard another woman address her as Betty.

"I'll keep that in mind," I said. "Sorry for intruding."

"So you're not interested in Lance?" the second one said. "He's a hottie." She leaned in closer. "And he's loaded, you know."

"Really?" Betty asked.

But I put up my hands. "All yours."

"Good, because you know what I'd like to do with Lance?" The second woman proceeded to tell us, in somewhat pornographic detail, and in a whisper so loud that I hoped her words weren't bouncing around the lobby outside.

Betty laughed. "Look at her!" she said pointing at me. "You'll have to forgive Joan. She wrote one of those kinky books and put it on Amazon and now she thinks she's E L James."

"I'll have you know my book has twelve five-star reviews," Joan said.

"Oh, you're a writer! You might know my sister-in-law, Cathy McCall?" I said, happily changing the subject.

"Cathy?" Joan said. "We were in a critique group together. I love her work." She thought for a moment, then wagged a finger at me. "Then *you're* the one in the harem costume!"

I put my hands up. "Never happened. That part was totally made up!" So much for changing the subject.

"Where do you think she got the idea?" Joan winked. "But, for someone who can pull off the Dance of the Seven Veils in the same scene where she finds a body? That deserves a prize."

"Like I said, never happened. Except for finding the body."

But Joan rummaged through her purse and pulled out a book and a pen. She hastily scrawled her signature on the title page before handing the book to me.

I glanced at the cover: a scantily clad female clasped close to a bare-chested Asian man, and both were standing behind a table containing a bowl of soup and one fortune cookie. "*Won Ton Desire?*" I read the title.

"A steamy tale of love and desire set against the backdrop of a Chinese restaurant," Joan said. "Which may or may not have been inspired by real-life situations."

Betty rolled her eyes. "Lo mein in all kinds of inappropriate places." She shuddered. "Really killed my taste for Chinese food."

"I couldn't take your book," I said, trying to play hot potato with it.

Joan put her hands up. "It's my pleasure. Besides, I already inscribed it to you."

I opened the cover. Just above her signature it said, "To harem girl."

"Thanks," I said, wishing I'd brought a larger purse with me. "So, you do this every week? The senior speed dating, I mean?"

"Almost every week," Joan said, turning to eye herself in the mirror. She adjusted a lock of hair, then leaned in for a closer look, clucking in disapproval at what she saw. "I was due for a color and perm."

"I know," Betty said, eyeing her own locks. "But I hear they closed the whole place down. Crime scene tape and everything. Not sure when they're going to reopen."

"You talking about Marya?" I asked.

"Yes," Betty said. "Said in the paper this morning that someone killed her."

"You both knew Marya?" I tried to keep my voice casual.

"Oh, yes," Joan said. "She showed up one day just to hand out coupons. The senior discount. Fifty percent off! She cut almost everybody's hair here. Hair here. That's hard to say."

"Or in Lance's case, hair not here," Betty teased. "But he's still hot."

Chapter 10

Before checking in with Lionel Kelley, I returned to the shop to ditch the racy book and put on my manager's hat and make sure everything was running smoothly. I also wanted to discuss Cathy's fiction endeavors with her—and make a plea for her to stop including me in them.

But when I walked in, Miles was also there, bent over his laptop at the counter.

"You're not on the schedule today," I said.

"I called him in." Cathy rushed from the doll room. "With Dad not around, I figured you'd be working the case too, and I needed help."

"But Dad doesn't want me working the case, remember?" I set my stuff on the counter, pulled Drew from his stalled swing, and took him into my arms.

"What's this?" Miles picked up the book.

"Better not," I warned. "I don't think you're old enough."

Cathy moved closer and caught a glimpse of the cover. "Seriously, don't open that one." Cathy squinted at me. "What are *you* doing with it?"

I explained all about senior speed dating and running into the author.

Cathy cocked her head. "I wonder why Kelley sent you there."

"I don't know. He's being very cagey about this whole investigation, but he was convinced something sinister was going on at this meeting. Not sure it's a coincidence, but Marya Young had been there, too, a few weeks back, handing out coupons."

"If it involves that book"—she pointed, but then pulled back her hand as if were covered in toxic slime—"if any part of that is real life, you should probably tell Dad. Or at least the health department." Her face blanched slightly. "Whatever you do, don't read the chapter about the duck sauce. You may never eat Chinese food again."

While we were talking, the bell over the door sounded, and a mother and young daughter came in and wandered into the doll room.

"Duty calls." Cathy went off to see if she could offer help.

I cuddled Drew close and blew a few playful raspberries into his chubby cheek, but remained next to Miles at the counter.

"I suppose," he said, "that you're interested in whether I came up with anything about Marya Young."

"Spot on."

He cracked his knuckles. "Did you have any doubts?"

"What did you find?" I leaned closer.

"On the immigration front, Marya Young was a citizen of these great United States."

"So the illegal immigration thing is a false rumor."

"Not so fast," he said, looking over his hipster glasses. "Immigration status is not something that's all that easy to find. But it seems Marya Young was the subject of a recent

Buffalo News photo, and they included her name in the caption." He turned his laptop to face me, and there was Marya's smiling face amid an eclectic group of all skin tones, many in their native dress. I squinted to read the tiny caption. "Citizenship swearing-in at the Theodore Roosevelt Inaugural Site."

Drew grabbed hold of the corner of Miles's laptop with slimy fingers. I lifted him back up. "Sorry about that."

Miles removed a cloth from his bag and wiped the drool away. "Par for the course when you work with babies or animals. No harm done."

"When was that article published?"

"Two weeks ago."

"Two *weeks*?" Two thoughts struck simultaneously. One, the idea that Irene and Lenora had about her marrying Ken to help in her bid for citizenship might have some validity. And two, it was truly sad that she'd worked and waited for so long, but was only able to enjoy her citizenship status for two weeks.

"Yeah," Miles said, catching my mood.

"Any idea when she moved to the U.S.?"

He tapped the counter. "That's a little trickier. Nobody was taking pictures for the local paper when she arrived. And I haven't found her name in connection with any crimes. Do you know her maiden name?"

"No idea," I said.

"Never mind. I can probably find it on their marriage license if I can narrow the county. Give me another day?"

"Absolutely," I said. "And thanks!"

# # #

Miles's favor deserved some reward, so I called in a take-out order for all of us and walked to Wallace's to get it.

The lunch crowd, as much as there is on a Monday, hadn't hit yet, but as I stood at the counter I heard a familiar pair of voices.

Dad and Mark Baker were seated at a booth, both leaning forward, deep in conversation. Neither man had seen me, nor did they look up as I approached them, so I sank into the adjacent booth, suddenly grateful that my father had never allowed me to go to concerts because my hearing was still fully intact.

"It would be premature to say I was investigating anyone in particular," Mark said. "Can we just leave it at that?"

"As a professional courtesy, would you tell me if any investigation pointed in Ian Browning's direction?"

There was a brief pause. "I can consider your position. Tell you what. I will say that I am not currently investigating Ian Browning. How's that?"

"Slightly reassuring. You don't like him for . . . whatever it is you're investigating?"

"Good fishing attempt. But no, I don't like him for whatever it is I'm investigating. Nor do I like him period. Too oily and self-assured. Is that why you invited me to lunch?"

"Not entirely. I need some advice. A little help on this investigation I'm working on."

"Read about that. That's a whole can of worms. You investigating Young?"

"Have to," Dad said.

"Think he did it?" Mark asked.

Dad let out a long breath. "Things weren't all that rosy in the Young house. He'd been checking up on her. I found evidence of that when we searched the place. He didn't trust her."

"Checking how?"

"Auditing her books, for one thing. He made no secret of that. But he'd also been keeping records of her spending, how much she had in her purse at any given time. How much she spent on clothing and groceries. Even kept a file on her whereabouts as if he had her under surveillance."

"Was he on to something or just whack-a-doodle paranoid about a pretty wife?"

"Wish I knew," Dad said. "He seemed like an okay guy, decent enough cop, but things changed when she came to town. Can't say I saw him as much after that."

"What do you need me to do?"

"I'd like if you could look over these financial records. See what you make of them. Maybe he was onto something."

"What does he say?"

"He was helpful at first, but now he's not saying much of anything. Except that he didn't kill her. He has two sisters who came to town. Didn't unpack before they hired him some big shot lawyer who told him to clam up. Meanwhile, I got a whole list of people who didn't care for his wife, but nobody can think of one who hated her enough to want her dead. Maybe something in that paperwork her husband was keeping will spark an idea. We also got all their joint financial records, if that helps."

"I'd be glad to look them over for you," Mark said, then paused as the waitress came to their table for refills and to drop off the check. She stopped by mine with a raised eyebrow, but I put a finger to my lips and shooed her on.

"You may be the money guy, but I got this," Dad said, and movement in the booth suggested he was reaching for his wallet.

If I stayed where I was, I'd be discovered. I eased my way out of the booth, took a few steps back, then marched directly up to them. "Well, look at that. Great minds think alike!" I said, perhaps a little too loudly.

"Liz," Dad said. "What are you doing here?"

"Picking up lunch for the crew at the toyshop," I said. "You *do* remember the toyshop?"

Dad stood. "I should ask if you remember the toyshop, blowing off a morning like that. Or did you not know that I'd hear about senior speed dating?"

My jaw must have dropped.

Dad wagged a finger at me. "And I don't care if Lance is older than dirt, if he's going to date my daughter, I want to meet him first." At that, he walked off, but not before he burst into raucous laughter that turned the heads of the bartender and every waitress in the place and amused the lunch crowd that had just begun to queue up at the hostess station.

I collapsed into the booth opposite Mark and stared down at Dad's plate.

"I take it there's a story there," he said.

I ran one of Dad's leftover fries through the ketchup while I waited for my face to cool down. "Maybe not one I'm ready to tell."

"Those are the stories worth waiting for." He sipped his Coke, then sat up straighter. "I was going to text you. You want to meet at the theater tonight, or should I pick you up?"

"It's just down the street. How about I meet you out front?"

"Question," he said. "Is this a date, or are we going as friends? Because I'm cool either way."

"Are you buying the popcorn?"

"Well, yes."

"Then it's a date."

When I stood up, I kissed him on the cheek, and now it was his turn for his face to flare.

Chapter 11

After lunch, I got up the nerve to see Lionel Kelley. Except he wasn't there, or at least didn't answer his door when I knocked. So I ended up back at the shop where I unpacked a couple of boxes of newly arrived inventory, including a rather nice edition of the Hardy Boys Mystery Game. Cleaned and priced, it was the star of our shelves. Joe was clearly the focus of the cover, looking straight ahead, but quieter Frank had always been my favorite.

Dad never returned home for dinner, so I kept it simple with grilled cheese and canned tomato soup, then dressed for my date with Mark. Without Cathy's help, I managed to pull together a rather cute outfit. At least I hoped I did. Green sweater, cheery holly scarf, jeans, and I even wore my nutcracker socks and snowman earrings.

And the nice thing about a movie date is that even if I didn't quite pass muster with the fashion police, the theater would be dark.

I pulled on a red wool coat and walked the block to the theater. The sun had set early, of course, but the shimmering Christmas decorations on every telephone pole and the steady light streaming from the businesses gave a luster of midday to Main Street. The oversized figure sitting on the roof of the five-and-dime was already decked out in his Santa hat. I could see why the town had been chosen to play host to a couple of holiday movies, even if we'd had a heat wave when they were filming and they'd had to borrow snowmaking equipment from a local ski resort.

A group of Dickens carolers were performing near the theater, and Mark didn't see me come up next to him. I tapped his arm with my mittened hand.

"Hi," he whispered.

I turned to listen to the rest of the song, which turned into a delightfully harmonic and upbeat medley, finishing up with a rather impolite and urgent demand for figgy pudding. Instead they received hearty applause and the clanking of coins into their bucket, including from Mark who pulled some bills from his wallet before he took my arm.

Conversation was a little awkward as we waited in line for our popcorn. First dates can be like that, at least any that I've ever been on. Anything witty that could have been said evacuated my nervous brain.

That's the other nice thing about movie dates: after the theater darkens and the screen lights up, you don't have to keep up a conversation.

Mark laughed heartily at the film, which featured a love-struck teenaged Shirley Temple crushing on Cary Grant, wreaking havoc with the budding relationship between Cary and Myrna Loy. Mark's laughter was infectious, and soon the whole theater was giggling at the comic situations and prat-falls. And any unease I felt at the first date vanished.

"I take it you've not seen this movie before," I said as we rose to leave.

"I haven't, but I think it's going in my top ten," he said. "It brings up something I did want to talk about, though. How about we find a nice place for a good cup of hot chocolate?" He glanced at his watch. "Who's still open?"

"I know a place not far from here with great hot chocolate."

"Lead on, then."

He didn't figure it out until we arrived at the toyshop. Miles had closed it up tight and set the alarm, so I entered the code before I popped on the lights.

"I do make a mean hot chocolate, and if you wanted a quiet place to talk . . ."

He wandered through the aisles a little before poking his head into the addition. "This is new."

"Dad's comic book room," I said.

"This must be right behind the barber shop."

I sighed. "Their old storage room."

"You can't see anything of the crime scene from here, can you?" he asked, getting down on one knee near a roughed-in electrical outlet where a glimmer of light was visible.

"No," he answered his own question then pushed himself up and brushed drywall dust from his pant legs.

"Are you working the investigation?" I asked as we climbed the stairs to the apartment.

He didn't answer until we reached the top. "Just assisting where I can. Looking into some financial records."

I opened the door and draped my coat on a kitchen chair while I gathered my ingredients: milk, sugar, pinch of salt, half-and-half, and cocoa from the Amish stand at the farmer's market. I doubted the Amish actually grew the cocoa locally, but it was still the best I'd had.

"It will just be a minute," I said. "Make yourself comfortable."

"Your dad home?"

"I somehow doubt it." I glanced down the hallway to his open door. If he'd come home and was sleeping, the door would be shut. "Probably out working the case. We never saw much of him in the early days of an investigation."

"He wouldn't have a problem with me being up here, would he?" He squinted at a few family photos in a collage frame, then pulled out a chair at the kitchen table.

I laughed. "I'm not exactly twelve."

"Let's see. When you were twelve, I was probably twenty-two or twenty-three."

I pointed my wooden spoon at him. "Now, if I were twelve and you were twenty-two *and* we were up here alone, you'd never see parole."

He leaned his elbows on the table. "That is, if I survived until the trial."

"Good point," I said.

I busied myself with the cocoa, and when I glanced around, Val had come out of seclusion and was sniffing Mark's fingers. "Careful, that cat can be unpredictable. I have the scars to prove it."

But Mark pet her and she leaned into him. She let him pick her up and set her on his lap.

"If the FBI doesn't work out, you might be able to get a job as a cat-whisperer."

"I'll keep that in mind."

"So, you're reviewing Ken and Marya's financial records . . ." I turned back to the hot chocolate. The key to the cocoa was heating the milk without boiling it. And I hoped the key to getting information would be to not seem so anxious to get it.

"Is that why I merited an invite? Not sure I should discuss that with you."

"Why's that?"

"You used to date the man. If the evidence points to him being guilty, how will you take it?"

"Like a cop's daughter," I said. "Just the facts, man."

His eyes narrowed slightly. "And if the evidence points to him being innocent?"

"Then that's good, right?" I poured the cocoa into two jolly Christmas mugs and slid one across the table.

"Wait!" Before he could take a sip, I retrieved the chocolate whipped cream from the fridge. "Not the same without the whipped cream."

"No desiccated mini marshmallows?" he said.

"Strictly for amateurs."

"Now you're talking." He put a deft swirl of chocolate whipped cream on top of his cocoa, then took a sip. When he leaned back with a contented sigh, he was wearing a chocolate moustache.

I chuckled and set a stack of napkins on the table.

He wiped the chocolate away, and a more serious expression overtook his face. "Tell you what. You can ask me one question about the investigation, as long as I can ask one question from you."

"An even trade?"

"I play fair."

I thought for a moment. "What all have you learned from looking into the couple's financial records?"

"Everything I've learned?"

I just smiled.

He took a fortifying sip of his cocoa. "For one thing, she was a very creative bookkeeper. Her husband apparently suspected her of some kind of shenanigans, and his suspicions seem valid enough. She had a lot of money coming in."

"I heard she was very popular."

"Among a certain clientele," he said. "Her appointment slots were always booked, but she gave huge discounts. I'm not sure how she could have turned a profit at all."

"Then where was she getting the money?"

Mark shrugged. "That's what her husband was apparently trying to figure out. That, and where it was going."

I lifted my mug up until it steamed my glasses. I guess I was hoping it would hide the eagerness in my face. I waited for him to go on.

"As fast as it came in, it disappeared," he said.

"Tax evasion? Some kind of money laundering?"

He rubbed the back of his neck. "Not like any scheme I've ever seen."

"How much money are we talking here?"

"Isn't that another question?"

"It's a clarification of the first question."

"Man, you are tough," he said. "Looks like two, three grand a month. Maybe more. Money comes in. Money goes out."

"And she's been here a year," I said.

"So we're talking possibly tens of thousands," Mark said. "Not exactly a huge criminal enterprise, if that's what it was, but it's something." He leaned his arms against the table. "Now my question."

"Shoot."

"If the investigation clears Ken Young of any wrongdoing in his wife's death, would you consider seeing him again?"

"Why?"

"Nope, that's a different question."

I took a long sip of my cocoa, then set the mug on the table. "I don't *think* so."

"You're not sure?"

"I liked Ken. And if Marya had never come to town and Ken had secretly gotten his divorce, who knows what would have happened? But honesty is a trait I value, and him not telling me he was married . . ."

"If it helps," Mark said, "it doesn't look like this year was much fun for him."

"Doesn't help at all." I sighed. "I don't want him to be unhappy, and I didn't want her to be unhappy, either. And I certainly didn't want to see her dead."

"You do know they're probably going to be talking with you officially."

"They took care of that this morning. Kind of surprised it didn't happen sooner."

"Probably because your father's driving the investigation."

"And driving himself to an early grave in the process," I said. "He just can't stay away."

"Liz, have you considered that he took this case *for* you?"

"What do you mean?"

"Look, one thing cops hate is investigating other cops. If the investigation clears Young, your father could be accused of a cover-up. If it condemns him, there'll be a big backlash from his supporters in the department. I'm going to lay odds that your dad's goal was to keep you as far away from the spotlight as possible for as long as possible. But he won't be able to do that forever, unless something else breaks in the investigation."

"Like figuring out where this money came from and where it was going."

The stairs leading up to the apartment sounded a familiar creak. Moments later, Dad opened the door. He looked at Mark, then at me, then down at the table. "Please tell me there's more cocoa."

I smiled. "Take a seat. I'll heat it up for you."

# # #

When Dad's cocoa was sufficiently hot, I joined the two men at the table and conversation came to a dead halt.

"Maybe I should head out." Mark started pushing himself out of his chair.

"Actually," Dad said, "I kind of wanted to talk with you."

Mark slid back down into his seat, but Dad did more slurping than talking.

"Should *I* leave?" I asked.

Dad sniffed, then stared at me for a moment. "If you don't mind, I could use a set of fresh eyes and ears."

If my eyebrows weren't attached, they probably would have bounced off the ceiling and smacked me in the face on the way back down. "You're asking me to help?"

Dad sat back. "Unofficially. I kind of figured I wouldn't be able to keep you out of it. Not for long, anyway. Better I can keep an eye on you. And I'd prefer you to be more of a sounding board, rather than chasing leads, red herrings, and the occasional goose on your own."

"Goose chasing?"

"And I'd appreciate your discretion." He winked. "No

sharing any of this with Lance or your other friends down at senior speed dating."

I rolled my eyes.

"I take it you discovered something," Mark said.

Dad rubbed his nose. "Well, we did get some background on the victim."

"On Marya," I said. "Victim" seemed so impersonal.

"From what Ken said before those two sisters of his arrived, from what they let slip when they got their dander up, and from what I learned from his former department, Marya has been in this country most of her life."

"Which explains why her English was so good," I said. "But she only became a citizen a couple of weeks ago."

Dad's head jerked in my direction. "How do you know that? Do you know how many hours it took me to find that out?"

I clammed up. No way I would throw Miles under the bus, especially if I might need to ride that bus a little later.

"As best we can figure," Dad said, "she was only two or three when she arrived, and not by the usual channels."

"What are we talking?" Mark asked. "Black-market adoption? Human trafficking?"

"Not adoption," Dad said. "There's reports of an adult sister who functioned as guardian. But she's like a ghost. No record of her much anywhere. Only a few people claimed to have met her."

"If they were illegal aliens," I said, "they wouldn't want to leave a paper trail."

"Still," Mark said, "most illegal aliens pay taxes. There should be records. You have a name on this sister?"

"That's about all I have." Dad pushed a paper in Mark's

direction, but I snagged it before he could complete the handoff.

"Anechka Besk . . . ry . . . ost . . . nov."

"Something like that," Dad said. "There's an office pool on how to pronounce it. You might have a shot."

I took out my cell phone and took a picture of the name, then handed the paper to Mark.

He stared at it for a moment. "I'll run it. And maybe some variations. She might have tried to anglicize, or at least shorten it."

"Appreciate it," Dad said. He leaned forward and rested his head on the table. "Unless we find a few other suspects and pretty quick, pressure is going to be on to arrest Ken Young. I think he knows it." He peeked up at me. "Any thoughts?"

"I wondered if it might be someone she encountered at her twelve-step program."

"That's a good thought," Dad said. "You know where she went?"

"The same one Mom went to," I said. "Only there's a Pastor Pete in charge of it now. I met him yesterday."

"Liz, you shouldn't be chasing down leads on your own."

"Well, *someone* shut me out of the investigation," I countered. "Besides, all I did was go to church. No crime in that."

Mark leaned forward. "Did you learn anything?"

"Not a lot. Pastor Pete didn't think Marya was relapsing or anything like that."

"Did you get a list of names of who else attends?" Dad asked.

"I asked, but they're all so . . . anonymous. I thought about attending a meeting, but now Pastor Pete knows me."

"He doesn't know me," Mark said. He held up his empty cup. "Hello, my name is Mark, and I'm a chocoholic."

"Hi, Mark." I took his cup and poured the dregs of the cocoa into it.

"Any other thoughts?" Dad asked.

"Well, since she was killed in the barber shop, maybe a client could have killed her." I mentioned the hair on the floor from the crime scene photo. "I couldn't make out the color."

"It was gray," Dad said. "And we have a client list." He shuffled through some papers. This time he slid it in my direction.

I scanned the names. "You want to know what's interesting about this list?" I said as I trailed a finger down the page. I looked up at him with what was probably a smug smile. "They were almost all at senior speed dating."

"Now *that* I'm not ready to check out," Mark said.

"And I don't think they'd welcome me back," I said.

We both turned to Dad. I won't repeat what he said.

# # #

While Dad went to find his much-neglected bed for a few hours, I walked Mark downstairs.

"This is a first," he said. "I've never had a date turn into a murder investigation before."

"Sadly, I think I have," I said. "Oh, you wanted to talk about something. Did we ever get to that?"

"Kind of. I was a little concerned about whether you were comfortable dating a much older man. When you turned it into a joke, I figured the answer was yes."

"I don't think of you as that much older."

"Is it my boyish looks or my perpetual immaturity that you find attractive?"

I swatted his arm and laughed. "Maybe both. But I should probably tell you that I do have some hesitation about getting involved with someone in law enforcement."

"Because of Ken?"

I shook my head. "Not entirely. I grew up in a cop's house, and I know the stresses it creates."

"Does that apply to accountants?" he asked. "My job is a bit less dangerous. Aside from a paper cut or two, I've had a perfect safety record." He pointed to his pinkie finger. "You can barely see the scar now."

"You make a strong case there," I said. "But now it's my turn. Ken had a problem with me getting involved in a case in the past. What are your thoughts?"

He moved closer to me. "Well," he said, trailing a finger along my cheekbone. "If you understand that I may not always be able to answer *all* of your questions, and as long as you don't take any stupid chances . . ."

He leaned in for a tender kiss that sent all the blood racing from my head down to my toes, then back again. Kind of like NASCAR but without the burning rubber, checkered flags, and—as Dad would always say—endless left turns. I felt a little dizzy, a little breathless. Either this was chemistry at work, or I needed a cardiologist, stat.

"I think it's kind of hot." He smiled at me, and the corners of his eyes crinkled. "Goodnight." And he was out the door.

Chapter 12

On Tuesday, Cathy took Drew for his checkup and vaccinations, meaning I was stuck in the shop selling toys. When not waiting on customers, I paced the aisles, itching to get out and continue my own investigation. After all, the clock was ticking. A murderer was out walking the streets, free to tamper with evidence or just skedaddle, while the police were busy compiling evidence—in their methodical, plodding way—possibly against someone once close to me. That my aging and supposedly retired father had to shoulder all the stress of leading the investigation didn't sit well on my stomach, which also churned with unanswered questions about Marya's background. And her sister's.

After all that time trying to keep Dad from going out and involving himself in police investigations, here I was, doing the same thing. I guess it's true: we become our parents.

I had my coat and boots on and car keys in hand when Amanda and Kohl came to relieve me at four. Of course Kohl was too young to be on the books, but he enjoyed the toyshop, especially sorting through all the comic books. Dad always let him keep a book or two every time he worked.

"Someone's in a hurry to leave," Amanda said as I paced the shop while they removed their coats. "Hot date?"

"That was last night."

"Do tell!" Amanda raised an eyebrow. "Did this Browning fellow sweep you off your feet?"

"No, this was Mark Baker. I think you've seen him. He's been to a few game nights."

"FBI guy? Older fellow?"

"He's an FBI accountant, and he's not *that* much older."

"Okay," she said.

"More than okay," I said. "He's a really nice guy."

"Still processing." She nodded. "Yeah, I can see that working. Is that where you're headed now?"

"Actually, I wanted to talk with Ken." I glanced at my watch. "And I need to be back in time for Cathy's doll meeting tonight."

"You're seeing Ken!"

"Not that way. Last night when we were discussing the case, I learned that Ken stopped talking to police. I hoped he might talk to me."

"Last night when you and *Mark* were discussing the case?"

"And Dad."

"On a date? Liz, not that you asked my advice, but you need to keep your father out of your love life."

"Working on that. You okay here by yourself?"

Amanda roughed up Kohl's hair, and Kohl rushed to straighten it. "I have my favorite guy to help. We're good."

# # #

Halfway to Ken's house, Dad's warning not to chase any more geese niggled at my brain. But I relegated it to the category of "optional parental advice," along with finishing broccoli before dessert and not dating Timothy Collins. (Okay, he'd been right about that last one.) But while Dad might not be pleased, I was determined not to let his overprotective instincts prevent me from helping keep Ken's neck out of the noose. Or mine, either.

Moments later, the door pushed open and Nancy stood there, drooling and panting. Okay, maybe that part was my imagination. On my way over, I'd nicknamed those two guard dogs that Ken called his sisters as Cujo and Mad Max.

Cujo, aka Nancy, squinted at me. "Liz, right?"

I nodded. "I hoped I might speak to your brother."

She swung open the door, and I followed her inside.

The front door led directly to the living room, so I pushed off my snowy boots and left them on the mat. Cujo and Mad Max were already seated on the sectional by the time I finished, and after wiping the fog from my glasses, I realized the sisters were glaring at me. At least Nancy was.

"He's not here," she finally said.

"We thought he might be with you," Grace added.

"You don't know where he is?"

"That's exactly what I mean," Nancy said. "He left early this morning before we woke up, and he's not answering his cell phone. The police . . ." Her eye twitched. "And by the police, I mean your father. He came by already, wanting to talk to him. We said Kenny'd just stepped out, but that was hours ago. Do you think they arrested him?"

"If they had, you'd likely be one of the first to know," I said, sliding into the stiff chair.

"One would think," Nancy said. "At least back home, someone would have the courtesy to call—not that we have much experience with that kind of thing, mind you. But up in New York?"

"You'll be relieved to know that the whole innocent-until-proven-guilty thing and the Constitution are in full effect here, too," I said.

"That's good to hear." Nancy picked a lint ball from her heavy sweater. Not quite sure why she needed it. The room felt as if someone had upped the thermostat to ninety.

"Look," I said, "I know you're having a rough time with all of this, but please understand that nobody is trying to railroad your brother. In fact, I was hoping he'd tell me a little about Marya." Then I remembered what Ken said about his sisters being closer to Marya than he was. Maybe, if I didn't seem too much like a "pushy Yankee," I could wheedle a little information from them.

"Why?" Grace asked.

I slipped off my coat. "If Ken didn't kill her—and I know he didn't—someone else did. Maybe there's something in her background before she came here that might give the police another avenue of investigation and clear Ken." And me, but I doubted they'd care too much about that.

"The lawyer advised him not to say anything," Nancy hedged.

I put my hands up. "I'm not asking for anything that would incriminate your brother. I'd just like to know a little more about Marya. Maybe before she married Ken."

The two sisters shared several glances, then Nancy finally said, "Grace went to school with her."

"You were friends?"

"Not friends, exactly," Grace said. "I'm not sure Marya had any friends. She seemed quite the loner, even back then. And

117

kids can be so cruel. We had no idea . . ." She trailed off and turned to Nancy.

Nancy scooted forward to the edge of her seat. "Grace is too hard on herself. We come from a small town, and families there go back a ways, with most tracing their ancestry to the Civil War and many to the Revolutionary. Just about everybody there is kin to everybody else. Friendly. Established."

And rampant inbreeding, I thought, but kept my tongue.

"Marya was different," Grace said. "She had that funny accent. Nobody knew much about where she'd come from or where she lived . . ." Grace trailed off and all was silent except for a large grandfather clock which continued to tick loudly as the pendulum swung back and forth. And back and forth. And . . .

"Where *did* she live, may I ask?" I hoped it sounded more polite with the "may I" tacked on. One thing I learned from being a cop's daughter is that interrogations could be most effective when the subject had no idea they were being interrogated. It would be nice to be on the other end of that whole process. So I put on my most innocuous smile and waited.

Finally, after a few more shared glances and when my fingernails were dug so tightly into my palm I worried they were going to pop out the other side of my hand, Nancy broke the silence. "Do you know anything about chicken ranches?"

When I put my dropped jaw back into alignment, I said, "You mean . . . prostitution?"

"Well!" Nancy barked, sounding more like Cujo by the minute.

Grace paled. "Certainly not! I mean literal chicken ranches."

"Where they keep literal chickens?" I asked.

"Of course," Nancy said. "And slaughter them and pluck

and disembowel them and get them ready for restaurants and supermarkets."

Grace had scrunched up her nose. "It's awful work. I did it for three days in high school when I was trying to save up for a car, and I decided my bicycle would be just fine."

"They could never get enough workers to fill all those jobs." Nancy pulled a throw pillow into her lap and smoothed the nap of it as if petting a cat. "So I guess they cut a few corners when it came to recruiting workers."

"Like checking immigration status," I said. "And maybe age. Did Marya work there?"

Grace shook her head. "The one good thing her sister did for her was keep her out."

"Anechka?" I said.

"Oh, good," Nancy said. "You know about Anechka then."

"Just the name," I said.

"She and a number of other workers and their families lived packed in these little rundown trailers near the plant," Grace said. "When you passed the bend in the road, it was really funny how similar the trailers were to the cramped chicken houses."

"And these other workers," I said, trying to speed up the conversation. "Did they also come from Russia? Legally?"

"Not sure about that," Nancy said, "but Marya told me once it was under false pretenses. Some thought they were coming as models, actresses, even teachers." She set the pillow next to her and fluffed her claw marks out of it. "Anechka thought she was bringing Marya to America with her for a better life."

"She was only a toddler when they arrived," Grace said. "She had a fairly normal life, as much as Anechka could provide on what she earned plucking chickens. They had plans to quit and find a better situation as soon as she paid them back."

"Pay who back? For what?" I asked.

"For the passage. The paperwork. The housing," Grace said.

And I guessed their silence.

"Anechka really did her best to provide for them," Nancy said. "And caring for her sister meant it took longer to pay back the—"

"Traffickers?" I wasn't about to excuse them with a polite word.

"And then there was the medication," Grace added, although Nancy shot her a foul look.

"Whose medication?" I asked.

Tick. Tick. Tick.

"Lemme guess," I said, running out of patience and having a pretty good idea of how this went down. "Anechka comes to this country under the guise of becoming a . . . ?"

"Russian teacher," Grace offered.

I winced. "And brings her little sister along in hopes of a better life."

"Her orphan sister," Nancy said. "Their parents were dead."

"Right," I said. "But after she arrived, she realized she'd been duped and was put to work long hours basically in a sweatshop."

Grace nodded.

"Where she proceeded to do her best to pay back the scumbag traffickers and raise her sister outside of their influence—which probably cost her more."

Now they were both nodding.

"You can see how this would take a physical and emotional

toll on a young woman," Nancy said. "And chicken needs to be kept cold, so that means working with sharp implements in a freezer all day. Fingers go numb . . . and then accidents happen.

"Usually Anechka tried to keep her hands in her pockets," Grace said, "but once I caught a glimpse and they were all swollen and bandaged. Anyone could tell she was in a lot of pain. You can't blame her for taking something for that. And to get through the day. Some quack at the plant handed them out like candy."

"Of course they did," I said. "So by the time Anechka had been here a year, she was probably pretty well hooked on . . ."

"Oxycodone and Diet Pepsi," Nancy said.

"So even if Anechka could find another job, which would be difficult given her lack of proper paperwork, she now had a drug problem. And they were her suppliers." An uncomfortable thought hit me. "How did Ken enter this equation?"

"Kenny was a rookie cop when he answered a call at the plant," Grace said.

"Anechka had passed out," Nancy said. "Some kind of fever it turned out, but Marya rushed over when she heard. There was an argument. Well, a fight, really. And when Marya was taken in, she had some of Anechka's oxycodone in her possession."

"There's no record," I said.

"She was still a minor," Grace said. "Her blood test came up clean, so she pled down to community service and was required to join a substance abuse program."

"Only things went catawampus after that," Grace said. "Kenny asked a few too many questions about the place. Questioned why the inspectors didn't flag any violations."

Nancy rubbed her fingers together in the universal sign for "show me the money." "It seems the chicken ranch was owned by the mayor's cousin. The more Kenny investigated, the more enemies he made."

"Talk was that Marya would be sent back to Russia," Nancy said, "even though she didn't even remember living there. Eventually though, folks just seemed to forget about it. Marya was convinced that Anechka made some kind of deal to keep quiet, and that the traffickers paid off officials so that Marya would be allowed to stay in the U.S."

"Fortunately," Grace said, "Marya enrolled in the cosmetology program at the high school. She cut all the girls' hair for practice."

"So after graduation she rented a space in an established shop downtown," Nancy said. "Since she was self-employed, nobody asked to see a green card, and she kept a low profile. After a few years, questions about her citizenship surfaced again. This time, Marya turned to Kenny for help. They must have hit it off. They . . . eloped." She shrugged, as if this were a perfectly normal, everyday solution.

Grace leaned forward. "They couldn't go after her then because she was married to a cop. But it hurt his career, I think. People under him started advancing faster, making more money."

"Probably why he ended up moving here," Nancy said with a sigh.

"And Marya chose not to come with him?" I asked.

The sisters clammed up. I'd hit a sore spot, and I swear that clock was ticking even louder. Getting them to open up more about this aspect of Ken and Marya's relationship would be challenging.

I leaned back, feigning disinterest. Maybe if I played on their natural desire to defend their brother?

"Of course men can be insensitive at times, chasing their careers without a thought to how their decisions impact others. Did he even ask Marya if she wanted to move . . . up to this frozen wasteland?" I adored it here, of course, but I thought that might play well with this crowd.

Grace bit her lower lip, but Nancy jerked her head up. "I'm sure Kenny *thought* he was doing the right thing. By then . . . maybe they needed a break from each other."

"A temporary one," Grace said. "After all, Marya kept on living in their house. We just felt they needed a little time apart to work out whatever."

"Of course, Marya was always sweet as she could be to us," Nancy said. "Kept doing our hair like regular. And for free."

"And *then* we heard talk of a divorce!" Grace said.

"Couples do divorce," I said.

"But with Marya not a citizen yet?" Nancy said. "I don't know what Kenny was thinking."

"So when the immigration people started asking questions," Grace said, "we told them that Kenny went on ahead and that Marya was staying behind to get the house ready to sell."

"It was the least we could do," Nancy said.

"After all, she did our hair for free."

"How were we to know they'd keep coming back?" Nancy said. "So we helped Marya pack up the house and put it on the market, and then sent her up here so she could prove that she didn't have one of those marriages of convenience." Nancy huffed. "I've been married for twelve years, and let me tell you, it's not always convenient."

"Of course when she arrived," Grace said, "she discovered . . ."

"That Ken had started seeing someone else." I sighed. "Look, you need to know that I wasn't aware that Marya even existed. Ken never told me."

"That doesn't seem like our brother," Nancy said.

"Kenny was always honorable, to a fault," Grace said.

"Eagle Scout," Nancy said.

"Returned money to the cashier if she accidently gave him too much," Grace said.

Nancy laughed. "Like that time at the Piggly Wiggly. She actually stood there and argued with him, mainly because she was too lazy to open her till."

"We just figured there were extenuating circumstances," Grace said. "For him to take up with someone else when he was still legally married."

"Extenuating?" I said.

Nancy narrowed her eyes. "Things are a little different up here, aren't they?"

"Different?" I paused to consider what they were hinting at.

"Where we come from," Grace said, "women are a little less gussied up, and they let men do the pursuing."

"We see how Kenny might have been flattered."

Ah, so I was the pushy Yankee temptress who lured their brother from the straight and narrow. And convincing them otherwise would be impossible, since they had the quorum. I pushed myself out of my seat. "And you don't know where Ken went?" I gathered my coat.

They rose, too.

"No," Nancy said. "I sure hope something we said helps our brother."

"And Marya. We adored Marya," Grace said, giving me a pointed look. "Despite their differences, we always thought she was perfectly suited to him."

Implying I wasn't.

"Anyway, thank you for your time." I shoved my feet into my boots, hopping to keep my balance. With my hand on the doorknob, I turned back to them. "Now if you good ladies will excuse me, I need to get gussied up and chase some men."

# # #

Still wanting to see the video footage that Lionel Kelley claimed he had—I was beginning to doubt its existence—I swung by his PI office. I pulled up just as he turned the key in the front lock. Coming or going, I couldn't tell.

"Glad I caught you!" I said as I climbed out of my Civic parked just out front.

Kelley's shoulders stiffened, and he spun around slowly. "Hello, Liz."

"You haven't been returning my texts," I said.

"You texted?" He pulled out his phone and flipped through.

"I wanted to report back on what I discovered at the library and pick up the video you promised."

"Senior speed dating? Already heard about it. Not the nefarious plot I was led to believe. And I'm afraid I'm not done with the video yet."

"A copy, then?"

"Perhaps, but I don't have time to fiddle with that now."

"I could make a copy."

He rolled his eyes. "Look. I'll try to have it for you tomorrow. Best I can do. Now if you'll excuse me." And with that he jogged down the sidewalk. Bad idea in the winter. Three businesses down, he lost his footing, skidded a bit, and bumped into an elderly shopper, upsetting her packages. And this was no sweet, old woman. She swore a blue streak at the top of her lungs and shook her cane while she did it. I watched a moment longer to see if she might whack him with the cane or bash him with her purse, but instead Kelley helped her pick up her packages, then they went on their merry ways.

When I arrived back at the store, Amanda and Kohl were almost finished setting up tables for the doll committee meeting. I pulled open the last two folding chairs and slid them in place.

"Should I fetch more from the back?" Amanda asked.

I scanned the room. Eight chairs. More than enough. Especially since one of the committee members had been murdered since the last meeting. "It's plenty. If we get a few more, I can always pull out more chairs."

"Great," Amanda said then instructed Kohl to put his coat on. "We're headed over to Jack's for dinner tonight. Would you like us to send anything back?"

"By Jack's you mean the restaurant?" I said.

"Yes, I guess I just equate Wallace's with him."

"Easy to do, especially since you haven't actually met his mother."

She shut her eyes. "Don't remind me. Meeting the parents. That's coming in the near future. We've chatted on Skype, but Jack was always there. She'll be here for the holidays, and I've heard she can be very protective of her son."

"I don't think you'll have any problems." I said. "After all, you have a couple of things going for you that I didn't."

She tilted her head.

"One, your father never arrested one of her boys, and two, you're not named Liz McCall."

She laughed until she saw that I wasn't. "You're serious?"

"Maybe she saw what we didn't: that Jack and I were never right for each other. But you and him and Kohl? It's like you all clicked from the beginning. I think she'll see that, too. You're just suited for each other."

As soon as those last words were out of my mouth, I thought of what Nancy (or was it Grace?) had said about Ken and Marya. They suited each other.

Here I was, another interloper, standing in the way of true love. Like an overzealous chaperone at the school dance.

I laid a hand on her arm. "Seriously, you'll be fine."

"Thanks, Liz. Enjoy your meeting."

Only after she had left did I realize that I never answered her that I wanted something for dinner. And since Cathy wouldn't be there until the meeting, that left me two long hours to man the shop on an empty stomach.

But the candy counter hadn't been sorted through in a while. So while the shop was empty, I sat down in front of it and started straightening things up and checking expiration dates. I scored when I discovered the Chuckles were expiring at the end of the week. I'd always liked the fruity, gumdrop-like candies which dated back to the 1920s, preferring them to their chewier German competition, the gummy bears, which debuted around the same time. I made a note to order more of each and pulled open a pack.

I don't know if it was the sugar rush or the chewing—I always used to snack while I studied for exams—but my thoughts were drawn back to the case.

Someone killed Marya Young.

And, perhaps inspired by the vintage *Let's Make a Deal* board game that was sitting at the counter, it seemed to me the killer was behind one of three doors.

Door number one. Ken. The Eagle Scout who wouldn't lie but never bothered to tell me he was married. His sisters had said the couple had problems. That's one reason why Ken had moved here and Marya hadn't. I also recalled him saying that he thought that she might have been up to her old . . . *something* again. Tricks? Habits? What were those, and what had he been looking for in her financial records? It was enough to cause that ruckus that I'd overheard. Had it been enough to turn him into a killer?

I didn't want to believe it, of course. But I'd known some perfectly nice people who I never thought would have crossed that line, yet they did. His sisters were welcome to keep their blind faith in him. I wasn't sure I could afford to.

Especially now, since he'd gone MIA.

My laughter echoed in the empty shop after the truth hit: Ken wasn't running from the law. He was running from his sisters!

And Door Number Two. Someone from Marya's past. She had a sister who'd been trafficked into this country to work in a sweatshop. Who knew where Anechka was now or what she was up to? Or even if she was alive. The traffickers or even those shady employers might want to clean up some loose ends and make sure neither of the sisters could expose them—by silencing the two women permanently.

And Door Number Three. Someone she met here. I had thought Marya hadn't made a lot of friends, but that might have been jealousy. She must have met people at the twelve-step group. Hopefully Mark would get a chance to check that out soon. And she endeared herself to a lot of people, especially a lot of senior citizens, by granting discounts. Any one of them could have done it.

Okay, I could rule out Lance.

And then there was Ken's suspicion that maybe there was someone else in her life.

And I could still rule out Lance.

I hadn't finished rolling the problem around in my head when Cathy rushed in and brushed a few snowflakes from her coat.

"No Drew tonight?" I asked.

"Parker is keeping him home. He's a little restless from his shots, I think."

"Hard for Mom to watch?"

"He hates it. He wiggles and cries. But it's over pretty quick. Better he's protected."

Glenda came through the door shortly after, her trusty knitting bag in one arm. I don't know that I'd ever seen her without it.

Lori Briggs arrived with Diana Oliveri, and the group remained rather reserved at first, the only sound being that of Glenda's knitting needles. I'd closed Val into the apartment to make sure that Diana wouldn't have to worry about any black cats crossing her path.

Cathy waited a couple of more minutes to see if anyone else would arrive, but no one did. She began, "I'm sure by now you all have heard what happened to Marya Young."

Everyone nodded, Diana made the sign of the cross, and Glenda sniffled, then dabbed the corner of her eye with the back of her hand—without letting go of her knitting.

"I had considered canceling," Cathy said, "especially since that means more work for even fewer people, but it's a worthy cause."

"It's for the children," Glenda said.

"That's right," Cathy said. "So let's see if we can get up to speed. First of all, does anyone have any suggestions on who might be able to do doll hair for us?"

Silence reigned, then a thought struck me. "When I talked to someone today, they mentioned that Marya learned to cut hair at her high school. Does anybody know if any schools around here have a similar program?"

"What a great idea!" Lori said. "I'm sure I could find out. And schools are always looking for community service ideas."

"You're deputized," Cathy said. "And I think we should add some kind of memorial to the project to keep Marya's name involved. She was very enthusiastic."

I nodded. It must have taken a lot of courage for her to come to the meeting.

"Do we have any update on funding?" Glenda asked, stopping to massage her hands.

Cathy pointed to me. "Care to handle that, Liz?"

"Um, yeah. I have a . . . meeting set up with Ian Browning this Wednesday evening."

Lori Briggs jerked her head up. "This Wednesday evening? You can't have a meeting with Ian then. It's the debut performance of *The Nutcracker* by the children's dance school. Mostly inner-city kids who could never afford the lessons. The Browning Foundation is one of the major sponsors. He has front row seats reserved. He has to be there."

"He did ask me if I liked *The Nutcracker*."

Lori squinted at me. "You're meeting with Ian at the performance?"

"He said something about dinner before."

Lori's jaw dropped. "Honey, that's not a meeting. That's a date. You have a *date* with Ian Browning. *You* have a date with the hottest bachelor in town!"

I wasn't so sure I liked the incredulous emphasis on "you" in the last sentence, but I sat up a little straighter. With a nonchalant shrug, I said, "I guess I do."

"You know what this means, don't you?" Glenda said.

"What's that?" Cathy asked.

Glenda shoved her knitting into her bag, cleared her throat, and sang a gravelly chorus of "We're in the Money." And everybody laughed.

Once Cathy regained control, the rest of the meeting progressed well enough. We hashed out a lot of details, and I managed to say "no" just often enough so that I was involved in the project without committing to do everything, something I'd struggled with in the past.

After a motion to adjourn, we offered more coffee all around and served the cookies Cathy had brought.

"Could I trouble you for a glass of water?" Glenda said. "I have to take a pill."

"Not a problem," I said and then retrieved a bottle of water from the refrigerator in the back room.

Before I could return, Lori waylaid me in front of the lunch boxes. "Sure you know what you're doing?" she asked.

"In regards to?"

"To dating Ian, of course. He travels in some awfully powerful circles."

"I thought everybody was for approaching the Browning Foundation for funding."

"Yes, but Ian . . . let's just say he's left a few girls broken-hearted. And rumor is he can get a bit handsy."

"At the children's ballet?" I said.

"Yeah, better not use mace. What about a Taser? I'll bet your Dad could hook you up."

And suddenly an evening at the children's ballet seemed more foreboding.

"I'll keep that in mind. And my dad on speed dial."

When I returned with the water, Glenda waved me off. "Sorry about that." She pulled an empty pill bottled out of her purse. "I must have forgotten to put the lid on tight."

"That's happened to me," Diana said. "Did they spill out in the bottom of your purse?"

I set the water on the table while they continued to rummage and went over to Cathy. "Nice job on the meeting," I said.

"Thanks. I wasn't sure how to handle that part with Marya. Are you going to be okay if we name the whole project after her?"

"Let me sleep on that," I said.

When I turned back to Glenda and Diana, they had emptied the entire contents of her large purse on the table.

"Found one!" Diana held a tiny pill on her palm.

"Thank goodness," Glenda said, then struggled to open the water bottle.

Diana helped her with that, too. I'd remember to at least loosen the cap next time.

"Thanks," she said again, washing her pill down with a dainty sip. "The arthritis is getting worse, I think."

As Diana and I both helped put everything back into Glenda's purse, I found a coupon with giant scissors and Marya's name on it.

"Did Marya cut your hair?" I asked Glenda.

"Yes." She looked forlornly at the coupon before crumpling it up with a sigh. "Hard to beat her prices. Or her work."

"She cut mine, too," Diana said, pushing a lock behind her ear. "Can't say I cared much for the woman, but her work was okay. She did perms and color, too. All the lowest prices around. *Everybody* went to her."

Lori sent her a bemused smile. "Not me. I go to Antoine's."

"Can't fault you for that. Antoine *is* dreamy," Diana said. "And the way he massages your scalp?" She closed her eyes and swayed ever so slightly. "I suppose I could go back to Antoine."

"Is there another hair stylist who lost a lot of business to Marya?" I asked.

"Are you thinking motive?" Cathy asked.

Lori grimaced. "I'm sure Antoine felt the pinch the most. But you can't possibly think he could kill someone."

"I couldn't say," I said. "I've never met him."

"Who does your hair?" Lori asked.

And I stood there stupidly with my mouth open, then gave a slight shrug, as if it was the most natural thing in the world. "My dad does," I half-whispered.

Glenda threw back her head and laughed so hard she nearly lost her dentures. "Hank McCall cuts your hair?"

Lori gave me a full inspection, circling me once, then tugging on the back of my hair. "He actually does a nice job."

"It's just that he's always done it," I said. "I suppose I ought to grow up and find someone."

"Sorry," Glenda said, once she'd recovered. She took

another sip of her water. "I shouldn't laugh. Your hair always looks nice. Just the thought of Hank McCall . . . well, it's not something you think the police chief does."

"Please don't tell him I mentioned it," I said.

"If that's the way you want it," Glenda said. "But I was about to ask if you thought he might do mine." She raised the water bottle in a toast, but Diana grabbed her arm in midair.

"Never toast with water," she said. "It's bad luck."

"Sorry." Glenda set the bottle down.

A wide-eyed Diana stared at the bottle. "I probably shouldn't tell you this, but toasting without drinking can mean seven years of bad sex."

Glenda chuckled. "Honey, at my age, I'll take what I can get."

After a little more small talk, Cathy and I walked the ladies to the door. As they shuffled through the snow to their homes and cars, I gave Cathy a hug. "You did a great job. Despite the setback with losing Marya, this is still going to work. So proud of you."

"Thanks," she said. "And let me know how it goes with Ian Browning."

"Will do."

And as I watched her head to her car, out of the corner of my eye I caught a glint of light through the shades at the PI office. When I turned in that direction, the light flicked off.

What was Lionel Kelley up to now?

Chapter 13

Dad arrived home midway through the ten o'clock news. I was hearing him in stereo because they were playing a recorded interview with him at the same time. I deserted the 2-D version, still spouting off the prescribed lines about "not commenting on an ongoing investigation," and found him poking through the fridge. He pulled out an apple.

"I'd be happy to make you something. Pancakes?"

"No, just hankering for something not deep-fried or slathered in sugar." He carried the apple to his recliner and sank back and lifted his feet.

"Home for the night, then?" I asked.

He leaned his head back and sighed, and I grabbed a throw blanket and tossed it to him.

"*You* are my favorite daughter." As soon as he'd spread the blanket across his lap, Othello leaped up for a pet.

Dad held out his hand for Othello to sniff. "I'm sure it smells like doughnuts and greasy burgers," he told the cat. "And sorry, no kitty bags."

Othello seemed unconcerned with this as he melted into Dad's gentle strokes. Soon I could hear his purr across the room.

"How's the investigation coming?" I asked.

"Slow," he said. "Liz, by any chance have you seen that old boyfriend of yours?"

"I wish you'd stop referring to him as my old boyfriend."

"Fair enough. But have you seen him?"

I wagged my head. "I went over to his house to try and talk with him today, but he was gone. Even his sisters didn't know where he went."

"Do you think they're telling the truth?" he asked.

I sat up a little straighter. I hadn't considered that they might be hiding him. But as I mulled the question, I began a slow nod. "They seemed genuinely concerned for him. So much so, they even talked to me."

"Learn anything?"

I shared with him all that I'd learned about Marya's background.

"Good job, kiddo," he said, his face beaming with approval. "Keep this up, I might have to put you on the payroll."

"We already have a family business, remember."

"And I hope you believe me that this time, I'm anxious to get back to it. Parts of me ache that I didn't know I had. As soon as this investigation is over, one way or another, I'm back being the congenial retiree you know and love."

"Glad to hear it."

He leaned back and closed his eyes.

"Dad?"

"Hmm?"

"Have you given any consideration to the idea that one of Marya's competitors might have been angry enough to kill her? She ran such steep discounts that she drove business away from other stylists."

He raised his eyelids, but only slightly. "You think one of the local stylists has turned into what, Jack the Clipper?"

"I'm being serious. And don't you dare tell me to *mullet* over."

"You're such a *tease.*" He closed his eyes with a satisfied grin. "Are you speaking in general terms, or is there a specific stylist you think might have wanted to give Marya Young the permanent . . . die job?"

"A couple of women mentioned someone named Antoine. I thought I might go check him out."

"And rob me of my favorite client?" he teased, then grew more serious. "Just don't accuse him of anything or ask too many overtly obvious questions. But I doubt there's anything there. Still, can you take someone with you, maybe?"

I instantly thought of Diana Oliveri, who'd been considering going back. "I think I can manage that."

He didn't reply. Moments later his breathing turned into a gentle snore.

I kissed him on the forehead and tucked the blanket in around his shoulders.

"I'll take that as your *parting* comment," I whispered.

# # #

The shop was hopping the following morning. I blamed a tour bus which dropped off its riders just a little too early for their lunch reservations, but without enough time to explore the huge five-and-dime. Our little shop swarmed with seniors.

One snowy-haired gentleman leaned over the enclosed case that held our tin soldiers. He tapped the case above one particularly bright metallic soldier. "I had a whole set of these. I used to line them up on the floor in battles for hours with my friend Timmy. We thought we were something, waging campaigns, sending in the artillery. We could almost smell the cordite in the air. I wish I could buy a set for my grandson."

I winced. "You can still buy sets of toy soldiers, but if they're for play I'd recommend recently manufactured ones. We only keep a few of these for collectors, and we suggest they be kept in a glass or Lucite case."

"To protect them?"

"In part. If they're stored in moist environments, like basements, the finishes easily dull. But more for safety. Many antique soldiers contain large amounts of lead. It's not too much of an issue for the collector who isn't likely to gnaw on them, but if you handled these a lot as a kid, you might want to be tested."

"Wow." And he backed away from the case as if the little men were about to jump out and wage an attack on him.

As he went on browsing through the rest of the store with his hands tucked behind his back, I cashed out the last of our Hayley Mills paper dolls, sold a stuffed Natasha (of Bullwinkle fame) doll to a woman actually named Natasha, and dickered over a remote controlled—via cable—Robbie the Robot, but we couldn't compromise on a fair price, so the bargain hunter left disappointed and Robbie remained on our shelves.

The biggest sale of the morning was a set of figures labeled "The Swingers Music Set." Despite the images on the front of the box bearing a significant resemblance to young versions of John, Paul, George, and Ringo, *and* the repeated phrase "Yeah, yeah, yeah" which was plastered all over the rest of it, no actual mention of "The Beatles" was found on this unlicensed item made in Hong Kong in the sixties. *Wink, wink.*

Before the rush, however, I'd managed to get a hold of Diana, then I'd called in two consecutive appointments for that afternoon at Antoine's.

I also texted Lionel Kelley seven times, asking him when I could pick up the promised tape. No response.

Finally, he texted back: "With a client. Will have to postpone until tomorrow."

That got me thinking. How many clients could a one-man PI firm have at a time? Might he be with the client who hired him to do the surveillance?

While I couldn't stay glued to the door, I peeked out as often as business would allow, hoping to catch a glimpse of this mysterious client.

During one of these checks, Cathy arrived with a squalling Drew in the baby carrier in one arm and a garment bag in the other. "Thanks," she mumbled, as I pushed open to door for her and took the carrier.

I wrestled Drew out of his snowsuit and tiny boots. "Going skiing, are we?" When I removed Drew's little ski cap, his hair was matted down to his head with sweat.

"Maybe I overcompensated," Cathy said, "but that wind cuts right through a person."

Drew settled down quickly once all the extra layers were removed and soon was content in his swing. I told Cathy about my plans to visit Antoine.

"That's a wonderful idea. A new hairstyle will go great with what's in here." She hung the garment bag on the shelf behind the counter and unzipped it. The effect was like Dorothy opening the farmhouse door in the *Wizard of Oz*. Everything in the shop seemed like grainy sepia compared to the vivid technicolor that was *the* dress.

I just stood there blinking at the silver-sequined cocktail dress that was reflecting all the light and colors in the shop.

"Too much?" she finally said.

My eyes took in the plunging neckline and the barely legal length. "Too much, and maybe too little, all at the same time. Cathy, where on earth would I wear that?" An apt question since you could probably see the glittery dress from space.

"On your date with Ian Browning tonight," she said. "Isn't that why you're getting a new 'do?"

"To watch a bunch of little kids on stage in tutus?" I said. "I thought I'd go casual."

Cathy's eyes widened. "Not on opening night, and not when you're going with Ian Browning. This performance is more than a podunk dance recital—the troupe has national recognition, and several dancers from it have gone on to professional ballet, and even to Broadway. They have an alumnus in *Hamilton*! Besides, opening night is when all the bigwigs will be there, and you're going to be seated next to the biggest wig of all."

I stopped to consider whether she was making a hair pun but decided she wasn't. I took a closer look at the dress then squinted up at Cathy. "Are you sure I should get so . . . gussied up?" I asked, painfully remembering my parting shot to Ken's sisters.

"Have I let you down? And since when do you say 'gussied up'?"

"Apparently ever since I started chasing men." I shook my head at the dress. "I hope he's wearing sunglasses."

On my next peek out the window, a shadowy coated figure was just leaving the PI office. He—or she—remained on the threshold chatting with Kelley long enough for me to grab my coat and tell Cathy I needed to run out for a moment.

He was a block ahead of me by the time I made it outside, and I had to walk at a pretty brisk pace to try to catch up.

With all the winter outerwear, I couldn't make a positive ID, but from the gait and height I was pretty sure I was following a man.

I made a mental note. Dark pants. Checked coat. Blue ski cap. I'd narrowed the gap to half a block when he entered the pharmacy.

Perfect. I'd be able to go in, maybe buy some aspirin or a candy bar—or better yet, wrapping paper—and get a chance to see him up close. I slowed my pace so I wasn't huffing when I entered the drugstore.

When I pulled open the door, the female clerk standing alone at the counter greeted me, barely audible over the upbeat holiday music. I waved back and then casually glanced down each aisle. The end caps were fully decked out for Christmas, and I passed by the replicas of the tree from *A Charlie Brown Christmas* and the "fragile" leg lamps from *A Christmas Story*. The next end cap featured personal grooming products scented like bacon. Bacon shampoo and body wash. They weren't particularly Christmassy, but they might make a fun gag gift for Parker. There were, however, no customers in the aisle.

And the next? Empty.

I casually scanned every aisle without seeing another person.

It wasn't until I arrived at the pharmacy at the back of the store that I noticed the checked coat hanging on a hook near where the pharmacist was filling a prescription.

The pharmacist, a man maybe in his fifties with a generous moustache, glanced up. I wasn't sure I'd seen him before. "Can I help you?"

"No," I said. "I just needed . . ." I turned around and grabbed the first item next to my hand, which upon closer inspection turned out to be wart remover. I guess it could have been worse. "Thanks anyway," I said, making a mental note of the name plate displayed on the glass of the counter: "Charles Barr, pharmacist."

I paid for my wrapping paper and wart cream at the front counter then added a peanut butter Lindt truffle to my purchase.

"Okay, Mr. Charles Barr," I said to myself on the walk back. "Why did you hire a PI, and what was so interesting to you at the barber shop?"

# # #

I waited in my Civic in front of Antoine's until Diana Oliveri pulled in behind me.

I'd almost lost my nerve as I scanned the extensive list of services placarded on the front of the building. Apparently Antoine did more than cut hair. He operated a full-service spa and offered mysterious, exotic treatments such as an Indian head massage, Famape, a Vichy shower massage, and threading. Some of his offerings sounded intimidating and others downright scary. I'd have to be careful what I agreed to.

"Remind me to check my birth certificate when I get home," I said to Diana when she joined me on the sidewalk. "Just to make sure I'm really a girl."

"Don't worry," Diana said. "There's a card explaining

everything inside, and it's okay to just get a shampoo and cut. It's all I usually do."

Antoine, it turned out, was a fairly slight man, maybe five seven, and straight as a board. He wore tight-fitting black pants and a short-sleeved black shirt that revealed extensive tattoos snaking up both arms. A black leather holster around his waist held his haircutting tools. He spoke without a hint of an accent, but threw out phrases in French, like *mon ami* and *bon vivant* and *ça va* at random intervals, which I suspected was more branding than heritage.

Then again, the only French I knew was *bon appétit* and *deja vu*. Oh, and *allons-y*, but I learned that last one watching *Doctor Who*.

"Come in," he said. "I have to apologize. My receptionist is . . . out getting lunch. Who's first?"

I pushed—I mean allowed—Diana to go first.

While he clucked and cooed and pampered her, and gave her that shampoo she'd been drooling over, I wandered his shop.

The front was dedicated to product displays and empty waiting chairs, which might soon fill up again now that his main competition was dead. Considering the cost of the storefront, plus all the fancy equipment and doodads used to accomplish whatever medieval torture went on here, he must have been hurt financially by Marya's undercutting prices.

And despite his claim that the receptionist "stepped out for lunch," there were no personal items at the front desk. A Styrofoam cup didn't have a hint of lipstick on it, and I couldn't imagine a receptionist at an upscale salon went without. The phone was set on the left side of the desk, and when I glanced at Antoine as he began working on Diana's hair, he was holding his scissors in his left hand.

My guess was that he'd had to let his receptionist go months ago. Along with his cleaning service. The haircutting area was freshly swept. That, he'd have to do quite often. But debris lined the walls in the waiting area, and cobwebs wove in among the chair legs. And running a finger along the tops of the pricy products all lined up on the racks left traces of dust on my fingertips.

Antoine was clearly hurting.

"*Enchanté, mademoiselle*," he said when he called me back. "Or is it *madame*?"

Okay, I knew that, too. "The first one."

Diana grabbed my arm and held me back while Antoine cleaned his station. "Don't risk it," she whispered. "In the old country we used to say if a broom touches your feet, no man will come to sweep you *off* your feet."

I somehow doubted too many of my problems with the opposite sex were broom-related, but I humored her and waited.

Once he finished sweeping, Antoine gestured toward his chair, and I climbed in.

"And what can we do for you today?" While he said this he gave my hair a thorough inspection.

"Just a cut today, please. A trim, really. Nothing too drastic."

"You don't want something a little fresher? A little more chic, perhaps, maybe for the holidays? Some special event?"

"Well, I do have a date tonight." Famous last words.

With that, Antoine was off and running. I'll have to admit, Diana was right about the shampoo and deep conditioning. Many more of those and my life might lose its G-rating.

I took my glasses off while he began cutting. Second mistake. I didn't realize that he'd gone way past the trim I'd asked for until the razor came out for the back of my neck. By then it was too late, so I held my tongue while he pulled out the straightening iron and went to town.

"Voila!" he said with a flourish, and I was finally able to put on my glasses and see what he'd done.

My hair, I had to admit, perfectly framed my face, making me look like I'd dropped those twenty pounds I keep talking about. The style, a bit longer in the front and super short in the back, was probably inspired by some model or actress. I had to admit that the overall effect was pleasing enough, but the stranger in the mirror wasn't quite me.

Diana came up behind me and gaped at my hair in the mirror. "Ooh-la-la."

"*C'est magnifique*, eh?" Antoine said, pivoting the chair so I could see the rest of it, what there was of it.

Antoine leaned in until I saw his face next to mine in the mirror. "Only for the date, we wear contacts, yes?" He pulled off my glasses. "And maybe we do the makeup, too. Fix the eyebrows a little?"

This wasn't really a question, and I squinted at his list of services to see how much the makeover would set me back financially as Antoine gathered his supplies.

"You sure you have time?" I hedged.

He pointed to the empty waiting room. "Slow afternoon. You caught me at a good time."

"I imagine things will pick up now," I ventured. "Considering what happened."

"I usually get a run just before the holidays."

"I meant with Marya Young," I said.

Antoine waved off my comment as if Marya meant nothing to him. "Apples and oranges. Marya cut hair cheap. I can't say I didn't lose clients. But good riddance. The competition made me branch out to a full-service spa."

"But now perhaps a few of them will trickle back."

"And if they do, they pay a bit more, eh?" He froze. "Who cut your hair? Was that . . . sheepdog look . . . Marya's work?"

"Oh, no. My . . . relative cut it for me. Just does a little on the side."

He forced my head back to the mirror. "You want to look like a sheepdog, you go to a relative who cuts hair on the side. You want to look like a sleek, beautiful woman? You come to Antoine. *N'est-ce pas?*"

I somehow croaked out an agreement but had to stop while he started working on my lips.

"Pout," he said, squeezing my cheeks so that my lips puckered. "And hold it there." He leaned back. "Pouting suits you. You should do it more often."

"Not sure my father would agree," I said. "Getting back to Marya . . ."

He put his hands on his hips. "Must we go there?"

"No," I said but went there anyway. "I just wondered how she made a living charging so little."

"At first, I thought it was bait and switch. Give discounts to new clients and then once they're there, charge them more. But the discounts just continued. She must have been making peanuts."

"Her husband seemed to think she had quite a bit of money coming in."

"That may be so," Antoine said, smiling at his work in the

mirror, just before whisking off the cloth that protected my clothing. "But she didn't get it by cutting hair."

# # #

I somehow made it through the rest of the afternoon without touching my face and hair. I avoided eating or drinking anything lest I mar my lipstick, although the high-grade stuff he used seemed like I might still be trying to scrub it off a week later. I did take a few selfies, just in case I wanted to replicate what he did later. I even did one pouting, just to see if it suited me.

I waited by the back door for Ian to arrive. I already figured Cathy would be aghast if I wore my old coat, and I'd be freezing waiting outside in the short dress and heels. Especially now with the bare neck.

I wasn't sure what kind of car to expect. Ian Browning was loaded. Would he pick me up in a private limo? Or maybe a sleek sports car.

When the Toyota Prius pulled in behind the shop, I almost ignored it. Not until Ian climbed out of the driver's seat did I push open the back door.

"Your chariot awaits," he said.

"I didn't know that was you," I admitted.

"This okay?" he said. "My father seems content to squander his money on one of those high-falluting gas guzzlers, but this one is my choice."

"No, it's fine with . . ." I stopped when I realized I was getting a head-to-toe inspection. A blush would have been welcome, considering the chill in the air.

"Did you do something different?" He gestured to his own head.

"Tried a new hair stylist."

"I approve." He pulled open the car door.

The conversation on the way to the restaurant felt stilted. I noticed that he avoided the self-park and chose the valet service, tipping them well. He straightened his tie. "They have to eat, too."

While Cathy might have chosen a show-stopping dress, she hadn't considered one aspect: how much it would ride up my legs when I sat down. At the restaurant, I could at least cover my lap with a napkin. Sitting front row in a theater full of children? I wished I'd brought a bigger purse.

"So," he said, after the waiter had taken our orders and menus. "This is the date that might not be a date, depending on whether or not we hit it off."

"I think that was the agreement."

"Then let's not waste any time." He leaned forward, resting his cheek against his palm. "Where have you been all my life? Right here, above the toyshop?"

I wondered if his question was a veiled *Sabrina* reference, but I left it alone. Instead, I told him about growing up as the daughter of the town's chief of police.

At the next lull, I thought about hitting him up for grant money, but that felt rushed. "So what is it that you do exactly?" I asked. "I mean I know about the foundation. And I know you're doing some work on Jack's place."

"Jack Wallace is one of my oldest friends."

"Mine, too," I said, leaving out the past romantic interest.

Ian squinted. "He's been hiding you from me, I think." He laughed. "But basically, I work for my father. It seems he's amassed a pretty penny and needed someone to manage it for him, eventually. So Mom and Dad spawned one heir, raised him with the best tutors and private schools, and sent him off to Harvard Business School. Am I boring you yet?"

I shook my head.

"So my job, at least right now, is to assume control of his various assets, drop by drop, to make sure I can 'manage them appropriately.' To my father's way of thinking, that means doing everything exactly the way he would—and bringing even more filthy lucre into the family coffers, of course."

"But you run a charitable foundation," I said. "That has to be costing you money."

He ran his finger along the blunt edge of his knife. "You call it charity. My father calls it a tax write-off. And he only put me in charge of that because he was tired of dealing with the begging."

"I see."

"By the look on your face, I don't think you do," he said. "I enjoy the foundation work. It makes some of the other pointless things I do more palatable. In fact, I'd like to do more of it." He leaned in with his elbows against the table. "The conglomerate my father built is a bit stale. Stuck back in the last millennium. Doing what they've always done. Business today needs a different feel. Less impersonal. More socially responsible. Millennials want companies to have hearts and faces and ideals."

"And you'd like to be the heart and face of the company?"

He leaned back in his chair. "Someone has to. It'll all be mine someday, so why not?"

"So the charitable foundation . . ."

"Puts a more human face on the Browning name," he said. "Look, like anyone in business, my father has made a few enemies. He's beaten competitors out of contracts, had disputes with former employees. When you start giving back to the community in a meaningful way, focus shifts from that negative past to the positive things you're doing now. And people get helped. It's a win-win."

I nodded, unsure what to say. I suspected "meaningful ways" meant with lots of fanfare and cameras, and that just wasn't how I was taught to help people.

"My turn," he said. "Is working with toys what you want to do the rest of your life?"

The question took me a little by surprise. "I'm not sure," I finally said. "Don't get me wrong. I do like toys. But the thing that makes my job special is working with family. Toys were my dad's hobby a long time before we opened the shop, and I like to see him when he's working on them. He's relaxed and care-free. Maybe a little bit boyish." I thought of the times I'd spent working with Cathy and Miles, and even Amanda and Kohl. And the game nights when we shared our shop with the community. "Yes," I said. "I think I do."

He took a sip of his water then stared at the glass. I doubted I gave him the answer he was looking for. Our food came, interrupting his reverie.

After a few bites, I carefully blotted my lips. "Can I ask you about our project?"

"No."

"No? I thought you said—"

"I said you could pitch me your project *if* we didn't hit it off. On the contrary, I'm enjoying getting to know you. And I never do business on a first date."

"Not even attend a charitable function?" I teased.

"Okay, you got me. I'm a hypocrite. But only because I was

in a rush to see you, and I had two tickets. Tell you what. You can pitch your project to me on our second date. Fair?"

I agreed, and small talk ensued. And by "small talk," I mean that Ian told me more about what he might accomplish when every Browning business was under his expert management, and I nodded politely.

When we reached the theater, Ian pulled down the mirror and adjusted his hair and tie before getting out of the car. It didn't take long to see why, as media cameras were soon focused on him. I tried to get out of the way, but he had a firm grip on my arm. So I flashed a smile, tried not to look too uncomfortable, and hoped that some kindly photo editor somewhere would crop me out entirely.

The *Nutcracker*, on the other hand, proved delightful. Just as Cathy had predicted, the dancers in the performance were talented and well rehearsed. I was happy to note that the glossy printed program, which bore the Browning Foundation name in several prominent places, was large enough to set on my lap, so I didn't end up indecently exposing the minors as I sat in the front row.

When we parked in the alley next to the dumpster, Ian turned to me. "Invite me up for coffee?"

I looked up at the upper floors and noted the light on. "I'd better not. Dad's home, and he's, well, armed."

"Armed?"

I chuckled. "It's funny now, but so tragic in high school. I'd come home from dates, and there he'd be, standing right in the window that looked out over our front porch."

"Lots of parents are like that."

"Cleaning their guns?"

"No coffee then." He climbed out of the car and opened my car door.

When we stood by the back door he looked up, noted that there was no clear line of sight from upstairs, due to the awning and the growing icicles, then he pressed me up against the door and kissed me.

Two thoughts struck me. One, he'd done this before, and often. And two, the metal door was cold.

"I'll text you." He winked.

"Goodnight, Ian."

Chapter 14

When I woke up the next morning, I had no idea what time it was. Gray clouds hung low, giving the effect of perpetual twilight.

The TV weatherperson droned on about lake-effect snow in the forecast, and Dad was still there when I stumbled out of my bed in my Wonder Woman pajamas and somehow made it to the kitchen.

"Why, Miss Prince," he teased. "Coffee?"

I pulled out a chair at the table and buried my head in my hands. "Why am I so tired?"

"I don't know," he said as he put a large mug in front of me. "Sleuthing by day, gallivanting with rich playboys by night. It'll wear a person out." He sat in the adjacent seat next to his open newspaper. "And don't think me insensitive, but what in the blazes happened to your hair?"

"Antoine," I said. "Marya's biggest competitor. Everybody said it looked amazing yesterday. I must have slept on it funny."

"At least," Dad said.

Finally my eyes focused on the numbers on the clock. Half past seven. "What are you still doing here?"

"I'm leaving in a few minutes. No hurry this morning."

"That sounds ominous. Is the investigation slowing down?"

"Unfortunately, yes. Initial leads are drying up, one by one. We even looked into your new buddy, Antoine."

I shook a finger at my father. "Don't make fun of me. He had motive."

Dad took a sip of his coffee. "You know what else he has? A clear alibi. He was out at some special Reiki certification class. Multiple people can verify it." He folded up his paper and creased it with his thumb. "What I really need to do is talk with Ken Young."

"He still missing?" I asked.

"Last night his sisters came in to fill out a missing persons report. As if we weren't already looking for him."

"Do you think something could have happened to him?"

Dad cocked his head. "You mean like whoever killed Marya came back for him, too?"

The thought tied knots in my stomach.

Dad scrubbed his face with his hands. "I'll make sure we consider that angle. At least it will appease his staunch supporters in the department, especially if I end up having to put out a BOLO. It gives us a new question, though. Who might want both of them dead?"

"Ken's not dead," I said.

Dad nodded, but his face wasn't all that convincing.

# # #

Dad was right about my hair looking awful, and traces of that lipstick were stuck in the cracks of my lips, giving the appearance of pink scales. I'm surprised he didn't run away when he saw me.

A shower did little to improve things. I spent the whole

time worrying about Ken. "Please don't be dead," I said a couple of times to my shampoo and conditioner bottles.

And when I finally blow-dried my hair, I'd made a new discovery. Straight and styled by a professional, the short cut might have made me look like a "sleek, beautiful woman," as Antoine put it. But styled by me? It all curled up, making me resemble a poodle. I'd gone from *ooh la la* to *oy vey*. Was it truly a step up from a sheepdog?

Cathy's eyes popped when I got down to the shop. "Tell me you didn't go out like that."

"Looked fine yesterday. At the stroke of midnight, apparently I turned into a pumpkin." I pulled out my phone and showed her the selfie.

She looked at the picture, then at me, then at the phone again, then at me. "You want me to try to fix it?"

I swallowed hard. "It's just going to have to grow out. My hair does what it wants, and I've made peace with that."

Cathy continued to stare at my phone. "Great picture, though. If you ever join an online dating site, use this one."

"Wouldn't that be bait and switch?"

Cathy shook her head. "It's still you."

While she held my phone, it buzzed with an incoming text. I'd had one from Ian already, telling me he enjoyed our date last evening and inviting me to dinner later in the week at the nearby country club. This one came from Lionel Kelley.

"Lionel's finally going to let me look at that video," I said. "Can you spare me?"

"No problem," Cathy said. "Amanda's coming in later, so we should have everything covered." She rolled a shoulder. "But about the doll."

"Still up to her old tricks?"

Cathy nodded. "I wondered if you'd mind if I took her to see Althena."

"Your psychic friend?"

"I know you're a skeptic, but what if Marya's still around and trying to send us a message through the doll?"

"So you're suggesting it's not the doll, but rather the spirit of my ex-boyfriend's wife, and you thought I might find that comforting?"

"Forget I mentioned it," she said. "But do you mind if I take the doll?"

"I'd be happy to see it leave the building. And if Althena should take an interest in it, feel free to leave it with her. Now I have to scoot."

I'd made it halfway to the door when she called after me. "Maybe you should consider a hat?"

I took her advice on the hat and added a scarf to prevent frostbite on the back of my neck.

Lionel Kelley was waiting for me. He pushed open the door to his office and welcomed me in as if he hadn't been ducking me for the last few days.

"So you have the tape?" I asked.

"About that," he said.

"Come on, Lionel. We had an agreement."

"Yes, but—"

"Before you finish, I should remind you that I review on Yelp."

He closed his eyes then stood up a little straighter. "Liz, my first duty is to my client, and he's agreed to allow you to watch the video."

I reached out my hand.

"But he asked that it not leave the premises."

He gestured to two chairs sitting in front of a television screen.

"I have to watch it here?" I reluctantly pulled off my hat and headed to the chair. I was surprised when Kelley joined me. "You're watching, too?"

"I've been through it several times, but I'm curious to see if perhaps your fresh eyes and different point of view might cast new light on it." He picked up the remote. "I'll go through it pretty quickly. Let me know if you need me to slow it down."

Soon the video began playing. I noticed with some relief that the focus of the camera was clearly the entrance to the barber shop and not the toyshop, but I wondered about the connection to the pharmacist, if he was the client that hired Kelley to begin this particular surveillance.

Within a minute or two, I had a hard time keeping a straight face. The black-and-white footage, especially at the speed Kelley played it, gave the effect of watching a Charlie Chaplin movie. Only these were mostly very old women going in and out of the barber shop at breakneck speed. By the time a darling little white-haired woman speed-walked her walker into the building, I lost it.

Kelley paused the video. "What is so funny?"

I pulled off my glasses and wiped tears away with the back of my hand. Kelley was still staring at me.

"You don't find it mildly amusing?" I said, mimicking the quick speed of the woman with her walker.

Kelley shook his head.

"Is the whole video like this?" I asked. "Customers going in and out of the barber shop?"

"Yes."

"And you showed this to your client?" I asked.

Kelley stretched his neck. "Yes. But don't ask me who that is. You know I can't tell you."

"Did anything in the video help you in your investigation?"

Kelley folded his arms across his chest and drummed his fingers on his upper arm. "It was another place where the subjects of my investigation frequented. So, yes."

I leaned forward. "You weren't watching Marya. You were trailing the old people?"

Kelley clammed up tight.

"That's why you sent me to senior speed dating. Why are you watching old people?"

"Will you quit saying old people? It's not like I was watching all of them."

I squinted at him. "Some of them, then?"

He gave a brief, hesitant nod.

"So you were trailing certain old . . . you were trailing the subjects of you investigation and happened to notice them frequenting the barber shop, especially when Marya was working there."

"Yes," he said. "That, and the mysterious group at the library we now know is senior speed dating. And I apologized about that."

"Anywhere else?" I asked.

"A few of them go to bingo night at the fire hall, but not all, so I focused on the other two."

"And you can't tell me which ones are your subjects of interest?" I gave him my best pouty look, since Antoine had suggested it was my strength.

"No dice, Liz," he said. "Do you want to see the rest of it, or no?"

"Yeah," I said, pulling an old envelope and pen out of my purse. While I watched the rest, I did my best to stifle any residue of laughter and jotted down the names of various women that I'd recognized. A couple I'd met at senior speed dating. Others I knew from game nights and from just living in the town for much of my life. If I were to talk to all of them, I suspected a substantial amount of tea in my future.

The video continued up until the day that Marya was killed. When people stopped going in and out, the tape stopped too.

"You don't have that evening?"

Kelley waved off the question. "Nobody else was coming. I didn't see the point."

I had him replay the last bit. Marya never left, but neither did anyone else go in. At least not until after his tape had ended.

"If you'd only let it run a few hours longer."

# # #

As I headed back to the shop, I spotted the ancient barber standing in front of the barber shop, its crime scene tape still intact. I wasn't sure anyone knew his name. The barber shop was called Ed's, but it had borne the name since the 1800s. That Ed was surely dead and buried. But everybody called the barber Ed by default, and he seemed fine with it.

"Ed" wagged his head as I approached. "You've been through this," he said. "How long can they keep me shut down?"

I shrugged. "Until they think they've processed the whole crime scene. It helps to show up at the police station every now and then and put a little pressure on them."

His eyes lit up under those thick, bushy white brows. "Will you talk to your father? I had a new stylist come by to see if she wanted to rent Marya's old space, and she had to peek through the windows. Not a very good impression."

"That's pretty quick," I said.

He rubbed his neck. "I've had to postpone my flight to Florida. I'd like to get this all wrapped up before I go."

"I wanted to ask about Marya," I said. "She seemed to have quite a large clientele."

"She kept busy," the barber said. "And she paid her rent, so I have no complaints. But that woman, she didn't listen to reason. No business sense. Senior discount." He shuddered. Or shivered. Hard to tell.

"You don't think she managed her business well?"

"Discounts," he said with an emphatic wag of his finger, "bring in *new* customers. You manage a business. You know these things. But *senior* discounts? They're on limited income. Social security. Have you ever met an old woman who tipped well?" He shook his head. "I don't get it." The barber jerked his head toward the road and whistled. "Well, will you look at that!"

I did, then wished I hadn't. The salt-splattered red pickup cruising down Main Street had a large multi-point deer lying in the bed.

Then it was my turn to shiver, just as a few stray flakes began to fall and swirl in the breeze.

I had a vague suspicion I knew where Ken Young might be.

# # #

I'm *not* a total idiot.

I texted Dad to let him know where I was going, and I stopped in at the shop to check on Cathy and let her know, too.

Then I changed into warm casual clothes, my chunky boots with the best traction, and took along my heaviest gloves, hat, and scarf. I even thought to grab a couple packs of those little hand warmers to stuff into my gloves.

Ken had pointed out his hunting spot to me on a drive during the summer we were dating. I'd only been half paying attention. He thought he'd negotiated a great deal on a bit of land to maybe put up a nice log cabin home, only to find out it was landlocked. It had no easement for a road, just a walking trail about a quarter of a mile long to get there. So he'd decided to keep the existing rundown cabin and just use it for hunting.

With no access road, the property would probably be appraised for about half of what he paid for it, and since he was embarrassed to be snookered by his own shrewd business move, he hadn't told a lot of people. I doubted Dad knew about it.

But Ken went up there to hunt when he needed to think. And with his wife dead and his home invaded by Cujo and Mad Max, I can imagine he craved the solitude of the place.

The potholed county route looked different now, coated in white, from how it did in the summer months, and I traversed the stretch of road several times, windshield wipers slapping, before I caught the entrance to the trail. Moments later I spotted the graveled parking area where his truck was camouflaged in a layer of snow.

I pulled up next to it, climbed out, and soon found the trail. It was hard walking. As a kid, I always enjoyed playing in the snow, and Parker and I would trample the whole lawn. We were supposed to be making snow angels and snowmen, but when our parents weren't looking, we'd been known to chuck a few snowballs—and ice balls—at each other. But that ill-fated day when we played *Princess Bride* using icicles as swords? That got both of us grounded.

As an adult, though, trudging through the heavy snow

took more effort than I recalled, and I was huffing a bit by the time the cabin came into view.

And I use the term "cabin" a bit loosely.

Even by tiny house standards, this thing was small. And rickety. There were no windows, just a solid door at the front. The green shingles might have been asbestos, and the roof was snow covered in spots, bare in others, with large icicles hanging down, a sign of poor or no insulation. But that also meant someone was heating it, and a bit of smoke wisped from the decrepit chimney.

I texted Dad again then slipped my phone into my coat pocket.

After climbing a set of rough steps, which looked like they'd been hastily constructed from two-by-fours, I took a fortifying breath and knocked.

No answer.

I tried again, and still no answer. Finally, feeling a little brave—or perhaps a little cold—I tried the knob and the door swung open.

Once my eyes adjusted to the dim light, I could see it was clearly no palace on the inside, either. Blankets were bunched up on a twin mattress on the rough plank floor. The only other furnishings were a folding camp chair, a small collapsible table—that looked on the verge of collapse—and, in the corner, a plastic bucket with a toilet seat attached to the top.

I'd found Hooverville.

I did an about-face and marched straight to the door, determined to leave. But when I pulled open the door, there was Ken Young. Carrying a chainsaw.

Chapter 15

"Liz!" Ken startled as he bobbled and then dropped the wood he carried under his arm. "What are you doing here?" He stopped to pick it up.

"Don't you know half the town is looking for you?"

He blew out an exasperated breath. "I thought it might come to that eventually." He stacked most of the wood onto the pile next to the cast iron stove and then added some on top of the glowing embers inside. The wood caught and flames kicked up hotter.

"Your sisters filed a missing persons report, and Dad was about to issue a BOLO. I need to tell him." I reached again for my cell.

"Wait," he said. "Before you do, we need to talk." He pulled open a small, battery-powered lantern on the table, and it lit up the room—well, that portion of the room in a three-foot circle from the lantern. "Have you had lunch?"

"Lunch?"

"It's a meal people eat, usually sometime around the noon hour."

"I guess I haven't."

"Then you're in luck," he said. "I make a great woodstove grilled cheese. Or pancakes. Come to think of it, that's pretty much the gamut of my cooking skills. Pick your poison." He snapped his fingers. "Or is poison a poor choice of words coming from a murder suspect? I, uh, am a suspect now, right?"

I inhaled through my teeth. "I'm afraid they're not coming up with many more leads."

He nodded. "Pancakes then? I have just enough real maple syrup for one more meal, and I'd hate for it to go to waste if I'm going to prison. Please." He pointed to the camp chair. "Make yourself comfortable."

I pulled off my outerwear and draped it on the back of the camp chair. Finally I pulled off the hat and did my best to smooth my hair with my fingers.

I sank into the chair. "Why are you holed up here?"

"Just a second. This is the crucial part." I watched as he eyeballed the ratio of water and pancake mix into a bowl and stirred it with a wooden spoon. He grimaced a bit then added substantially more pancake mix. "Hope you're hungry."

Only after the first three pancakes were bubbling up on the cast iron skillet did he answer. "First of all, I'm not 'holed up here.' I'm innocent until proven guilty, and I have a perfect right to come and go as I please."

"Without telling anyone? Your sisters were worried."

"And if my sisters knew about this cabin?" He stabbed the air with the spatula. "I'd have no place to get away and think. Look, my gut instinct is to help the police. That shyster they hired told me to clam up, and then he claimed he was tied up and couldn't talk for a few days. But I'm sure I'll have a bill long before then. Meanwhile, someone killed Marya." His voice cracked. "If anyone has a shot at figuring out who that might be, it's me. I needed to think."

"Fair enough."

He turned back to the stove and flipped the pancakes, sending off a hearty sizzle. His shoulders slumped. "I didn't mean to lose my temper with you."

"You must be under a lot of stress."

"That may be so." He slid a heaping plate in front of me, along with a bent metal fork and a jug of maple syrup bearing the label of a local farm. "But of all people, you don't deserve it."

I paused to consider what he meant.

"Go ahead while they're hot. I'll have the next ones."

I slathered syrup over the whole plate. "Have you thought of anything helpful?"

"It must have something to do with the money."

"I'd heard that you were going over Marya's business records."

The next batch went into the pan before he answered. "Does that seem creepy? That sounds creepy, even to me."

"I assumed that you wouldn't have done it without good reason."

"Thanks for believing that," he said. "At first I thought I was losing my mind. I bounced a check trying to pay a bill when I knew there was enough in the account. I checked the balance online, and almost the whole account was cleaned out. Then it magically reappeared. Marya tried to shrug it off as a bank error, but I backtracked and found she'd made a whole series of withdrawals and deposits. No explanation. But after I confronted her, she left the account alone.

"Then one day I knocked over her purse by accident. She

had almost a thousand dollars in cash stuffed into her wallet. I volunteered to make a bank deposit for her, told her it wasn't safe to carry so much around. I was trying to be helpful. But she just got defensive and nervous. She was up to something. Something she didn't want me to know about."

"You thought it might be something illegal?"

His shoulders sagged. "I must have gone over every piece of paper in the house a dozen times. Every account. Every record. And I still don't get it. Money came in from nowhere and vanished just as fast."

I avoided his eyes and dug into my lunch. "Mark Baker has those records now."

He wrestled with some bags in the corner and returned with another camp chair, which he propped up on the opposite side of the table. "Probably for the best. Sharp man. Maybe he can turn up something. It can only help me."

Even in the dim light, I noticed him eating his pancakes with a spoon.

"Do you get more syrup that way?" I asked.

He looked down at the spoon. "Only one set of utensils. Don't get much company here. Not invited company, anyway."

"That sounds ominous."

"Everything was all topsy-turvy when I got here. Not like I remembered it, and I swore I had more food. Maybe it's just my imagination, though. Or maybe some kids found the place. I'll have to get a lock. Assuming . . ."

I let that comment slide. Assuming he didn't go to prison.

"Back to Marya," I said. "You'd been following her, too?"

He let his spoon fall onto his plate. "You know that?" He stared down at his puddle of syrup. "Yeah, I guess I was.

Caught her lying. Told me she was going to the library on an evening when I knew the library closed early. I thought maybe there was someone else. That maybe she was giving *him* money."

"Did you find evidence of infidelity?"

He shook his head. "Look, if I'm going to have to tell everyone about this, I might as well practice on you. In case you haven't guessed, Marya and I weren't particularly close lately. She came up here saying she wanted to make amends, but it became clear that she was just trying to get immigration off her back. I understand that. She had a long battle." He looked up at me. "You know about any of that?"

"Your sisters told me. They also told me repeatedly how the two of you were *perfectly suited* to each other, but I suspect they were trying to get under my skin."

Ken rolled his eyes. "Sorry about that. They loved Marya. She could be a charmer when she wanted to. Didn't hurt that she cut their hair for free. They might have been more taken in than I was." He winced. "That sounds bitter, doesn't it?" He scrubbed his face with his hands. "I was furious. Not that I wanted anything to happen to Marya, but I was so angry that she'd come up here, tried to cozy up to me, turned everything upside down, and then was sneaking around, involved in who knows what. Now she's dead, and I'm trying to remember the good things, and that's painful. But so is remembering the bad things. And I feel guilty every time I get angry."

He released his clenched fists. "A year ago, I'd thought I'd closed that chapter of my life, and that you and I were starting something new. I was tempted to tell her I'd moved on." He looked up and his eyes glistened in the lantern light. "But the costs were so high for her. Arrest. Deportation to a country she had no memories of. I couldn't just walk away. But we had separate bedrooms, you know. That part of our marriage was long over. I want you to know that."

I shrugged. "Not sure that's any of my business."

"I hoped you'd understand." He stared down at his plate. "Marya was so young, so vulnerable. I guess I fancied myself as some valiant knight rescuing the damsel in distress. She was grateful. I was flattered. Somehow we both mistook that for love—or at least, I did—but after a few months that fairy tale disintegrated. On the day she got her citizenship, we celebrated with ice cream and divorce planning."

"Yet you were still together."

"Filing immediately could have raised eyebrows. If someone at INS decided that we'd entered into the relationship just to evade immigration laws, we both could have been charged. Seems the government considers that fraud."

Before I could respond, the cabin started creaking.

"Don't be alarmed," he said, "the wind must have kicked up."

"You still should have called my father. To let him know where you were."

"My cell's dead. Not that it would do me any good here. No reception."

I pulled my cell out of my coat pocket. And no, the little icon that lights up when there's phone reception—which is like, always, except after that time I dropped it in Val's water dish, but rice brought it back—wasn't there, and I also had a nice little "unable to deliver" notice about that last text I'd sent Dad.

"I think the hills interfere with the signal," he said. "Sometimes you can't get a connection even at the road."

"Dad's going to worry. I need to get back." I turned to Ken. "Will you come, too? It'll look better than if he has to come get you."

He smirked and gestured to his meager surroundings. "As lovely as this place is, I guess I can't stay here forever. Let me just do the dishes and douse the fire."

Doing dishes proved complicated with no running water, but after he'd heated a pan and I helped him wash the sticky plates and utensils, he doused the fire. In moments the deep chill seeped into the cabin. We donned our winter things and he pulled open the door.

The sky loomed dark, as dark as if it were night, and snow had drifted up against the door, maybe as high as my waist.

"Did you happen to listen to the weather forecast before you came up here?" he asked.

"It said something about lake effect, but you know they always over blow those things."

Thunder crashed nearby and Ken pushed the door shut. "I have playing cards."

"Sure we can't make it?" I pulled open the door again. The knob had left a visible imprint in the compacted snow. This time it took both of us to shut the door against the wind, and not until it blew a little of that drift inside.

"This is bad," I said.

"Yeah," Ken said. "I'll bet Jim Cantore is out there somewhere, dancing in the thunder snow."

"I'd meant being stranded. Dad's going to be . . ." I trailed off because I wasn't sure what he was going to be. Angry? And if so, at whom? Me, for coming out here? Ken, for laying low?

Ken relit the fire then started to shuffle his cards.

I walked my phone around the cabin. Once I thought I

saw a single bar light up, but I couldn't get it to repeat. I began to wonder if it might have been a trick of the light.

So we whiled away the hours playing cards. Every game I could think of, ending with cribbage. I made a makeshift cribbage board on an envelope I had in my purse.

"What's that?" Ken said, pointing to the names I had written on the other.

"That," I said, "is a list of some of the customers who saw Marya in the days leading up to her death."

He took it and read down the list.

"Mean anything to you?" I asked.

"I know a few of them," he said. "I've seen their names in her appointment books."

"The barber thinks she pursued the wrong clientele and gave too many discounts to turn a profit."

"I've thought as much myself." He continued to shuffle.

I swallowed hard. "You said something once, or rather started to say, you were worried she'd gone back to her old habits."

He said nothing, just dealt the cards.

"What did you mean by 'old habits'? You never explained it."

"That's because I don't know," he said. "She told me there were a few things in her past that it might be better I didn't know. I gathered she had been involved in something sketchy, maybe downright illegal. She assured me that was all over. That she only did what it took to survive her situation."

"What did you think she was involved in?"

"She was busted for drug possession back in high school." He rearranged the cards in his hand. "At the time she said they weren't for her, that they were her sister's. She told me later she was trying to help wean her sister off the drugs. I know it's near impossible to quit a lot of those things cold turkey, so

I guess I believed her. Now I'm not sure. Maybe Marya was using. Maybe selling. Maybe buying. Who knows?"

"Anything lead you to think she herself had a drug problem?"

He shook his head. "She kept going to the twelve-step programs, even after the court order expired. I wasn't sure what to make of that since she claimed she never used. Maybe she found support there. But I never found anything in the house." He sighed. "Not for lack of checking. The more lies she told and secretive she seemed, the more tyrannical I became. I started searching her purse whenever she took a shower." He winced. "I never thought I'd become that husband. Not sure why I did it."

"Because you still cared about her."

"Or maybe I just cared about me."

I rubbed his hand. "Now you're just being hard on yourself. If that were true, you never would have taken her back."

The creaking and groaning of the old place grew more incessant. He glanced up. "This isn't letting up anytime soon. I'm afraid you're stuck here for a while."

I closed my eyes. Being stranded during a snowstorm was a real, albeit infrequent threat when you grew up in what was known as the "Snow Belt" south of Buffalo. I'd been snowed in for an extra day at Jenny Hill's slumber party. That was fun at first, but when we ran out of ice cream and new questions for truth or dare, the party became a little boring. We were all glad—and that went double for her haggard parents—when the plows finally made it down her street.

But that was better than the time we got snowed in at home when I was eight. Dad had to work, as usual, and Mom sneaked off to "pay a few bills." Of course, she went on a bender, and Parker and I survived the whole weekend on Pop-Tarts, peanut butter sandwiches, and unheated cans of SpaghettiOs.

But this was a first, being stuck in a wilderness cabin with a man I once dated. On some level it could be considered romantic. I glanced at the bucket in the corner with the toilet seat attached and sighed. So *not* romantic.

When I looked back up at Ken, he was staring into my eyes. "Have you considered that this might be providential? That maybe the weather is luring you and me back together?"

I set my cards back down on the table and folded my hands in front of me. "What would you like me to say?"

"I'd like to hear you say that you know I didn't kill Marya, that people can change and a relationship can be restored."

"I know you didn't kill Marya," I said then stopped.

"And?"

"And yes, I believe that relationships can be restored. That is, if they were ever healthy in the first place. If you're talking about you and me . . . You and I were just getting to know each other when I learned that everything you told me, everything our friendship was built upon, was a lie."

"I regret how things turned out. I meant to tell you. I was about to tell you when Marya showed up."

"But you didn't."

"And I am sorry." He placed his hand over mine. "Is there no hope of redemption?"

I pulled back my hand, took off my glasses, and rubbed my eyes. Playing cards in the low light was beginning to trouble them. I kept my eyes closed when I continued, in part because it was easier not to see his face.

"Ken," I said, my voice wavering just slightly. "There's

always hope of redemption. I wish you well and I hope you find it. But you and me? I don't know."

When I opened my eyes, Ken was nodding. "Give it some thought and time," he said. "I don't mean we start right now and try to pick up where we left off. But maybe, after a reasonable period . . . Meanwhile, I think we need to get some rest."

I looked around to figure out how that might be possible.

Ken stood and put another log in the fire. "I suppose I could take the mattress and you could take the loft."

"There's a loft?" I looked up. I had thought that someone just hadn't bothered to finish putting in the plywood ceiling.

"There's another twin mattress up there, already made up. And another pot, if you need one. There's instructions on the side, if you're unfamiliar."

"Thanks," I said, as he propped a ladder that I'd mistaken for empty shelving up against the side of the loft.

When I reached to the top, he handed me up another battery-powered lamp, then stood on the steps like a rejected Romeo.

"Good night," I said.

He climbed back down the steps, and I inspected the space. I found the pot and managed to read through the directions in the dim light. Seemed easy in theory, but still not private enough to suit me. I glanced around to see how I might improve upon the situation.

The loft, I decided, must have served as the main sleeping area for the original resident, who could have been an outlaw, a revenuer, or perhaps Laura Ingalls, who used the creaking and groaning space as an inspiration for writing the book *The Long Winter*, which I'd found heartily depressing when I'd read it in the fifth grade. But the loft was a little better furnished than the lower level. There was even a roughly framed-in closet which I thought might make for an excellent place to put the pot, so that I could take care of my most pressing needs more privately.

The door stuck when I tried to open it, but there was no visible lock, so I pulled harder. Every time I made headway, it pulled back shut, like it was held by elastic. Too tired to process the physics of this, I left off applying pressure, then all of a sudden gave the door a quick yank.

And stared into the surprised, frightened face of Marya Young.

Chapter 16

I screamed.

Marya screamed, and when she did, I realized her face appeared a little older and more haggard than I'd ever seen it. But considering she'd just been murdered, how could she be in the closet? Or screaming, for that matter?

I screamed again.

Ken raced up the ladder, and I positioned myself behind him.

"Anechka!" he said.

"Anechka?" I repeated, peeking out from behind him.

"What are you doing here?" Ken approached the closet.

Anechka stumbled out. The resemblance to Marya was still striking, but Ken's lantern illuminated the differences: a harder jaw, paler skin, and deep fatigue underscoring her eyes. I caught just a glimpse of her hands. Marya's were always dainty and well manicured. Anechka's were disfigured and scarred. But a glimpse was all I got. She jammed her hands into the pocket of her boxy sweater.

"Why are you hiding in the closet?" Ken asked.

"You didn't know?" I asked Ken.

He shook his head but never let his gaze veer from Anechka.

"I was sleeping when you first arrived," she said. "I could tell it was not Marya down there, but I did not know who it was. Marya told me to stay hidden."

"You saw Marya?" Ken asked. "How long have you been here?"

"Is hard to say. One day runs into another. But she has not been here in days, and then you come. I did not know what to think."

"So you haven't heard what happened," I said.

"What?" She shifted an uneasy gaze between Ken and me.

"Maybe you'd better come downstairs and sit down," Ken said, offering her his hand.

# # #

A rough night followed. Not only did the storm beat incessantly on the little cabin, but Anechka didn't take the news of the death of her sister particularly well. She went from wailing to self-recrimination, then back to wailing, then to questioning Ken's involvement and making awkward suggestions about what I was doing there alone with him so soon after her sister's death.

Ken used his skills in interrogation to get her to recount her story. She hesitantly related how she had called her sister for help and Marya had sent her a bus ticket, picked her up at the station, and took her straight to the cabin. Anechka couldn't place the exact day she arrived, but it was long before the snow fell.

"What happens now?" she asked, her face turning even more ashen. "Will you have to tell anyone I'm here?" Her eyes widened and she scanned the room wildly, as if plotting a course to escape.

"Now," Ken said, "we have breakfast."

In the middle of our grilled cheese—since we'd finished the pancakes—a snowmobile engine revved outside.

Ken pulled the door open and was met with a wall of white that had packed up against it. He grabbed a shovel and started putting snow into his dishpan, since he had no other place to put it.

But he wasn't the only one clearing. Soon light appeared through the snow, then a porthole opened, revealing a blue sky on the other side. Moments later my father stuck his head in the hole.

He looked at Ken, then at me, then did a double take at Anechka.

"Ken Young?" he said. "Would you please come with us? I'd like to ask you some questions regarding the death of your wife."

# # #

My trip to the station was on the back of a snowmobile driven by a rookie cop I knew only as Jenkins. At first I clutched the folds of his jacket loosely, but by the time he got up to speed, rocking the snowmobile precariously on the uneven trail and even going airborne over a few dips, I had my arms crossed around his chest, holding on for dear life.

A couple of hours later my adrenaline levels returned to normal as I paced in the office of the chief of police. I wasn't sure who that title belonged to: my father or the man my father was currently letting sweat it out in the interrogation room.

"You know, the waiting game isn't going to be very effective on him," I told my dad. "He's wise to those tricks."

"It gives *me* time to cool down, though." Dad plopped into his chair and leaned back. "What were you thinking?"

"That Ken was missing, maybe dead, and I got a lead to where he might be. I just followed it."

"You should have—"

"Let you know? I texted you that I was going to try to find Ken's hunting lodge."

"But not where it was, or that you were holed up with him there all night!"

"I tried. What would you have me do, MacGyver a homemade cell tower out of a ladder, three spatulas, aluminum foil, and a roll of duct tape?"

Dad held his tongue for a moment. "You know I just want you safe, right?"

I put my arm around him and gave him a hug. "I was safe. Ken's not a killer. That rookie Jenkins on the other hand . . ."

"What did he do?"

"Gave me quite a wild ride on the way back. I think he was doing it on purpose."

Dad's jaw took on a serious grimace. "Sorry about that. I should have figured something like that would happen."

"What's his beef with me?"

"You gotta remember, he joined the force under Ken's administration, and it's natural that his loyalty is to him. He's pretty sure his boss isn't a killer."

"But why take it out on me?"

Dad just sent me a painful smile.

"Because he thinks I might have killed Marya." That revelation nearly knocked the wind out of me.

"You make a convenient scapegoat. And not only that, I'm also a threat, trying to usurp his boss's authority. It's been tense around here." Dad scratched the back of his head and exhaled a lungful of frustration. "To be honest," he said in a measured tone tinged with sheepishness, "I didn't see your first message until late last night. Between the murder investigation and the stress in the department, I didn't know you were gone until Cathy started calling every five minutes." He leaned his elbows on his desk and buried his face in his hands. "Do you know how many men, how many man-hours, how much special equipment, it took to find you in that little love shack of his?"

"Love shack?" I folded my arms, perhaps a little petulantly. "Well, sorry for the inconvenience. I guess it doesn't matter that I found the man your whole department was looking for?" I jabbed a finger at him. "And Anechka!" I looked around. "Where did she go, anyway?"

"We sent her straight to the hospital to get checked out."

"She must have been hidden in that loft, without much food or water, for days."

He threw his hands up. "And now there's immigration to deal with. What a mess."

"Sounds like someone wouldn't mind getting out of the cop business and back into the toy business."

"There's a big difference between chasing a few leads and allocating the resources of the whole department. I'd forgotten what a headache it could be." He looked around to make sure nobody was listening in. "Not to mention every man that came on board under Ken's administration thinks I'm out to railroad their boss and steal his job."

I hugged him. "You're doing a good job, but maybe you see now why I didn't want you involved so much?"

179

He finished the hug with a hearty clap to my back and pushed away. "Do you see now why I didn't want you chasing down leads on your own? Your involvement in this case doesn't exactly earn me any respect in the department. And you. You were stuck in that cabin all night with a suspect."

"With *Ken*. He's a friend. At least he was once."

He winced. "And you also might want to check in with Mark Baker."

"Mark?"

"He was here when we started the search. In fact, he was the one who found the deed to that property tucked away in the couple's financial records."

"So he knows . . ."

Dad treated me to a particularly awful toothy grin. "Just that you were off looking for Ken Young, and that you were gone all night."

"Swell," I said. I'd plugged my phone in to recharge when I reached the station, and I picked it up now to find multiple texts from Mark, Dad, and Cathy. "Apparently my social life just blew up in my face."

Dad placed his hand on my upper arm. "Welcome to law enforcement."

# # #

Cathy, of course, was relieved to hear from me and assured me she had the store covered if I needed to get some sleep. I texted Mark, then sent another text explaining the first text, then stared at my phone hoping it would buzz. When it still hadn't ten minutes later, I broke down and called him, but it went to voice mail, so I left a message that sounded confusing even to me. And I knew the whole story.

On zero sleep and a boatload of caffeine, I finally left the police station and walked, no, marched between the walls of plowed snow directly to the pharmacy. One, I needed pain relievers for a headache that threatened to burst my skull apart, and two, if Lionel Kelley was going to continue being cagey, I was going straight to the horse's mouth.

I waved at the clerk again at the front counter then made my way through the sparsely populated aisles to the back of the store. Charles Barr was with a customer, so I sat in the small waiting area and tried out the automatic blood pressure machine. I think I broke it.

I paced. Took a seat. Paced again. Tried a different seat. Flipped through a magazine without seeing any of the pages, and then, when I didn't think I could stand it any longer, the customer left with her little white bag, and I went up to the counter.

"Mr. Barr?" I said, pointing to the name plate.

"How can I help you?" he said with a smile. I had a feeling that smile wouldn't last very long.

"My name is Liz McCall," I started. I watched his face for any sign of recognition.

If he knew of me, he didn't let on. Instead, he went over to a small collection of prescriptions already filled and started looking at the names. "I don't see anything . . ."

"No, I'm not here for a prescription," I said, then ran a hand through what was left of my hair, post Antoine. "This is awkward. Let me try again. I manage Well Played, the toyshop right next to the barber shop."

His moustache twitched a little as recognition dawned.

"I noticed Lionel Kelley watching the shop, and I know he's working for you."

"Did he tell you that?"

"No, he was adamant about not revealing his client. I happened to see you come out of his office." I didn't mention that I'd practically glued myself to the glass. "I know you don't have to say anything at all to me, but I'm not sure you understand what's at stake here. A young woman has been murdered. My boyfriend—I mean my ex-boyfriend—might get arrested for it. Her sister's in the hospital and may get deported. My boyfriend—I mean, my *friend*—won't text me back, and I got this awful haircut."

To my horror, my voice cracked, and tears started streaming down my cheeks. I needed sleep. Bad.

His moustache twitched again, and he cast a nervous glance toward the front of the store. "Look, don't cry. I'll talk to you. But not here. I have a break in twenty minutes." He pushed a tissue box toward me. "How about I meet you somewhere."

"The tea shop?" I suggested.

"Fine," he said softly, and then a little more loudly, probably for the benefit of the counter clerk, "and have a nice day!"

# # #

Rather than go home and clean up, which would have been the rational thing to do, I went straight to the tea shop.

I had mixed feelings about this place. I loved sniffing all the small demo canisters of loose tea. I set out to try something a little bit different with every visit, and this time I picked out a lovely blueberry something or other. The words were blurring as I tried to read them. I sure hoped the tea had caffeine.

The only thing I had against the tea shop was that it replaced the cupcake shop that closed last year, and I still mourned the loss of my favorite sugar fix.

Once I'd paid for the tea, I sat at a table and lingered over the steamy aroma so long that my glasses fogged over. Not that I needed to see what was going on around me. More thoughts than I could handle were roiling around in my head.

I'd ticked off an awful lot of people.

Lionel Kelley would be miffed that I'd confronted his client. But at this point, I didn't care what he thought, and if he raised too big a stink over it, I could always remind him that I was privy to his . . . passion for ponies.

Dad was ticked at me. I replayed the whole scenario in my head. At first I wasn't sure what else I could have done. But after the caffeine hit I realized that, yeah, maybe once I'd found Ken's truck, I could have driven back to the station and dragged someone out there with me. Not that I was in danger, except for maybe that cabin collapsing under the weight of the snow. Or a heart attack when I opened that closet door.

Anechka? I wouldn't call her ticked at me. She seemed terrified, mostly. Sure, when she'd learned that I had briefly dated her brother-in-law, I got a few dirty looks, but I'd grown used to those. Maybe after she was treated at the hospital she could supply my father with information pertinent to the investigation. I doubted it, though. Even if Dad could ease her fears enough to get a coherent statement, Anechka hadn't even known that Marya was dead. Still, she might be able to shed some light on her sister's activities in those last few weeks, the ones that had made Ken so suspicious.

Ken wasn't ticked at me either. He'd seemed so hopeful of, after a reasonable mourning period, resuming our relationship.

Jenkins and some of Ken's other loyal officers might more happily see me strung up for killing Marya.

But Mark. I pulled out my phone and turned the volume

way up so I wouldn't miss a text or call, and set it on the table in front of me.

And then there was Ian. As I looked at my phone I realized that my date with him was no longer "tomorrow." I'd have to get some sleep to deal wisely with that. Still, Ian was a good conversationalist, especially when talking about himself. I figured I could get him going and not have to worry about constructing full sentences out of my sleep-deprived brain.

I'd started my second cup of tea by the time Charles Barr slid into the seat opposite me. He didn't remove his jacket, and he didn't look like he planned to stay long.

"I called Lionel before I came, and he said I don't have to tell you anything."

"That's probably true," I said. "I hoped you'd want to."

"Why would I? The little matter I had Lionel looking into had nothing to do with the death of that woman. And you're not even with the police."

"Also true," I said, "but the police might want to decide for themselves if your 'little matter' is relevant when I tell them what I found out. They'd come to your place of work, perhaps, ask you to accompany them, give you a truly lousy cup of coffee, then make you wait forever until they grill you for all the details. If, on the other hand, you tell *me* what the investigation was all about, I could pass that information along, and if it's not relevant to the murder investigation, you might not have to have that conversation with them at all. Wouldn't that be better?"

While he paused to think it over, I said, "Would you like a cup of tea?"

"Earl Grey, hot," he said, leaving me wondering if that was his preference or if he were a *Star Trek: The Next Generation* fan.

When I returned with his tea and a refill of mine, he seemed more ready to talk. He'd taken off his checked coat and laid it across the next empty chair. After a glance at his watch, he began.

"Okay, the first thing you need to know is that I've only worked at the pharmacy for three months. The last place I worked got swallowed up by a huge conglomerate, and my job went to a perky new grad named Debbie who was happy to work for three-quarters of my salary." He lifted the tea to his mouth and took his first cautious sip. "Mmm. This is good."

I nodded.

"I'd used up all my severance by the time I scored the job here. Just the kind of place I was looking for. Not too many independent drugstores left these days. Only, the mom-and-pop shops tend to have moms and pops. The clerk at the desk? She owns the place with her husband. She's my boss."

"Which is why you didn't want to talk there."

"I don't want to lose this job too."

"Yet you're fearful that you may."

At this he started into a full-fledged fidget. "You need to understand that I didn't do anything wrong. I'm careful in my work. I've never experienced anything like this before."

I leaned forward. "Like what?"

"Complaints."

"Look, I know customers can be difficult at times, especially when they're sick."

He took a deep breath and let it out slowly. "I've received complaints that I've shorted people on their pills. Multiple complaints. I can see maybe making one mistake, not that it's ever happened before. At least not to my knowledge. I'm usually the one who *catches* mistakes. Like the time the doctor accidentally prescribed the adult dose of a medication for an infant." He sat up a little straighter. "I might have saved that child's life."

"Nice work," I said.

"I take pride in my work. Not like certain teenyboppers named Debbie. So the first customer who came in complaining, I apologized profusely. The amount of painkillers is all controlled, so it was a nightmare getting the okay from the doctor and insurance to cover the missing pills, and I had to eat the co-pay myself. But we worked it out, and I thought it was all over.

"Then the next week it happened again. Different customer. I was suspicious, but basically did the same thing. Fortunately it was a different insurance company and different doctor. But two days later . . . I didn't know what I was up against. I started counting pills out loud, just to double check." His eyebrows furrowed. "I'm nearly positive I'm not the problem."

"So you thought maybe the clients . . . ?"

He leaned forward. "It happens. People strapped for cash have been known to sell their medication. Kids sell their ADHD meds at school to students who find it helps them study, and then they raid their grandparents' medicine cabinet. There's always a street market for opiates. I thought that might be happening here. But all of a sudden? I figured there might be some kind of conspiracy. So I gave the names to Kelley and hired him to check them out. See where they might gather together."

I rested my elbows on the table. "And he found they met together at senior speed dating, and most of them had their hair cut by Marya Young."

"It probably sounds absurd," he said. "All these people are older, respected members of the community."

"There might be a live one or two in there," I said, thinking of my writer friend.

"Do you think the police will still want to talk with me?"

I paused for a second then nodded.

He slid back into his chair with an exasperated sigh.

"But," I said, "don't wait for them to come to you. When you get off for the day, go straight to the station and tell them all this yourself. It's better if you volunteer it." I took a sip and found myself smiling as I set my cup down. "Tell them Liz McCall sent you."

Chapter 17

I somehow dreamt I was Laura Ingalls Wilder trying to survive the ferocious, long winter by binding hay to be burned to keep us warm. And then Doctor Who came to rescue me. But it wasn't Doctor Who. It was my Doctor Who ring tone.

"Hello?" I croaked into my cell phone.

"Hi, there."

"Mark." I pushed myself up to sit on the bed and wiped the sleep from my eyes. "What time is it?"

I glanced at the blurry clock, then I bobbled my glasses when I tried to pick them up and they fell between the bed and the nightstand.

"A little after four," he said. "Sorry I didn't get to return your texts or calls until now. I was tied up at work."

Now I regretted sending him so many. Desperate, much? "I just wanted to make sure you knew I was all right. Seems there was a bit of confusion." I winced.

"All I heard is that you found Ken Young," he said.

Relief flooded me.

"And then got snowed in with him in some rustic hunting lodge."

"Not what it sounds like," I said. "And we weren't alone. We found Anechka."

"Marya's sister?"

"It seems Marya was hiding her. Could that have anything to do with the money situation?"

"It would take money for food and supplies, but not the kind that her hubby was tracking in and out of her accounts."

"I have a lead where it might be coming from." I told him what I'd learned from Charles Barr.

"Does your father know this yet?"

I shook my head then rolled my eyes. I must've been only half awake if I thought he could see either. "I recommended Barr see Dad and tell him himself."

"So you're thinking Marya was what? Buying pills from older customers and reselling them? That's quite an operation. I guess it might explain where the money came from."

"But not where it was going," I said.

"Still, it's progress. What are you up to tonight?"

"Tonight?"

"I thought maybe we could have dinner and go over a few things."

"I can't tonight. I'm . . . pitching the doll project to the Browning foundation." I winced. True enough. But I neglected to tell him it was with Ian over dinner at the country club. And that Cathy had rummaged up another humdinger of a dress, this one from a local consignment shop where the owner said I could consign it back after the evening was over as long as I didn't damage it.

"Tomorrow night?" he said.

"Tomorrow is game night at the shop," I said. "Unless you wanted to catch a quick dinner before? Might have to be takeout though. I need to put some hours in at the shop, or as my own boss, I might have to dock my pay."

"Well, we wouldn't want that. Tomorrow night, then. Have a good meeting."

I felt like a rat when I hung up the phone. Tomorrow when we had dinner, when I could see him face to face, I'd clarify all those half truths.

Cathy showed up at five thirty with a bin of beauty products, determined to do something about my hair. "I'm not as good as Marya was," she said. "Or Antoine, even though I don't think the cut works for curly hair. But I think I can improve on what you've been doing."

"Yes, ma'am," I said, and let her at it. She worked silently, and I might have dozed off once. By six thirty, I was almost a new woman. She'd tamed the poodle into gentle waves, but not stopping there, went on to see that my nails were freshly groomed and colored and that my makeup looked better than Antoine had done—more natural, which seemed to suit my personality better.

I leaned in closer to the mirror. "I can barely make out the dark circles under the eyes."

"I'm still waiting on details of that, you know."

"I know." I closed my eyes. "Not sure I want to rehash all that then go out with Ian. Can we save it for later?"

Cathy agreed, but her somber tone suggested she'd rather have the gory details now. "Oh, I gave the doll to Althena."

"Good riddance."

"And she gave it right back. Apparently dolls creep her out. She said she sensed some kind of negative energy associated with her."

"I'll buy that. It gives me the willies, too."

"But nothing more than that. Unless I set up a session and pay her."

I started to shake my head, but she cautioned me to hold still.

"Which I'm not going to do," she finished, mumbling through the bobby pins she held in her mouth. "There." She did a three-sixty walk around me and nodded approval at the glittery hair ornament she'd strategically placed over the most unruly patch of hair. "You're so much easier than doll heads."

"Thanks?" I stared at my reflection in the mirror. "Seriously, thanks for helping. Keep this up, and I might have to name you my official fairy godmother."

She put the hair goop on the bathroom counter. "Keep this. You may need a couple more gallons until that cut grows out." She winked. "Let's think of it as Bibbidi-Bobbidi-Goo."

I groaned. "Dad would be proud of that one."

"He's a bad influence."

The dress of the evening was classic, classy, and a little more subdued. And thankfully a tad longer. I gave it a swirl in the full length mirror. "I might have to keep this one. How much was it?"

"Would you consider it an early Christmas present?" she said.

"I'd love it."

"Good, you're set for the next three Christmases."

"Yikes!" I said. "We'll figure that out later."

Cathy had left by the time Ian arrived, not with the practical Prius. A big honking limo snaked its way around the dumpsters and other obstacles in the narrow back alley. And by honking, I mean quite literally. Not an impatient Manhattan taxi kind of honk, but one of those musical car horns. I think he was going for "Jingle Bells."

As I stepped outside, Ian stood next to the car, tapping the final line of the carol into a small keyboard. He held the last note which blared and echoed in the alleyway. "It's nice to know that all those pricy music lessons didn't go completely to waste."

"What's this?" I pointed at the limo, the chauffeur of which was standing stiffly with the back door propped open.

"My father insisted," he said, then squinted at me. "You look lovely tonight. Mom and Dad are sure to approve."

"Your parents?"

"Are joining us for dinner at the club. Didn't I mention it?"

"No, I don't think you did."

"Huh," he said. "Well, I guess that means there's less time to be nervous about meeting my folks, then. I think you're going to get along just fine."

Great. My "you're very nice, Ian, but I don't see us having a future, but let me tell you about our doll project" speech was just pre-empted by the dreaded meeting-the-parents date.

I climbed inside the limo and slid across the plush seat. Once Ian joined me, I said, "You know, I don't think I've ever ridden in a limo before. We were supposed to have one for Cathy's bachelorette party, but it never showed, so we piled eight grown women into my Civic. Some party."

Ian wagged a finger. "I don't know. Perhaps all the best parties begin with eight women in a Civic."

Ian spent the rest of the trip pointing out all the doodads and whatnots of the luxury limo, ending with another chorus of "Jingle Bells" just as we pulled up at the country club. The stone building was awash with thousands of twinkle lights draping every tree down the long drive and around the building itself.

"It's beautiful."

"Never been here, either?" he asked.

"Not at Christmas," I said. "One year the mayor gave Dad golf lessons. He didn't have time himself, so he set it up so my brother Parker and I could both have a few lessons. I never took to it, but Parker still plays occasionally."

The valet held open the door then Ian helped me out of the car, and we made our way into the club's restaurant.

Lush poinsettias decked the massive stone fireplace, and red linens graced the tables. It didn't take long for me to figure out who Ian's parents were. Not only were the two of them sitting at a four-person table close to the fireplace, they were probably the least welcoming people I could have imagined.

Marvin Browning most closely resembled a rotten lemon. Shriveled and slightly jaundiced, but without the softness. Still, his handshake was so firm it might have sent recipients to the nearest orthopedist for x-rays.

His wife seemed a little more approachable. She was impeccably dressed in a black suit with white trim, which accented her snowy hair, fashionably styled in a chic bob. In fact, I was pretty sure I'd seen that bob before, coming out of the barber shop on Lionel Kelley's surveillance tape.

She squinted momentarily after I escaped her husband's vise grip but greeted both Ian and me with wan smiles and air kisses.

"We were about to send out a search party," Mr. Browning—and no, he did nothing to encourage more familiarity—staunchly told his son. In fact, he told the whole room.

But his wife—"call me Valerie"—waved him off.

"They're right on time," she said, pushing her watch in her husband's face. "Grumpy old fool."

Ian slipped ahead of the waiter to pull out my chair, next to his mother and opposite his father.

"Lovely dress," Valerie said. "Who designed it?"

"I'm not sure," I said, trying to figure out how to describe the dress. Used? Previously loved? "It's . . . vintage."

"It's very becoming on you. More than that number you were wearing in that picture in the paper, I think."

"My picture was in the paper?" I said.

"If what I hear is true, you'd better get used to it."

I looked over at Ian, but he was knee-deep in a business conversation with his father.

"I think I prefer your hair this way, too," she said.

"I tried a new stylist, but I'm afraid he didn't work out." This gave me an idea. "Your hair is lovely. May I ask where you go?"

"I'm afraid I'm in search of a new stylist myself. Mine no longer cuts hair."

"Retired?"

"Actually, the poor girl got herself killed."

"I think I did see something about that," I said.

Ian took this moment to join our conversation. "Don't be so cagey, Liz." He turned to his mother. "Liz's father is with the police."

"With the police?" Her eyelids started twitching. What, a cop's daughter not good enough for their heir apparent?

"Afraid so," I said. "Actually, he retired several years ago as chief of police, but he's been *reactivated*, I guess you could call it, for this investigation."

"How novel," Valerie said. "You've never dated a police-man's daughter before."

Mr. Browning laughed so hard he choked, but recovered with a sip from his water glass. "What you need to keep you on the straight and narrow, my boy."

"I thought you'd like that," Ian said.

A few more questions followed. They seemed like casual conversation, but before our dinners arrived, they'd learned where I went to college, my area of study, and a brief sketch of both my dating history and my current aspirations. If I'd have known, I would have worn my blue interview suit and brought my résumé.

And then it hit me. I wasn't Ian's choice, nor was I the type of girl—that glamorous model type—he was normally attracted to. I was Ian's best attempt to please his parents. And it became clear that a mature, educated woman with working class roots was just what they'd ordered for him.

"Nothing wrong with starting at the bottom," Mr. Browning said, with the first smile I'd seen on him all evening. "When I started my business, I didn't have two nickels to rub together. But I worked hard, lived frugally, invested everything. I've made some friends in the business, and I've made some enemies, but I arrived where I wanted to be."

I nodded.

"But it grounded me," he continued. "Ian, he works hard and he's a smart boy, but he needs that grounding."

And suddenly I panicked. I had to do something before I got the "welcome to our family" speech. I wasn't sure if Ian had said something that suggested our relationship was more advanced than two dates, or if perhaps Ian assumed the same, but I needed to set things straight.

Unfortunately, when I panic, I get clumsy, and when I turned to address the misconception, I upset my full and unwanted glass of wine. It ran down the tablecloth and puddled in my lap.

"Good heavens!" Ian leaped out of his chair. Of course, everyone in the restaurant was now watching.

Milliseconds later an observant waiter reached our table with extra napkins which absorbed much of the spill.

"I should probably visit the ladies room and see what I can do," I said.

"I'll go with you," Valerie said.

In the rest room, which I was relieved to find unattended, I blotted a little more of the stain, then Valerie suggested rinsing it out. I was trying to figure out what kind of contortions I'd need to get the full skirt of the dress into the sink when Valerie suggested I take it off. So I went into a stall, removed the dress, and handed it to her over the door.

I'd considered going out there to help, but I'd worn only a half slip, and my beleaguered bra wasn't quite ready for prime time.

"How's it coming?" I asked when the water finally stopped running.

"I think I rinsed out most of it," she said. "I'm afraid it's dripping wet, though. I'm going to set it in front of the hand dryer. Would you like to come out and sit while it's drying? I'm sure nobody will come in."

"I'm not totally . . ."

"Want my jacket?" Without waiting for a response, she hoisted her jacket over the door. I put it on, and clutched it up tight.

Once freed from my three-by-five-foot prison, I inspected the dress, held suspended over the hand dryer by Valerie's clutch purse. The skirt looked much better. I gave the dryer another cycle and joined her on the sofa in the small anteroom.

"Thanks so much," I said. "I feel like an idiot. And I hate to keep you from dinner just to help me."

"No worries," she said, kneading her hands. "Happens to everyone. How clever of you to choose something washable. Besides, the men'll be talking business nonstop. I should be thanking you for the relief."

"Aren't you involved? In the business, I mean?"

"If you ask Marvin, my job is to spend what he makes."

"I somehow doubt that," I said.

"I guess I'm old enough to be comfortable with the role of the woman behind the man. Things are a bit different today. Women have careers of their own. The corporate wife with her mad skills of arranging dinner parties, entertaining clients, smoothing ruffled feathers, and getting various stains out of expensive clothing has gone the way of the rotary phone and party lines. I'm becoming obsolete."

"I think that perhaps you're appreciated more than you think. I, for one, am very thankful for your help."

The dryer stopped again, so I excused myself, rearranged the garment, and gave it another cycle.

"I must admit," she said, "you're not like the girls Ian usually brings home."

"What, poised, attractive, and capable of getting through a meal without a single catastrophe?" I shrugged it off. After all, even though half the women in the town might consider Ian the catch of the day, I was still inclined to throw him back.

She laughed. "I find it refreshing. So, tell me about yourself."

"I think we covered that at dinner."

"Not the résumé. What are your passions, your hobbies? What makes you tick?"

"Family is important to me. I like my work. It wasn't what I set out to do, but I find I enjoy the shop."

"Are toys all that lucrative? I mean, there can't be that many serious collectors."

"We've had our lean times. Fortunately, our clientele isn't limited to the serious collectors looking for that rare find. Though we are thankful for them. We get a lot of casual browsers who come in just for a look. But then they see that toy they played with as a child, and then another, maybe something they haven't thought about in years. We make a lot of impulse sales that way. I guess our primary market is nostalgia. My dad always said that just about everyone can say they once owned a vintage toy collection if they've lived long enough."

"I'll have to come check it out, then. I do think I have a couple of my old Madame Alexander dolls in the attic."

"Thinking of selling?"

She laughed. "Guess I'm just curious if they're worth anything."

"There are a fair amount of Madame Alexander collectors out there. Value, of course, would depend on the specific models and their condition. My sister-in-law, Cathy, runs the doll department. She could probably tell you." And then lightning struck. It might be the perfect opportunity to pitch the doll project to at least one Browning.

"That sounds like a lot of fun," she said, after I explained the rehab project. "Is there still room on this committee?"

"You want to help on the doll committee?"

"You've seen my mad stain-removal skills. If nothing else, I'm sure I could help with that. I'm surprised you haven't pitched the idea to Ian's foundation."

"To be honest, I've been waiting for the right moment."

"That can be awkward, considering you're dating and all. Tell you what, how about I put in a good word for you?"

"I'd . . ." It wasn't exactly how I'd pictured this going. "I'd appreciate that. Thank you."

My dress took just one more cycle before I declared it dry enough to wear, during which I gave Valerie the details about our next meeting.

"Looking forward to it," she said.

# # #

I'd barely opened the shop the next morning when Amanda and Cathy showed up.

"Did I make a mistake with the scheduling?" I said.

"No, I'm not working today," Cathy said, settling Drew in his swing.

"Couldn't get enough of my charming personality and witty one-liners then?" I asked.

"Well, there's that. But I really wanted to hear more about *the date*."

"Ooh, *the date*," Amanda teased. "Forgive me, but who was this with? There's so many men seeking your attention, I've lost track."

For that, I threw a sock monkey at her.

"Seriously," Cathy said, "romance aside, I'm more interested in whether you pitched the doll project. Unless there are juicier details to share."

Amanda leaned forward against the counter, her face resting on her hand. "I'm all ears." She set the sock monkey up next to her. "So's my friend here."

"If you're looking for juicy details, I'm afraid to disappoint you. Our evening ended with just a chaste peck on my cheek."

"From Ian Browning?" Amanda said. "The town's quickest mover?"

"Was your father watching from the window while he cleaned his gun again?" Cathy asked.

I laughed. "That was a long time ago."

"Jack?" Amanda guessed.

"'Fraid so," I said. "Make sure he tells you the whole story. But no, this time *Ian's* parents were watching from the limo."

"I thought you were going to end it with Ian and pitch the doll program," Cathy said.

"Well, it's hard to break it off with a guy on the second date when he's already progressed to meeting the parents. But I did pitch the program to Valerie Browning. In fact, she might be coming to the next meeting."

"Does that mean you'll be seeing Ian again?" Amanda asked.

"Not entirely sure," I said then shared my theory that Ian was looking for a girl his parents would approve of. "Last night felt more like a job interview."

"Ouch," Cathy said.

"On the bright side, when I do get a chance to tell him I'm not interested, it won't leave him brokenhearted and despondent."

"Speaking of broken hearted and despondent, I'm still waiting to hear more about that night with Ken."

"Night with Ken?" Amanda said then covered the sock monkey's ears.

"And his sister-in-law," I added.

"That much I got from Dad," Cathy said.

I walked over to Drew's swing and pulled up the sock that he'd kicked loose. "You, sweet boy, are the only man in my life not giving me any trouble."

With that, he threw his drool-slobbered toy giraffe on the ground. I picked it up, wiped it against my pant leg, and placed it back on the tray. When I turned around, Cathy and Amanda were frozen in place waiting for me to go on.

"Fine." I sighed. "Ken seemed to think that maybe we could pick up where we left off."

Cathy's eyelids shot up. "Does he now? Are we baking a cake with a file in it for him?"

"He's not under arrest," I said. "At least not last I heard. I don't think Dad has enough to hold him unless something incriminating came back from forensics. He might be out already."

"And how did you leave it with Ken?" Cathy asked.

"Let's get past the investigation first. I still don't think he killed Marya. Meanwhile, I thought I'd try to sell some toys," I said. "If that's all right with you."

"What, no big dates on your social calendar today?" Amanda asked.

"Maybe a little one," I said. "Mark Baker is bringing dinner over before game night tonight." As I said it, I felt my anticipation growing. No, it wasn't a gourmet dinner at the club, but on the flip side, I didn't have to dress up and I could wear flats. Win-win.

"Sounds nice," Cathy said.

"Hey," Amanda said, "wouldn't it be funny if Ian and Ken showed up, too?"

Neither Cathy nor I said anything as we both stared at her. She pointed at the monkey. "It wasn't me. He said it."

Chapter 18

When Mark arrived with takeout, I had just finished setting up for game night. The tables and chairs were all arranged at the front of the store. Tonight's theme, chosen weeks earlier, was mystery games. Of course, there were several different editions of Clue, or Cluedo, as the original British edition was called, but I also pulled out some playable—in other words, not in pristine collector's condition—versions of both the Nancy Drew and Hardy Boys games, an old Perry Mason game, and even Scooby-Doo. I rounded it out with some newer mystery games from my personal collection, like Scotland Yard.

I stared at the fun, colorful boxes. Solving a real crime was no lighthearted game, no mere mental puzzle, though sometimes the techniques were the same. Gather evidence. Uncover secrets. Put the pieces together. Eliminate suspects until you've figured out the killer.

Unlike the vague, faceless Mr. Boddy (or Doctor Black in the UK), whose death begins the game of Clue, Marya was once alive and breathing, strolling around the town in those incredibly high heels of hers, with no inkling that soon her death would launch a real and dangerous game of whodunit. If she'd realized that her death would cast suspicion on her husband, would she have buried her secrets as deep?

Or deeper?

"Earth to Liz," Mark said, waving a hand in front of my face.

"Sorry." I crumpled up my Mighty Taco wrapper. "I was thinking about this whole thing with Marya."

"Worried about Ken?" he asked.

I jerked my face to look at him. "I'm worried there might be too much circumstantial evidence. Maybe not enough to convict him, but nothing to clear him either. That maybe this whole thing might always be hanging over his head."

Mark leaned his arms against the table. "You don't have enough faith in your father."

"That's not true," I said. "If anyone can get to the bottom of this, he can." I winked. "With a little help, of course."

"Are you talking about you or me?" he asked.

"You, me, and, oh, his whole department." I laughed.

"Fair enough," he said. "Tell you what, since you uncovered quite a bit of evidence—and found Ken—I decided to quit slacking off. I unearthed a few things myself. Although I'm not sure they help your friend."

"Do tell."

"First, I visited Marya's twelve-step program."

"Learn anything?"

"Well, you can't interrogate anyone at one of those things. I fibbed and said that Marya had told me about the group, and when she died, I knew I had to get help."

I rolled my eyes. "That's quite a lie to tell in church."

"It's not a lie when you're under cover."

"Is that in the Bible?" I teased.

"Should be. Look, do you want to know what I found out, or not?"

I nodded.

"Nobody had much to say about Marya, but I managed to snap a few pics of license plates, so I think I know who all was in the group. I ran a few backgrounds."

"And?"

"And a few of them have records."

"Is that surprising?" I asked. "They're in a twelve-step program."

"No, but what's surprising is that it includes Pastor Pete."

I sat up a little straighter. "Think he might have something to do with Marya's death?"

Mark gave a brief shrug. "He'd have to be pretty devious to go into the ministry so he could have access to a twelve-step group so he could then do what? Buy drugs? Sell drugs? Seems a stretch."

"Unless he became a pastor sincerely, but then relapsed."

Mark clicked his tongue as he considered. "I guess I could check with the prison and his former parole officer and see what they have to say about him. Meanwhile, we still don't have a handle on where all Marya's money came from or where it went. We're only assuming drugs because of Lionel Kelley's investigation."

I shook my head. "I can't imagine any of those sweet old people selling their drugs to Marya."

Mark shrugged. "You'd be surprised what some people will do for money."

"Then why cast more suspicion on it by accusing the

pharmacist of shorting their prescriptions? And who was she selling these drugs to?"

"That I don't know."

"It would have to be someone she came into regular contact with. It's not like she peddled them on a street corner. Ken was tracking her. He would have known."

"Possibly she acquired the drugs and sold them to a dealer."

I squinted. "I still can't see all those old people selling . . . oh!" And the brainstorm hit.

"Get up!" I told Mark, and then pushed him to the door. "I'll be Marya. You be a customer coming to get her hair done."

Mark ran a hand through his hair. "What?"

"Humor me." I pushed his chair into the middle of the open space and said, "I'm ready for you now."

Mark started toward the chair, stopped, and then finished his walk with a decided wiggle. He eased into the chair, sat primly with his legs folded at the ankles, and fluttered his eyelashes at me.

"First, Marya would ascertain what kind of cut the customer wanted."

"I was thinking maybe a bouffant."

"Would look lovely on you, I'm sure." I held up a finger. "The next step would be to shampoo your hair." I set up another chair a few feet away.

"Do all your dates end up this way?"

"Seriously, I think I'm onto something."

"Okay." He pushed himself up and moved to the second chair. "I must warn you. I have a sensitive scalp."

"You know what you don't have, though? A purse."

"It didn't go with my shoes."

"But Mrs. Attenborough has a purse."

"Who's Mrs. Attenborough?"

"Right now, you are." I looked around and found a vinyl Barbie and Skipper carry case and shoved it into his hands.

"You can set your purse right there, Mrs. Attenborough." I slid another chair next to his. "Or if you'd prefer I can hang it up in the back for you."

"Oh," Mark said, sliding the purse onto the chair next to him.

"Now lean back and close your eyes."

Mark slouched with his head dangling over the back of the chair.

I stood between him and the purse and pretended to shampoo his hair. "I'm not sure exactly when she did it, maybe when the conditioner was in or something, but in that position, with the danger of getting product in her eyes, Mrs. Attenborough wouldn't be able to tell if Marya rummaged through her purse. It makes more sense than all of her customers selling her their drugs."

"You know what?" Mark gave my arm a tug and pulled me closer, then kissed me. "See, that's how all your dates should end."

"Why, Mrs. Attenborough!"

# # #

That game night might have been our best attended ever. True to Amanda's prediction, Ken showed up. To my dismay, he'd brought Mad Max and Cujo with him. Ken's appearance might have been the reason my father "took the night off" and came to game night, reminding me of when Ken had done the same thing once.

Jack and Amanda were both there, as were most of our regulars, such as Lori Briggs and Glenda and her knitting needles. The one first-timer, sneaking in just as we were about to begin, was Lionel Kelley. He took a while to pick a seat and ended up with Lori Briggs at the table next to Glenda's. Glenda had been a client of Marya; I'd seen her on the video. I wondered if he'd followed her in.

Despite the attendance, game play was otherwise subdued. No one joined Ken and his sisters. I wasn't sure if everybody stayed away because of the cloud of suspicion still over his head or if they didn't want to face his guard dogs.

Midway through his game of Scotland Yard, Lionel Kelley stood up slowly and winced. When nobody else seemed to notice that, he clutched his back, stooped over a little, and let out a pathetic sound, somewhere between a whine and yelp.

"What's wrong?" Lori asked.

"My back," Lionel said. "And rats! I forgot my pain meds."

Everybody just traded glances.

Finally, Lionel asked, "Does anyone have anything?"

Nancy rummaged through her purse and came up with a bottle of Tylenol. Someone else had Advil.

Lionel pushed them away. "I need something stronger."

With that, Ken shot my father a look, but Dad waved him off.

Kelley practically hovered over Glenda, but she kept on knitting without looking up.

"Ma'am?" he said. "Do you have any pain meds I could borrow? Or buy from you? I think the going rate for Oxycontin is eight bucks? One pill?"

"Hank!" Glenda yelled, jumping from her seat. She waved

the knitting needle toward Kelley, like an Olympic fencer parries with his sword. "Arrest this man!"

At this my father cracked up.

Ken jumped to his feet. "I might be suspended, but I can still make a citizen's arrest. And if you're not going to do anything about this, right here in your own shop—"

"Hold your horses," Dad told Ken. "I think I know what this is about." He turned to Glenda. "Kelley was just testing you, I think, to see if you'd sell drugs."

"Me?" Glenda said. "A drug dealer?"

Now the whole room was snickering.

Lionel's face grew red, and I almost felt sorry for him. He was only a little off from the truth.

"No one thinks you would sell drugs," I assured her. "But did you have some go missing?"

She reclaimed her seat, but looked wary. Of Kelley or of the question? "There was that bottle that spilled out in my purse," she finally said. "I never did find all of them. I had to go back to the doctor and he gave me a sample to last out the month."

"You didn't sell them to Marya Young?" Kelley asked.

"Hey!" Ken said. "What is this?"

Dad looked at Ken. "Back at the station I asked you about your wife's accounts and, in particular, your audit of the funds going in and out. You suspected something."

"But he just called my wife a drug dealer." Ken advanced on Kelley, who stumbled backward.

Dad hurried to place himself between them. "Knock it off!" He turned to Ken. "What he says doesn't matter. What matters is the truth. Did you suspect your wife's extra funds might have come from drugs?"

Ken held his tongue, but his face betrayed the answer.

Nancy and Grace jumped up. "I told you it was a bad idea to come here," Nancy said, tugging on her coat.

Grace picked up Ken's jacket and handed it to him.

Ken sent one last look toward me—a plea for help?—then his sisters hustled him out the door.

Lionel paced, then turned back abruptly and wagged a finger at my father. "What I say does matter. Just wait until I crack this case." And then he was gone.

Lori, now missing her game partners, put down her clue sheet. "That means I win, right?"

# # #

The evening ended a bit early, and Mark stayed to help my father and me put everything back to rights.

"This little theater performance tonight reminded me that I never finished telling you what I learned about Marya's money habits," Mark said. "Before Mrs. Attenborough most rudely interrupted."

"Since when do you report to my daughter?" my father said. "And who in the blazes is Mrs. Attenborough?"

"Liz, you need to tell him your theory," Mark said. "I think it's a good one."

"Only if I can sit down." Dad set up the chair he had tucked under his arm.

I retold the theory, without the dramatic demonstration— or the kiss—and Dad bobbed his head.

"Makes better sense than a lot of ideas that have been thrown around." He turned to Mark. "How does that jibe with what you've learned?"

"As best I can narrow down, she bought cashier's checks totaling twenty thousand dollars over the past few months."

"Twenty grand?" Dad said. "From drugs?"

"Maybe not all of it. She was also robbing her hubby blind. There's a lien on the house that I'll bet he knows nothing about."

"Wow," I said.

"And if she made some from selling whatever drugs she stole from her clients . . ." Mark said. "Not sure if that accounts for everything. Still working on it."

"But where did it all go?" Dad asked. "And does that have anything to do with who killed her?"

"Twenty grand could be plenty of motive," Mark said.

But it didn't answer the question. I stooped to pick up a game card that someone must have dropped.

"Go back three spaces." Story of my life.

Chapter 19

With Christmas only a couple of weeks away, Sunday proved a busy day at Well Played. Cathy was home for the day, but Amanda and Kohl were working. Dad had Kohl sorting through comics, dividing them up by universe, character, and date. He excelled at the task, even if he did stop occasionally to read. Then again, we were paying him in pizza, so not sure we had any right to complain.

It was when I took the pizza box to the dumpster in the back alley that I caught movement out of the corner of my eye.

"Hi, Lionel," I said. An educated guess.

"Hi, Liz." He poked his head from his vantage spot in the walkway near the back of the barbershop. He gestured to the pizza box in my hand. "That empty?"

I opened it up. "There's sort of a piece left, but someone pulled all the pepperoni off." Cup-and-char pepperoni, while not unique to the area, was all the rage. Whether it was the casing or the thickness or the way heat was applied from the top, those little cups of, well, pepperoni grease, with the crisp, almost bacon-y edges . . . Okay, I admit it. It was me who pulled them off the last piece.

Lionel waved me over. "Beggars can't be choosers. Bring it here."

I walked over to where he'd set his camp chair. On a portable table were a pair of binoculars, an insulated mug, and a box of Timbits. His open duffel bag was loaded with high-tech equipment his mother had purchased.

"With Marya dead," I said, "is there any point to watching the barber shop?"

"Maybe. Maybe not," he said, taking the slice. "But"—he tapped the top of his head—"I get paid by the hour either way. Who knows? Maybe some of Marya's associates don't know she's dead."

"Lionel, it was plastered all over the news."

"Yes, but do Russians watch the same news?"

"Probably. I don't think there's a special newscast for Russians. *If* Marya had associates, why would you think they would be Russian too?"

"Instinct." Kelley nodded sagely. "I can't explain it, but it's in the gut of many of us in law enforcement."

"You're not in law enforcement," I said. "You're a private detective."

"Doesn't mean I lost it," he said. "Besides, I minored in Cold War studies in college. I'm wise to how they work."

"Didn't the Cold War end when the Berlin Wall went down?"

"That," he said with a derisive roll of the eyes, "is what *they* want you to believe. Just watch. By the time this is all over, the Russians will figure into this somehow. Mark. My. Words."

# # #

When Dad came home for supper that night, I mentioned my conversation with the xenophobic private eye.

"We don't have someone on it twenty-four/seven, but we've been watching the barber shop, too."

"For the Russians?"

"For any associates who might go there looking for something. And Kelley's idea might not be as far-fetched as you think."

"That Marya had connections with the Russian mob?"

"That's going a bit too far," he said. "Nothing in our investigation so far leads us to believe that Marya had any connection to organized crime."

"That's what I thought."

"But Anechka's appearance raises questions. Why was she hiding out in that cabin?"

"You haven't been able to get anything out of her?"

"No, and you wanna know why? Those two sisters of Young felt sorry for her and hired that same dad-blamed lawyer they hired for Ken. So, watching the barber shop to see if someone comes back looking for something is one of our best options. It's why we haven't released the crime scene yet, but don't tell our barber friend."

"He's a bit hot under the collar," I admitted. "And frankly, I know how he feels."

"Ask yourself this," he said. "Why was she killed there? It's probably the biggest argument your buddy Ken has going for him. If he were to kill his wife, it would make more sense to do it in the privacy of his own home. Or up in that love nest of his."

"Quit calling it a love nest."

"Murder someone up there, and they might never be found. Look, I'm not saying cops don't sometimes turn violent, especially in domestic situations. Sad, but it's been known to happen. Maybe it's the stress of the job—not that it excuses it."

"But Ken wouldn't—"

"Hold on," he said, "if Ken *were* to kill someone, I think he'd be a whole lot smarter about it."

"So, you're thinking it has something to do with the drugs?" I asked.

Dad shrugged. "An addict begging for a cheap fix. Marya wouldn't give it to him, or maybe they couldn't reach an agreement. He strangles her with a hair dryer cord. Could happen. Especially if Marya was cutting hair in the front and dealing drugs in the back alley. Right under my nose."

"We need to improve security back there," I said. "I realized the other night coming home from my date with Ian that you can't see anything by the back door from the upstairs apartment."

"You used to hate when I just happened to see you come home from a date."

"That was when I was sixteen. And there's a big difference between being a bit overprotective and cleaning your guns in front of the window."

"Well, guns must be kept clean."

"Every time I went out?"

"You got me. Just putting a little fear of God into them."

"And a little fear of Hank McCall into them too."

He dropped the fork back onto his plate. "But why the concern now? Did Browning get fresh?"

"Not exactly. Nothing I can't handle."

Dad drummed his fingers on the table. "Those words don't exactly reassure me, you know. You seeing him again?"

"I think so," I said. "Because of his surprise meet-the-parents stunt, I never got a chance to let him down gently."

"That's important?"

"If we still want him to fund our doll project, yes. Not that I think I'm going to leave him broken hearted." I shared with him my theory of me cast in the role of nice-girl-who'll-please-the-parents.

"If you do go out with him again, let me know. The gun's going to need cleaning sometime soon. But I'm sorry things didn't work."

"I'm not. I can finally focus on one relationship that seems to have potential."

Dad jerked his head up. "Did I miss something?"

"I told you I was seeing Mark."

"You told me you were seeing Mark, but I didn't realize you were *seeing* Mark."

He stared at me. I quirked an eyebrow and stared right back. He opened his mouth several times to begin a sentence, but closed it again without uttering a word.

"Let's have it," I said. "Is he a little old for me? No, I don't think the age difference is that big at this stage. Am I ready for a relationship with someone in law enforcement? Maybe, especially since he's basically an accountant. But it's still early days."

Dad didn't say anything, just beat out a rhythm on the table. Finally, he cleared his throat. "Might not be too bad, at that. I always thought he was a good egg."

"Not a good toy name, though, huh?" I said, remembering Dad's joy of welcoming "Chatty Cathy" to the family. Not that she'd been pleased that he'd pegged her as such during a formal toast at their wedding reception.

He scratched his chin. "I don't know. There's Marx Toys. And they made a lot of great toys. And *Baker*. There's the Easy Bake Oven, of course. Oh, and the baker from the Fisher-Price Three Men in a Tub." Dad nodded. "Yeah, he'll do nicely."

"Glad you have your priorities straight," I said.

# # #

Early Monday morning, when I collapsed some spare boxes to take out for recycling, I thought of Lionel Kelley. Just in case he was still out back waiting for the Russian invasion, I decided to take him a cup of hot coffee. And maybe invite him in to check out some new My Little Ponies that came in via an estate sale. There was a mint-in-box "Fizzie," one of the rarer twinkle-eyed ponies, and Kelley might be just the twinkle-eyed collector who'd appreciate it the most. As long as we let him carry it out in a plain, unmarked bag.

I could make out his boots just protruding into the alley from his "secret" hidey-hole.

"Lionel, I brought you a—"

But he wasn't in those boots, which were sitting next to his empty chair. His duffel bag of techno-gadgets, his coat and hat, and almost all the rest of his clothing were scattered throughout the passageway. And flush against the cold, brick wall, Lionel Kelley was suspended in his, well, underclothes. His hands were bound with rope and tied to a non-functioning security light, and his feet were dangling, not quite able to reach the ground. Duct tape covered his mouth, but he was conscious and wriggling and trying to say something to me.

I ripped off the duct tape first and he screamed.

"Liz. Down. Down." The words were barely recognizable, he was shivering so badly.

I looked for a way to get him down, tried to untie the ropes, but couldn't budge the knots. Kelley's weight had pulled them even tighter against his wrists. I ran back to the shop and retrieved the box-cutter.

The blade broke as I tried to saw through the rope, and I had to stop and change it, but within ten minutes he was hopping on his bare feet in the snow and gathering his boots and clothing.

"Come in and get warm," I told him, picking up his pricy equipment bag.

When we were both in the back room, I pulled the door to the shop closed and called my father at the station.

"Keep him there," Dad said. "And lock the doors. Stay out of sight and keep the shop closed until I tell you. I might not be able to get there right away. We got a situation going—wait, does he need medical attention?"

I pulled the phone away from my face and addressed Kelley. "Do you need medical attention?"

He was still shivering, but he shook his head and went for the coffeepot.

"He says no," I said into the phone.

"Okay, then stay right there. Promise me?"

"I promise."

I set open a folding chair and made Kelley sit in it while I poured the coffee for him, then helped him steady both hands around the cup. I walked through the shop to make sure no customers had come in when I was distracted, then I locked the door and flipped the sign to "closed." Taking a moment to scan the street, I was a bit unnerved to see Pastor Pete strolling on the sidewalk with his neck craned in my direction.

A shiver ran up my spine. Was he watching the shop? Or did he have something to do with the attack on Kelley? Maybe he was back to finish the job. Or maybe he was just walking down the street. No crime in that. Dad was right, though. I needed to stay out of sight, even if only to stop fueling the paranoia.

I sprinted through the shop and ran up to the apartment to grab my *Lego Movie* blanket (yes, it's awesome) for Kelley. He clutched it tightly around himself. I even bumped up the thermostat a couple of degrees.

When the shivering stopped, I pulled open another chair and sat opposite him.

"Thanks, you might have saved my life." He took a long sip of the coffee. "Although, I was working on the ropes. I probably could have gotten myself out, eventually."

Yeah, right. "How long were you strung up like that?"

"I don't know. What time is it now?"

I checked my cell. "Ten after seven."

He rocked a little in his chair. "Two hours. Maybe three. I'm still a little hazy how it all happened."

"What do you mean? What *did* happen?"

"I was surveilling the back of the shops, and I had just gone behind your dumpster to, well, you know."

"I know what?"

"Relieve myself."

"You've been peeing behind our dumpster?"

"Everybody pees."

"But not behind *our* dumpster."

"Liz, it's a stakeout. All cops—"

"Don't go telling me I wouldn't understand peeing because

218

it's a cop thing, all right? Because I might have to hit you. My father's been a cop longer than you've been alive, and he doesn't go around peeing behind people's dumpsters."

"Oh, yeah? You ask him about stakeouts. I'll bet he's peed behind plenty of dumpsters. Now, do you want to hear the story or not?"

I bit back a sharp retort and calmed my voice to the point it sounded like a harried nanny pushed past her patience. "Yes, Lionel. Please tell me the story."

"Fine. I had just finished, you know, and I swore I saw a bit of light coming from the back door of the barber shop. Just a sliver, like a door opening or closing. Then it went dark."

"Someone turned the light off?" I said. "Or closed the door?" Good heavens, Lionel was right about the criminal returning to the scene of the crime.

"I mean someone conked me on the head." He reached up and gingerly touched the back of his head.

"Lionel." I jumped up and examined the spot he pointed out, and sure enough, he had quite a goose egg already. I pulled out my cell phone.

"What are you doing?" he said.

"Remember your training," I said. "All head wounds get checked out. Especially if you lost consciousness."

"I don't think I did."

"But you just said everything went dark."

"Dark, hazy, blurry. But I was awake. It's almost all better now."

"I'm still calling you an ambulance."

I made the call, answered a few questions, looked deeply into Lionel's eyes to examine his pupils to see if they were unnaturally dilated, and waited for help to arrive.

"So you didn't see who it was?" I asked.

"They must have come on foot, because I didn't hear anyone drive up, and there had to be more than one of them to get the jump on me like that." He sat up straighter. "You know what this means, don't you. I was right! It had to be the Russians."

"Did anyone speak? With an accent or in another language?"

"No, I only saw the one guy. And he never said a word."

"You just told me you didn't see anyone."

"I didn't *make out* anyone. He had on one of those ski masks that covers the whole face. But I remember the eyes. Deep, piercing, Russian eyes. If I ever see those eyes again, I'll know."

# # #

I texted Dad to update him that Kelley was on his way to the hospital and then did a poor job of cooling my heels in the closed shop. I jumped every time someone jiggled the handle trying the front door, but otherwise I hung out in the back room, peering through the small, square window in the steel door, trying to see if the police had arrived yet. And pacing. I did a lot of pacing.

Why had I promised my father I wouldn't leave the shop? Now I was more curious to see if someone had broken into the barber shop and what they might have done there. And if they might still be inside!

Then again, I'd already seen Pastor Pete rubbernecking the shop. Who else might be lurking nearby? Perhaps Dad's advice to lock the doors and stay out of sight was prudent. As if on cue, someone—hopefully an impatient customer—banged on the front door. Too bad honoring my promise to stay safely out of sight kept me in the dark about what might be happening just next door.

During one of my trips back and forth across the small

room, I noticed Kelley's bag of gadgets still by the door. But it wouldn't be right to go through his things.

Then again . . .

Kelley had gone through our stock at the toy show last year without our permission. And he'd kept me waiting unnecessarily when he promised I could watch the video tape. Add the fact that he'd sent me to senior speed dating—not to mention the dumpster-peeing incident. I was pretty sure he owed me the chance to see if something in the bag could help figure out what was going on next door.

One of the first things I came across was the camera with a long flexible tube—the one that looked like something you could use for a do-it-yourself colonoscopy. I found the on switch and a Bluetooth button. Within minutes, my phone asked if I wanted to connect with the endoscope—at least now I knew what to call it. As soon as I clicked "yes," images appeared on my phone.

The next step was finding the right-sized hole. I went back into our still incomplete comic book room and knelt down next to the roughed-in electrical outlet. There was a little space on the side, and after a few tries, the camera went through.

It took me a while to figure out how to manipulate the camera to see anything, but eventually I was able to scan the room and even record the video scan to my phone.

I saw only the new, smaller back storage room of the barber shop, but it had obviously been ransacked. Bottles, tubes, and tubs of pricy hair product had been pushed onto the floor. I could read some of the labels, not that I knew what they did. Hair food. Pomade. Primer. Masques. Shields. Vitalizer. Soother. (Maybe those two could duke it out.) And hair bonding glue. Glue?

The only item I could have picked out of a lineup was the single aerosol can of Aqua Net. My mother always had one or two of the exact same cans of hairspray sitting on the bathroom vanity.

I couldn't see around the door to get a glimpse of the rest of the shop, but I suspected it was torn apart too.

Someone had been looking for something. Money? Drugs?

Once I saw everything I could, I pulled back the endoscope so that I imagined it was flush with the other side of the wall. No sense alerting anyone to the fact that I was just on the other side of the drywall. I pushed myself off the ground and dragged a chair into the room, so I could continue to monitor any developments in the barber shop—at least in the store room of the barber shop.

I realized I must have left the apartment door open, probably when I came down with the blanket, because Othello wandered into the comic room. He checked out the endoscope, still jutting from the electrical outlet, giving it a sniff, then a rub with his cheek.

I picked him up. "Sorry, fella. That's gotta go back to Lionel Kelley."

After the brief distraction, I glanced back at my cell phone to see if anything had changed.

A giant eyeball was staring back at me. And Lionel Kelley's words echoed in my head:

Deep, piercing Russian eyes.

Chapter 20

I pulled on the endoscope, and to my horror, the endoscope pulled back.

Whoever was on the other side of the wall was playing tug-of-war with me. And just a minute earlier, I'd felt so clever. Now I could end up strung up half-naked in the alleyway. Or worse. How did the Russian mob dispose of people? Lionel Kelley would know.

I dropped to the floor and crept out of that room, lest someone start shooting through the wall. After all, just dry-wall separated me from whomever was now in the barber shop, and anyone who watched HGTV knew you could just kick right through that.

In the wider open space of the shop I felt more exposed, so I kept on crawling until I was hidden from view behind a display rack of building blocks. I strained to hear any sound above the pounding of blood in my ears. After about thirty seconds, my pulse was beginning to slow, then the pounding on the front door began again.

Why was Dad taking so long to get here? I reached for my

phone to call him again and realized that my cell was still in the comic book room.

Could I make it to the shop phone? Not without being seen from the front windows.

I wrung my hands trying to corral my panicked thoughts then looked around for anything that might be used as a weapon, or at least a deterrent.

The glass case where we displayed our toy guns was at the end of the aisle. We'd had to keep them padlocked because many old toy guns were so realistic we worried they could get someone shot. In fact, Dad only sold them to serious collectors he knew would keep them secured. And I did still have the shop keys in my pocket.

Careful to stay out of sight, I crab-walked over to the case, jiggled the key in the lock, and carefully and quietly eased away the padlock and lifted the hasp. Worried that someone from the street might see the lid of the case rise, I elevated it by infinitesimal increments. My arm muscles began to burn then trembled from the strain. When I'd raised the lid about four inches, I visualized the stock of the case, then made a quick reach for the Mattel Fanner 50, one of the most realistic cap guns ever made. Once I had the gun in hand, I let the lid fall closed, collapsed back against the display rack, and rubbed my aching arm.

More urgent pounding at the door echoed through the shop.

I examined the toy gun in my hand, ripped off the price tag, and practiced holding it.

Why couldn't I be content selling old toys? Now here I was: on the verge of confronting a possible killer with only a shop full of toys to protect me. If only Dad were here. But that thought left me shaky. Would they go after my father when he arrived?

I caught movement out of the corner of my eye, but it was only Val, headed toward me. Then the cat, who normally had nothing to do with any of us unless maybe it was time to eat, lifted a paw to climb up on my lap. I pushed her away, but that just made her more determined. Moments later she extended all her claws trying to steady herself on my thighs.

More sounds came from the door, but not the banging sound from earlier. This sound was even more terrifying: the sound of the lock clicking open followed by the bell over the door ringing. Then a few slow footsteps.

I tried again to push Val off my lap, but she hissed in protest and dug in her claws even tighter.

The footsteps stopped and I froze, trying not to breathe.

For one brief moment I wondered if throwing Val at the intruder would be more effective than the toy gun, but I pushed aside the impulse. Despite her quirks, she was beginning to grow on me. So I let her rest on my lap while I picked up the cap gun and aimed it at the end of the aisle.

More footsteps creaked. I swallowed hard, wondering who might soon round the corner of the aisle. A Russian mobster? Pastor Pete? Some other resourceful killer?

I tabled my regrets for becoming involved in this case; anyone who could so easily enter locked doors, inflict terror, and disrupt so many lives needed to be stopped. I steadied the toy gun with two arms.

But the face that peered around the corner was the rookie Jenkins, in uniform.

"Whoa," he said, lifting his hands. "You don't want to do that."

"How did you get in?"

"Your father gave me the keys."

"Dad's here?"

Jenkins nodded. "Can you put down the gun?"

"How do I know you're telling me the truth? You seemed pretty anxious to kill me on the back of that snowmobile."

"Look," he said, eyeing the gun, "sorry about that. We were out all night looking for you, and I might have been a little agitated. I shouldn't have done that."

"Liz!" Dad called from the door.

"Back here!"

Jenkins retreated into the shadows when Dad rounded the corner. "She pulled a gun on me."

Dad rolled his eyes and took the toy from my hands. "It's a cap gun. And it's not even loaded. Liz . . ."

"I didn't know who came in."

Dad turned to Jenkins. "You didn't announce yourself? Police?"

Jenkins hung his head.

Dad wagged a finger at him. "Would have served you right if she'd shot you." He held out a hand and helped me up before leaning in closer. "You and I will talk about this later." He stepped back. "And am I right in thinking that little camera was your doing?"

I could feel my cheeks flame. "You said not to leave the shop."

He rolled his eyes and turned to Jenkins. "Let's get the photographer in there and start taking some new pictures."

Jenkins seemed happy to hightail it out of the shop.

Dad leaned closer. "What were you thinking?"

"About the camera or the cap gun?"

"Let's start with the camera."

"I was thinking that I wanted to see what was going on, just to be that fly on the wall. And then I noticed that Lionel Kelley left his equipment."

"And if the killer was in there and caught you, you'd be one dead fly. Not to mention, if Jenkins had been following his training, he might have shot you." Despite the seriousness of his tone, the corner of his mouth betrayed his amusement. "I should put you over my knee and give you the *swat* you deserve."

I groaned. "What gave me away?"

"When you pushed the camera through, you left drywall dust on the floor." He scratched his chin. "You know how to make a *pest* of yourself."

"You're not mad?"

"How could I be? Jenkins needed to be taken down a peg."

"You're talking about the man who'd be happy to see me arrested for murder."

"Won't come to that. I'd quit first."

"Then nothing would be stopping him, would it?"

"Take heart, kiddo. I don't think there's any need to start trying on orange jumpsuits. There was a huge break in the case today. First time that it feels like we're making any headway."

"Really? Was this the 'situation' you mentioned on the phone?"

"Yes, that shyster the sisters hired finally showed his face. When he actually talked with Anechka, he decided it would be better for her to cooperate with authorities, especially when her drug test came back positive for opiates. It may have been impressed upon her that an undocumented illegal alien drug abuser who wouldn't cooperate with police would soon find herself on a slow boat back to Russia."

"So she talked?"

"Sang like Ethel Merman. Turns out she wanted to make a break from her employers and move up here with Marya. Only when she gave notice, the people who smuggled her into the country got nervous she was about to blow the whistle on their whole operation. They intimated that they had friends high up in the government. If Anechka either came back to work or paid them off, they'd 'find' her paperwork and she'd be free to stay. But if she blabbed, they'd turn her over to immigration and she'd be deported. Marya figured the cabin would be a good place to hide her."

"Will she be deported?"

"Maybe. Eventually. But in the meantime, I'm going to want her as a witness, and so will the FBI, the DEA, and ICE. We had a whole boatload of alphabet soup involved in this. And police in two states."

"Did Anechka say any more about what Marya was up to or who might have killed her? Could it be the Russians? I'll never live it down if Lionel Kelley was right about that."

"Anechka was mostly locked up in that cabin detoxing," Dad said. "Marya tried to handle the situation, maybe paying off the traffickers—we're still trying to work that out. But she didn't share with her sister much of what she was doing."

"Anechka wouldn't have liked it if she found out her baby sister was dealing drugs."

A shadow fell over Dad's face. "That's where it gets a little strange. Anechka admits that Marya supplied her with oxycontin, trying to wean her off the drug by tapering off the dosage gradually."

"That rings true," I said. "Ken's sisters told me that Marya had tried to do the same thing before. The addiction kept Anechka dependent on her employers."

"Anechka also admitted that Marya lifted a few pills from her clients. And based on the numbers that Lionel Kelley was investigating, it probably doesn't amount to much more than that."

"But the money," I said. "The larger amounts of money going in and out of her hands."

"We're back to the drawing board on that," he said. "I'm not sure where it came from. But at least I think we know where it was going."

"The traffickers?"

Dad smirked. "I think so. I had guys pull all the security cams on Main Street on the days that Mark Baker said Marya likely transferred cash. We caught her coming out of the barber shop between clients and getting into a pickup with Carolina plates. Guess what they found parked at that chicken plant in NC? So things are coming together, piece by piece."

"Except *who* killed Marya. And why. If she was paying them off, they'd have no motive to harm her."

"That's the *fly* in the ointment," he said. "Maybe, since her husband was the chief of police and he was following her around, they thought he was getting too close."

"Then why not target him?" I said. "Going after Marya would be like poking the bear."

"Still, that's a lot of suspects, a lot of witnesses, and a few folks looking to trade information for lighter sentences. Someone will end up implicated. I suspect it won't be Ken, and it certainly won't be you. After everyone is interviewed, maybe something will pop there."

"Pop. Fly? Are we moving puns into baseball now? Can I cry foul?"

"Nah. That one was unintentional. So you're off base."

"Standing in left field?" I said. "Catching flies?"

"Home run."

# # #

By the time Dad gave me the okay to open the shop for business as usual, Cathy was due to start her shift. I filled her in on the morning's events. I may have downplayed the part about pulling a cap gun on a police officer.

"Lionel Kelley in his tighty whities? Oh, that must have been a sight."

"Actually, the fledgling private eye is a boxers man," I said, glad she'd latched onto that detail. "Oh, and remember me saying I thought we had a feral cat problem in the alley? Turns out we do not."

"Sure? That ammonia smell by the dumpster was pretty intense."

"Trust me." I held up my hands. "You do *not* want to know the whole story."

But with Cathy to mind the shop, I texted Mark and asked if he was free for lunch.

"It would have to be in Buffalo," he replied. "Only have forty-five minutes."

"Meet you at your office?" I asked.

"Sounds good."

# # #

I'm not fond of traffic circles, so the half hour trip grew a little bit dicey at the end, but my GPS guided me there, even if I did get a great view of the McKinley monument by circling it about three times. I'm even worse at parallel parking, so I was glad to find Mark waiting outside the concrete and glass FBI building. He hopped into my passenger seat and buckled up.

"Where are we going?" he asked.

"Dinosaur Bar-B-Que okay?" I asked. "How strict is that forty-five minutes?"

"It's been known to be flexible, especially if brisket is involved," he said. "Lead on, McDuff."

The restaurant wasn't that busy on an early Monday afternoon, and our food came out quickly. Mark, as predicted, ordered the brisket. I'd contemplated getting the Carolina pork sandwich, but considering what was going on with Ken, Marya, and a certain chicken plant, I decided to avoid it. And the chicken, for that matter. I opted for the Tres Niños, a plate with a generous sampling of brisket, ribs, and pork, which turned out to be a wise choice. I think the adrenaline expenditure had left me ravenous.

"I have to say," Mark said, "I've never had a woman ask me out before. I'm afraid you'll find me terribly old-fashioned."

"Are you offended that I asked you?" I said.

"Oh, no. I'm glad you did. I just hope you don't mind if I pick up the check. I've also been known to open doors and stuff. Not sure where you stood on that."

"Mark, as an accountant, you probably know all about the struggles of small businesses, right?"

"In college I wrote a thesis on it."

"Then you know I'll be happy to let you pay. As for doors, I don't mind a little pampering now and then. But if it's cold outside, I'm not going to wait on ceremony."

"Gotcha. I think we're good."

"I have to admit something, though. I had an ulterior motive for inviting you to lunch."

Mark leaned forward. "Sounds intriguing."

"Don't get too excited. I just wanted to know if you could tell me something about the investigation."

"Are you sure you want to keep going with this?"

I narrowed my eyes. "Yes, why would you ask?"

He blushed ever so slightly.

"Who told you?"

"About you holding off Jenkins with a cap gun? You gotta figure everyone in law enforcement in the county is talking about it. Don't be too embarrassed, though. You actually came off much better than Jenkins."

I shook my head. "Which gives him another reason to hate me."

He pressed a hand on mine. "You must have been scared to death. Look, Liz, this isn't fun and games anymore. That's why I asked if you're sure you want to continue."

I nodded. "It was never fun and games. But this one seems worse. Maybe it's because someone in the police department, someone we trust to keep us safe, might be involved. The chief is suspected of murder. I know my dad has to investigate him, but because of that, a lot of the younger officers don't trust him. Jenkins is a police officer, but today he terrified me. And it goes beyond the fragmented police department. Pastor Pete is a minister, but I saw him loitering on the street near the shop. And that made me afraid."

"I'm still looking into Pastor Pete," Mark said. "His parole officer said he had no problems, and I also put a call into the prison chaplain. He said Pete found the light in prison, was a model prisoner after that, and got his degree from an online

Bible school while he was still incarcerated. The chaplain is fairly certain his reform is genuine."

"Which still leaves open the possibility that he relapsed when he got out." My shoulders sank. "It's just impossible to know who to trust. It's like some demented version of the *Sesame Street* song about all the "People in Your Neighborhood," except any upstanding member of the community might be a stone-cold killer out to get you. Mark, this needs to end, and I can't see that happening until Marya's killer is behind bars. So will you help me?"

"What would you like to know?"

"Dad told me that you'd narrowed down two dates where money was most likely transferred, and that they think they have video of the handoff."

"It was a good break," he said. "I, uh, *might* be able to clue you into something even your father doesn't know yet."

I sat up in my chair. "Really?"

"Shortly after the second payoff, Marya filed an I-130."

"Oh."

"You have no idea what an I-130 is, do you?"

"Not a clue."

"Since Marya was now a citizen, she could petition that Anechka become one, too. But only if she could prove their relationship. My working theory is that she paid off the traffickers to cough up the paperwork she needed to file the form."

"Nice," I said, then sighed. "And sad. With Marya now dead, what happens to Anechka?"

"No idea. That," he said, "is a little beyond my pay grade."

"Can you tell me what days Marya paid off the traffickers?"

Mark paused for a moment, dabbing a bit of his honey cornbread into the remnants of sauce on his plate. "I don't see any harm in that. I don't have them on me, though. But I can text you when I get back to the office." He leaned back in his chair. "Can I ask you a question in return? Why didn't you just ask your father?"

"And deny you the opportunity of Dinosaur brisket?"

"Seriously."

"Well, besides needing to get away from the shop for a little while, I wanted to see you."

He reached across the table and took my hand. I just hoped it wasn't too sticky with all the barbecue sauce. "I wanted to see you, too."

He glanced around, then assured no one was looking, leaned in for a kiss.

"Mark," I said, after I caught my breath. "You got barbecue sauce all over your tie."

Chapter 21

The dates of the money transfer reached my phone long before I reached East Aurora. In fact, I think I heard my text notification ping several times while still circumnavigating Niagara Square.

The next part of my little, unofficial investigation wasn't going to be nearly as pleasant. But when I got back to the shop I texted Ken Young anyway, asking if he had Marya's appointment book.

He called me back a little later.

"I had her account book that has record of all her payments. But your father took that. The barber might have her appointment book."

"What's the difference?"

"They shared a phone number in the shop, and the stylist working that day would schedule all the appointments in the same book."

"Do you think it's locked up in the barber shop?" I asked.

"No idea," he said. "Why? What are you working on?"

"Just a theory," I said. "Probably won't turn into anything."

"I've seen you work those theories of yours. Let me know if you need anything."

I assured him I would, told him to take care of himself, then deleted his number from my contact list.

"Goodbye, Ken." I closed my phone.

I called Dad next.

"Not sure I want to talk with you right now," he said.

'What did I do?"

"Sent me chasing a few of those geese of yours. They sure don't make little old ladies as nice as they used to. I swear one of them pinched me."

"Little old . . . ohhh. You went to Senior Speed Dating. Did you . . . get many numbers?"

"Plenty. Let's just say I gave your buddy Lance some serious competition. Unfortunately, that's all I got."

When I asked about the appointment book, he said, "Yeah, I think one of my guys brought that in. Wanted to run down the names of everybody who had an appointment the day Marya was killed."

"May I see it?" I asked. "I can come in. I can wear gloves. I promise not to damage any evidence."

There was a long pause. "Tell you what. How about I send you a PDF?"

"You'd do that?"

"Only for my favorite daughter. Just promise you won't go brandishing it around. And if you have any brainstorms, don't get in over your head."

"I just want a peek at the appointment book."

"Fine. Give me a few minutes and I'll e-mail it to you."

I must have checked my e-mail every thirty seconds after that. Finally the file came in. While Cathy dealt with customers,

I was behind the counter, hunched over my laptop, staring at the almost illegible names. Some were scratched out. Others included more information, such as what kind of service the customer needed.

I set up a spreadsheet and typed in the names and times of everyone with an appointment on the days just prior to the two suspected money transfers, then looked for any customers on both lists. Because if Marya *wasn't* selling drugs to get all that money she was alleged to have, then it might, just might, have come from one of her customers.

Why one of her customers would give her exorbitant sums of money was a mystery to me, but that's what this was, anyway: a mystery that needed a solution.

"Huh," I said, staring at the spreadsheet while Cathy worked nearby.

"What's that?"

"Turns out, there were three women who saw Marya just before she apparently handed off money to . . ." I didn't know what to call them. "The Russians?"

She came up behind me. "Anybody we know?"

"We know all three. At least I do."

Cathy started to read over my shoulder. "Diana Oliveri, Joan Toscano, and . . . whoa. Valerie Browning? Your future mother-in-law?"

"Hah! In her son's dreams."

"So you think one of them might have killed Marya?"

"Or gave her the money. If we could figure out who and why, we might be a step closer."

"Well, Diana and Mrs. B should both be here tomorrow night for our doll club meeting. Promise me you won't make any accusations."

"Give me some credit. I'm just going to poke around, as subtly as I can, and see what I can dig up. If I find out anything useful, I'll pass it on to Dad. Now I just have to figure out how to bump into Joan."

Cathy winced.

"What?" I asked warily.

"I know where she's going to be tonight, but you're not going to like it. At my last writers group at the bookstore I noticed a poster. Joan's doing a reading and a signing tonight at the Monday night Between the Covers Book Club."

"*Won Ton Desire*?" I said. "They allow her to read that in a public place?"

"They put up a sign saying that nobody under twenty-one would be admitted."

I scrubbed my face with my hands. "She's going to ask if I read it." I peeked through my fingers. "Isn't she?"

Cathy looked at her watch. "Book club doesn't start until seven. You'd have time to start it."

"Go with me?"

Cathy sighed. "Tell you what. If Drew is being good for Parker, I could probably sneak out for a little while."

I hugged her. "Thank you!"

# # #

The Between the Covers Book Club shared quite a few members with the senior speed dating group. Cathy and I found seats in the last row behind a lot of white hair.

Our row filled up when Irene and Lenora claimed the last two seats.

"I told you we should have gotten here earlier," Irene chided her sister.

Lenora poked me in the arm. "Should be a good one tonight."

"You're here for *Won Ton Desire*?" I asked. "I should warn you, it's a bit steamy, and I'm only part way through it."

Lenora waved me off. "You don't have to warn me. I already read it."

Irene leaned over her sister. "Don't let her fool you. She read it twice!"

"And I don't think it's any steamier than last month's book," Lenora said. "*The Swashbuckler's Secret Soulmate*."

"You two come every month?" I gestured to the packed house. "Are meetings always this well attended?"

Lenora bobbed her head. "There's a few more here than normal. We don't always have an author come."

"Usually we just all sit in a circle and trash the book," Irene said. "But I guess you can't do that when the author is here. And I had some choice comments about this one."

"You didn't care for it?" I asked.

Irene winced. "Haven't been able to stomach Chinese food since."

Lenora sighed. "And we had a coupon."

By this time the room had quieted down, and Irene's comment kind of hung out there. If Joan heard it, she was gracious enough not to respond. She went to the podium and began her reading. It didn't take me long to realize that she'd picked the part about the orange chicken sauce. I did my best to let my mind wander anywhere.

I began to mentally review what I knew about Marya's activities, just before her death.

She'd been stealing pills from her clients' purses. Perhaps she'd targeted the senior crowd because they have more aches and pains than the general population. She gleaned just enough not to be noticed, she thought, but enough to help slowly wean her sister off the drugs she'd been force fed.

". . . pushed all the food off the table with a mighty crash, and turned and stared at her with those deep, piercing eyes."

I shivered—it reminded me of the deep, piercing Russian eyes Lionel Kelley claimed he saw under that ski mask. Someone had come back to the barber shop looking for *something*. Drugs? Money? Large sums had apparently crossed Marya's hands. Money that Mark had theorized she needed to procure Anechka's full freedom. Marya had met with a representative twice, presumably passing these funds. But killing her would be like killing the goose that laid the golden egg.

"He dipped his finger in the orange chicken sauce . . ."

And that money had to come from somewhere. If Marya didn't sell drugs, then where did it come from? Was she stealing it like she stole the pills, from customer wallets?"

And who would carry that much cash? Valerie might, despite her thrifty choice of stylists.

"She watched in rapt expectation as the sauce trickled down his finger."

Of course, Diana owned her own business. From my own experience, I knew that didn't always mean you were awash in cash, but her store had been there for decades and enjoyed a regular clientele. She might have had a deposit in her purse, for all I knew.

"He flipped on the radio, and Vanilla Ice began to play."

And then there was Joan. How much did authors make, anyhow? I'd bet Cathy would have some idea.

"His eyes twinkled mischievously, and he winked. 'Rice, rice, baby.'"

Irene elbowed her sister. "She stole that from Weird Al."

Of course, this sent up a stir of murmurs, but Joan raised her voice and continued her reading, undaunted.

I went back to active avoidance. One thought stopped me cold. If Marya had stolen money from any of these three ladies, why wouldn't they have reported it? I was still missing something.

"She never did find her shoe." With that, Joan stopped her reading and closed the book.

The group applauded.

"Now I have time for questions," she said.

One woman's hand went up. "That part on page ninety-seven—is that even physically possible?"

"Oh, yeah," Joan said. "But I don't think we'll demonstrate it."

Cathy and I waited until everyone else had lined up for the signing before we joined the end of the queue. The store had pretty much cleared out. Everybody was leaving with their books and a small gift from Joan: fortune cookies.

Joan looked up from the table. "You already have my book," she said to me. "How are you enjoying it?"

"It's certainly eye-opening," I said.

"But *I* don't have your book," Cathy said, sliding a copy across the table.

"How sweet," Joan said. "I remember you from writers group." She paused with her pen suspended above the page. "That's . . ."

"Cathy, with a *C*."

"That's right. I had to stop coming to that group. They weren't friendly to what I was writing." She looked over her glasses. "But then again, the group met in a public place. I can understand why those parents complained. How's your book coming along?"

"Still revising," she said, "although I have a little one at home now, and he's rather demanding of my time."

Joan set down her Sharpie. "Don't be hard on yourself. It's more important to raise your family. I didn't even begin to write until after all my kids were out of the house. By then I had more . . . life experience to draw from, if you get my meaning." Just in case we hadn't, she punctuated that statement with a sly wink.

"I wanted to ask you something," I said.

"If it's about page ninety-seven, I'll be honest with you. I don't know if it's possible or not."

"Not sure I'm there yet."

"You'll know when you get there," Joan said.

"Something to look forward to. But I really wanted to ask you about Marya Young."

"What about her?"

"One of the things the investigation revealed is that Marya may have dipped into a few clients' purses while they were distracted. Did you ever think you were missing anything from your purse after an appointment?"

"Like money, you mean?" she said. "Well, once I thought I had another five in my purse, but that could be me. I'm a little scatterbrained when it comes to finances. Using the whole creative side of the brain, I think."

"Five dollars?"

"And if she took it, the joke was on her, because that was her tip anyhow. But from the tone of your voice, you were thinking something more?"

"Do you carry prescription medications with you?"

"Never," she said. "Maybe the occasional essential oil. Jasmine. Sandalwood. Ylang-ylang."

I'd never heard of Ylang-ylang, but from her tone I figured it might be wise to end the conversation before she enlightened me. But not before I snagged a few of her remaining fortune cookies.

Chapter 22

Dad was still AWOL on Tuesday, working the case. Waiting on customers, usually a task I enjoyed, did little to advance the clock.

Overcome by curiosity, or maybe even boredom, I even sneaked a peek at page ninety-seven of *Won Ton Desire*. That was a mistake. I wondered how much lasting damage it would cause if I bleached my eyeballs.

Later in the morning Mark texted and asked what I was doing that night, but I had to tell him I was tied up with the doll club meeting.

"Could you skip? Play hooky?" he texted.

"Wouldn't be fair to Cathy," I said, although my mind was more concerned with getting another chance to talk with both Diana and Valerie about their experience with Marya.

Mark's frowny face emoji preceded a couple more flirty texts and a GIF of David Tennant saying hello.

By the time Cathy arrived for our meeting, I'd set up all the tables. She pulled off her scarf. "I'd planned to help set up. You ready for tonight?"

"For the meeting?" I gestured at the fully set-up room. "Did I forget anything?"

"You know what I mean. You're going to interrogate Diana and Mrs. Browning."

"I'm not going to interrogate them. That's the quickest way to get them to freeze up. What we need to do is gently push the conversation in that direction. You can help, you know."

"How's that?"

"Marya was part of the committee, so it wouldn't be hard for you to bring her up, and maybe I can ask a few casual follow-up questions and see how they respond. And if the conversation veers off topic, there'll be two of us to swing it back around again. Keep it nice and simple, and there's a better chance something will slip out."

"Wow. I don't know what scares me more, how well you've thought this out or how devious you've become."

"Just a sixth sense that I have from all my years in law enforcement, however vicariously. I think Dad used the same technique on me and Parker. Felons, kids. He insisted the same techniques worked on both."

Lori Briggs arrived first. "I thought maybe you'd cancel. I heard about the break-in next door."

"Yeah," I said, "Dad said it was ransacked pretty good."

"I also heard you found Lionel Kelley naked in the alley."

"Not exactly naked," I said. "I guess the gossip network got that a little wrong."

"Too bad," she said. "Made for a better story. Anyway, I started brainstorming fundraising ideas, just in case the Browning Foundation doesn't come through."

"Not sure you have to worry about that," Cathy said, and tilted her head toward the door.

Valerie Browning was being helped from the passenger seat of the Prius by Ian.

"Why, Liz McCall," Lori said. "Nice catch."

"Valerie should be a good addition to the committee," I said.

"I was talking about Ian," Lori said, fanning her face.

"Too bad she's thinking of throwing him back," Cathy said.

"Why on earth would you do a thing like that?" Lori asked.

"Because we're as compatible as champagne and barbecue," I said. "Not sure why he hasn't seen it yet, but sooner or later it would end badly. Best to end it early."

"But not before he funds the doll project, right?" Lori said.

Before I could answer, Valerie and Ian came in the door. "What a quaint little shop!" Valerie said as her son helped her with her coat. She wandered a few aisles and went on to explore the doll room with Cathy on her heels, ready to give the grand tour.

Ian pulled me aside. "Mother is very keen on this project and insisted I come hear what it's all about."

"I told you from the very beginning that I had a project I wanted to pitch."

"I thought maybe that was your coy way of getting my attention. Tell you what. I can't stay for the meeting tonight. Have dinner with me tomorrow, and you can pitch to your heart's content. I'll listen fairly and impartially."

Another date? Before I could answer, he surprised me with a passionate kiss, and then was out the door.

Cathy had just come back in from the doll room, and her jaw dropped.

Lori hid her reaction with a polite cough.

And Mrs. Browning beamed a most satisfied, motherly smile in my direction.

That brief prelude threw me off kilter. By the time Diana Oliveri arrived, I'd forgotten I even had a plan. Good thing Cathy ran the meeting. She did a remarkable job of encapsulating the whole project for Valerie, who asked intelligent questions such as whether we were officially incorporating as a nonprofit and which 501.3 program we'd be applying for.

"I'm not even sure how that works," Cathy said.

"You'll need to have that in place," Valerie said, "just to open up the business account, which you'll need before you officially apply for a grant."

Cathy and I looked at each other. Our little doll project had just gotten a whole lot more complicated, care of the state and federal government.

"Let me see if I can draft a mission statement and bylaws," Valerie offered, "and run them past my attorney, okay?"

"That would be wonderful!" Cathy said. "I know we've been just talking about organization, and it's all been theoretical, but"—she picked up a box and opened it—"I thought maybe it would be a good time to get our hands dirty and rehab a few dolls." As she started unloading her box, the women grouped around her and I kept to the fringes.

"This one basically needs a good cleaning," she said, picking up a bedraggled smiling blonde doll.

"I'm good at stains," Valerie said.

"I can testify to that," I said. The dress she cleaned looked about as good as it did when I first took it off the hanger.

"I used to clean Ian's dolls—excuse me, action figures—with toothpaste and an old toothbrush. It works wonders and doesn't remove the paint."

"You're hired," Cathy said. "Getting the grunge off the dress and the loving off the face would help a great deal." She handed the doll toward Valerie. "Want to give it a go?"

"I'll be happy to try," she said. "Of course my hands aren't as strong as they once were. Might have to do it a little at a time."

I looked at her fingers and then remembered her kneading her hands after rinsing my dress for me.

"Arthritis?" I asked.

"Afraid so," she said. "Hazards of growing older."

"Sorry," I said. On the other hand, with limited hand strength, she'd just pretty much cleared herself in Marya's death. I doubted those hands could strangle anyone, even using the hair dryer cord.

Diana, on the other hand, was a big hefty woman, used to working hard all her life.

"Of course you should take your time," Cathy said, "Unless you'd rather I find someone else."

"No," Valerie said, taking the doll and holding it possessively. "I'd love to do my part."

Cathy turned to Lori. "Any luck finding replacement volunteers to help with the hair?"

Lori shook her head. "I tried a couple of schools. Still waiting for guidance counselors to get back to me."

"What's this about?" Valerie asked.

"Our original volunteer . . . uh," Cathy began, then turned to me.

I sighed. Hopefully not too dramatically. "Yes, Marya."

"Oh," Valerie said. "Marya would have done a lovely job."

"We could always ask Antoine," Diana said. "I'd be happy to approach him."

I bet she would. "He didn't seem like the volunteering sort," I said.

"Well, Marya never struck me as the sort, either," Diana said. "And yet, she volunteered."

"Did you have many dealings with Marya?" Cathy asked.

"Other than getting my hair cut, not really," Diana said. "She came in the store once and handed around her coupons to my quilting group."

"Mostly seniors?" I said.

Diana nodded.

"She came in and did the same thing at my knitting group," Glenda said. "I mean, I appreciate a discount, but I thought it odd that she never asked permission first."

"And the knitting group was also mainly seniors," I said.

"What are you getting at?" Diana said.

"She also handed out coupons at senior speed dating. It wasn't just that she had a lot of senior clients. She was specifically targeting them."

"Targeting us!" Glenda said. "But why?"

"Well, *I* heard," Cathy said, putting on her best gossipy tone, "that she was stealing from people's purses." She gave an exaggerated nod. "Drugs. Maybe money."

A few gasps followed.

"Did any of you ladies ever miss anything?" I asked, trying for my best innocent tone.

"Of course not!" Diana said. "Just because we're getting up there doesn't mean we're all easy marks."

"I certainly wouldn't have suspected her of anything," Glenda said. "And here she was, married to the chief of police!"

"If you ask me, the whole thing was hinky from the very beginning," Lori said. "Evil through and through, that bimbo."

"Do people still say bimbo?" Glenda asked.

"They must," Lori said. "I just did."

"Well, now," I said, thinking that Lori, whether she intended to or not, had just set me up to play good cop to her bad cop. "Sometimes there's reasons for things. From what I hear, Marya had a pretty rough childhood, smuggled into the country by traffickers, and I guess maybe she needed money pretty badly."

"Who doesn't have a past, or things to overcome?" Diana said. "You work hard, and you do things the right way. That's the American way I know. None of this, 'Why, I married an American. I guess I'm an American.'" She finished that last part with a finger to her cheek, a fair approximation of Marya's accent, and a tone so thick with sarcasm you'd need a jackhammer to remove it.

It was apparent that Diana resented Marya's "easy" road to citizenship. Could Marya have said or done something that compeled her to violence?

While the vehement comments continued, the only one not participating was Valerie Browning. Perhaps she considered herself above what she thought of as petty gossip. But that approving smile had dimmed considerably to a tight sneer.

The meeting ended on a happier note, with less talk of Marya and more talk of getting dolls in the hands of needy children. As the group emptied out, Lori lingered behind, looking through the dolls that nobody had taken with them.

"Liz, can we talk frankly?" she said.

Cathy glanced at me. "I should probably head home to check on Parker anyway."

After she collected the rest of her things, I pulled out a chair across the table from Lori. "Something wrong?"

She pushed an invisible piece of lint off the table then looked up at me.

"I know things haven't been all that rosy for you in the romance department these last few years," she began. "And that can make it tempting to fall for the first fast-talking, good-looking hunk who throws a little attention your way."

I winced. "I thought you called Ian a good catch."

"I've teased you, but that was before I realized it had gotten serious between you two."

"Serious?"

"I saw that kiss," she said. "And from the way Mrs. Browning eyed you up, I'm going to lay odds she's been catalog shopping mother-of-the-groom dresses."

"Oh, please. I've gone out with him twice, and mainly because I wanted to get grant money for this project."

"She's here because of you, you know. And that kiss Ian planted on you, he was staking a claim."

"I've done little to give him hopes of having one. Oh, Lori, I don't know what to do," I said. "I went to one party. One party. Just looking for a chance to meet him and pitch the doll project. He keeps putting it off and asking me out. Then meeting his parents. How did it snowball into this?"

"Look, it's probably none of my business, but the Browning family is used to getting what they want. Businessmen, politicians, everybody just caters to their whims. Zoning boards change their votes. Permits are fast-tracked. If this isn't what *you* want, you better start putting up a struggle, otherwise you're going to be carried in the current. Right to the altar."

I took a deep breath then let it out slowly. "I'll make it clear to him tomorrow."

"I guess I shouldn't throw away the info on fundraising I gathered, huh?"

"Thanks, Lori."

\# \# \#

Dad was already snoring in his favorite recliner when I got upstairs. Too many hours working, too little rest. I pulled a blanket around him, and he smiled in his sleep then went back on snoring.

I didn't get a chance to check my phone until after I'd fed two hungry cats and climbed into my warmest pajamas.

"Dinner tomorrow?" from Mark.

"Just got back," I texted. "If you're still awake, call me."

I climbed into bed with the phone and stared at it, willing it to ring.

Othello hopped up next to me and meowed once loudly until I acknowledged the chewed up toy mouse he'd dropped next to my pillow. I stroked his soft fur, and he eventually quieted and curled up for a catnap.

I'd started to nod off, too, when the Tardis landed—in other words, my phone rang.

"Hello?" I said.

"So, dinner tomorrow?" Mark said.

"That's one of the things I wanted to talk about. I'm afraid I can't make dinner tomorrow. I have a dinner meeting with Ian Browning."

This was met with silence. Finally, he said, "I heard something about you and Ian. Not sure I wanted to believe it."

"I'm not interested in him," I said. "That's something I hope to make clear to him tomorrow night."

"Do you have to go out with him to do it? After all, I heard there's fifty ways to leave a lover. Probably more now because of technology. Texts. E-mail. Fax. They really should update that song."

"It's more complicated than that," I said. "Cathy's counting on the Browning Foundation to fund her doll project, and now Mrs. Browning is involved."

"Not sure if it's the jealous suitor or the FBI accountant talking, but I wish you'd steer clear of the whole clan. I don't trust them."

"Something touching your investigation?" I asked.

"That, you know, I can't talk about. Just be careful. They're a powerful bunch, and that power can be a bit mesmerizing."

"Trust me, I never had any intentions of getting involved with Ian."

"So you have been dating."

Now it was my turn to stretch the silence. "Just twice."

"I guess we never discussed anything exclusive. Look, if you want to call it quits—"

"No!" I said quickly. "Not with you anyway."

"Oh, should we be discussing something exclusive then?"

"I'd . . . be open to the idea. How about dinner Thursday? I'll even cook."

"Really? You make more than a killer hot cocoa then?"

"Can't claim to be cordon bleu, but I do manage to keep my father and me alive."

"Will he be there, too?"

"Probably not," I said. "He's been working long hours on this case."

"Not that I mind your father. I like him, in fact. But there are a few things I want to make sure we talk about early on."

"If there's a Mrs. Mark Baker that you haven't told me about, somewhere in another state, so help me—"

Mark laughed. "Nothing like that. But especially considering what happened, I want to make sure there are no surprises."

"Sounds good," I said, although the words terrified me. What deep, dark secret was Mark going to spring on me?

Chapter 23

When I made my way to the kitchen the next morning, Dad was just standing up after feeding Val and Othello. He clutched his back and winced.

"You okay?" I asked.

"I will be. It seems *someone* let me sleep in the chair last night."

"What did you expect me to do? Carry you to bed and tuck you in?"

"You could have woken me."

"You were dead to the world."

Dad sucked air through his teeth. "Maybe not the best choice of words."

"How's the investigation going?" I pulled out the biggest mug I could find in the cabinet, the one with a jolly snowman. He wore a badge and directed traffic, and some of the guys in the department had bought it for Dad a few years back as a gag gift. I filled it with coffee and slid into my seat at the table.

"I kind of wish I knew," he said.

"What happened to your big break? With the FBI, ICE, and I-forget-who-else swooping in."

"I could tell you if they returned my calls. I managed to

get the name of the man Marya was in contact with. Someone named Bobkov."

"The guy in the pickup? Let's call him Bob."

"Works for me. But they also uncovered a few details about Bob that threw a king-sized wrench into our investigation."

"Why a wrench? And *don't* say because he's a real tool."

Dad chuckled. "Now *I* don't have to. Seems the Feds are more interested in *nailing*"—he cleared his throat—"that whole trafficking ring than they are in helping with our little old murder. If I want to question him about the money Marya handed off, I have to wait in line. But they did say someone *saw* Bob in North Carolina just a couple of hours after Marya was killed. He was in jail, in fact. Seems he got *hammered* and ran his pickup into a tree."

"So he didn't kill her."

"Sounds like we can't pin our murder on Bob, after all."

"Do we have a picture of Bob?" I asked.

"It's about all we do have," he said. "If you want, I can text you a copy when I get to the office."

"I'd appreciate it," I said.

"On the *level*?"

I touched the tip of his nose "Right on the bubble."

# # #

When I reached the shop, I realized I'd become so disconnected from the business that I had no idea who was on the schedule or where I'd put it. When Miles arrived with his laptop under his arm, just a little after ten, I decided it must be him.

"Sorry I'm late, boss."

"Only a couple of minutes. I won't dock you." I winked at

him. "This time. I was wondering if you could do me a favor. Work a little magic with your keyboard."

"I'm going to have to put a tip jar on the counter if I keep getting requests like this. You know, search engines are free to use. Have been ever since Al Gore invented the Internet."

"But you always seem to find so much more than I do. What's your secret? Voodoo?"

"Boolean search terms."

"I'm still assuming that's a form of Voodoo."

"It's a way of typing in what you want to search for and eliminating what's irrelevant. That, and I sacrifice a goat once a week." He laughed and cracked his knuckles. "What do you want to find?"

"Anything you can dig up on Joan Toscano, Diana Oliveri, and Valerie Browning."

"This about the murder?"

"More about money," I said. "And Dad always said to follow the money. Oh, and I have a video on my phone that I want to get onto my laptop. How hard is that?"

"Not hard at all," he said. "Just give me your phone and laptop."

I handed over my phone and pointed to where my laptop was under the counter. "I suppose you need the passwords?"

He looked up at me over his glasses. "Only if you want to make it easy."

"I'm glad you're on our side," I said, and left him to it.

Cathy came in a little after noon carrying a garment bag.

"Oh, my personal stylist is here," I said. "I'm beginning to think I'm some kind of important celebrity or something, with all this attention to my appearance."

"What Cathy's *actually* saying," Miles said, "is that you have no fashion sense of your own."

Cathy put her hands on her hips. "Now, we weren't supposed to tell her that."

"And I shouldn't tease you, either," I said. "I do appreciate everything you've done. What are we wearing tonight?"

"Another great score from the local consignment shops! Since he didn't tell you where you were having dinner, I thought we'd go with a classic." She unzipped the bag. "And you can't get more classic than the little black dress."

"How little are we talking?"

Fortunately, not as little as I feared. Still, the sleeveless dress with the halter top and asymmetric hemline wasn't something I would have chosen, especially in the dead of winter.

"Ha!" I said. "After all this, wouldn't it be funny if Ian took me for pizza and bowling?"

"He's not going to take you bowling," Cathy said.

"He's got to lighten up sometime, doesn't he? Well, tonight's my only chance to find out. If all goes to plan, this will be the last date with Ian Browning."

"I'm going to miss all this, I think," Cathy said. She put an arm around my shoulder. "It's like having a real live fashion doll."

"You still have Drew and a whole shop of dolls to dress. And a creepy, haunted doll to give you messages from the beyond."

"Ah!" she said. "Miles, show her."

Miles reached underneath the counter and pulled out the matryoshka.

I took an unconscious step back. "Do we have to?"

Cathy laughed. "This *will* make you feel better." She nodded to Miles.

Miles set the doll on the counter, then started banging his fist next to it, and the doll slowly rotated on its base. "Seems it's not quite even."

"Oh, Miles, you're brilliant," I said.

"I get that a lot." He chuckled and went back to his work on my laptop.

"So nothing supernatural," Cathy said. "Turns out the vibrations were caused by people strolling around the shop, maybe the workers in the comic room."

I pointed a finger at her. "A much better explanation than poltergeists or Marya's ghost. But, uh, can we still keep it in the doll room?"

"Sure." She gathered her things. "Let me know how it goes tonight. I want to know if you think we still have a chance at funding after you drop the bomb."

"Will do."

"Hey," Miles said. "Video's up." He turned my laptop around, and my footage from the inside of the barber shop played on the screen.

"What's that?" Cathy asked.

"The inside of the barber shop storage room after it was ransacked," I said. "I wanted to see it on a larger screen."

Cathy leaned in. "They sure made a mess, didn't they?" She leaned in closer. "Can you back that up?"

"Sure," Miles said.

"Pause it there." Cathy pointed at the screen, letting her finger rest just under the Aqua Net can. "See that?"

"Yeah, I noticed that earlier. My mother used to have the same can."

"Everybody's mother used to have the same can," she said. "I didn't know they made it anymore, with the whole chlorofluorocarbon scare. But I was looking for some wig shampoo at the drugstore the other day."

"Wig shampoo?"

"For the dolls. I've been looking up what other doll rehabbers do, and most say they like fabric softener for detangling, but a couple swear by wig shampoo if the hair is dirty."

"Go on."

"I found it right next to the Aqua Net."

"So they do still make it," I said.

"Yeah, but the whole can is different."

"So the barber shop had an old one?"

"A really old one," she said. "I wonder when they changed it."

"Is that a request I hear?" Miles said, putting up his hand to his ear. Soon he was typing away. "Whoa," he added, just a moment later.

"Now you're just showing off," I said.

"Look!" He pushed the laptop around, and there was a can, identical to the one on the floor of the shop.

"Very good," I said.

"No, read the description."

Cathy and I both leaned in, read the page, then looked at each other.

"It's not hairspray," I said.

"It's a safe!" Cathy said.

# # #

I texted Dad immediately. I was dying to know if the innocent looking hairspray can really was a safe, and if so, what might be inside. From the website—which also featured diversion safes made from Coke cans, household cleaners, and shaving cream—I saw how the bottom could be unscrewed. Not sure how much you could fit inside an ordinary hairspray can. Jewelry, papers, photographs? Or in Marya's case, maybe even those pills she pilfered. Or money.

While I had my phone out, I also reminded Dad that I was still waiting for a picture of Bob.

"Bob's your uncle," he answered. "Tied up, will get to it later."

I texted back. "Bob's your suspect. Need me to untie you?"

But he didn't respond, so I assumed he was mired in police work.

I still hadn't heard back from him when I stood staring in the mirror at my reflection wearing that little black dress hours later. Truth be told, I was going to miss having a personal dresser and considered keeping Cathy on retainer, at least for important events. Especially since she didn't charge me anything except the cost of the clothing.

The only time my phone buzzed, however, I got a Cary Grant GIF from Mark, with the caption, "Seeing me in your dreams?"

I texted back, "You or Cary?" and then shoved my phone into the little black clutch Cathy had also found.

I slipped on my black wool dress coat. No way I was going out tonight without it.

"You look . . . warm," Ian said, as he climbed out of his Prius to open the passenger door.

I was tempted to ask if none of the other girls he dated ever wore coats, but in the end I just thanked him. The easy banter I enjoyed with Mark just wasn't there with Ian.

And no, Ian did not take me bowling, although we passed the bowling alley and I looked at it wistfully.

I'd never been to the restaurant he pulled into and then handed his keys to the valet. I wasn't sure how to pronounce the name, and I certainly hoped the menu choices were in

English. When I saw they weren't, I pulled a classic film move and asked Ian to order for me. "Anything but snails," I added.

As the waiter went away and I awaited my culinary surprise, Ian turned to me. "So, tell me about this doll project that has my mother all fired up."

And I finally got to pitch the doll rehab program.

When I finished, he gave one long sniff. "One thing I don't understand, though. Why not just buy new dolls? It would be less work, and when you consider all the materials, it probably won't be much more expensive."

"But rehabbing saves the dolls," I said. And I wished Cathy was there for this part. She was so much more eloquent about the cause.

Ian brushed a bit of road salt from his sleeve. "I guess that works too. Tell you what, if Mother is for it, I can't see how I could go wrong. Get the grant application together, and I'll make sure it's fast-tracked."

"Wonderful!" I said. "And I'm so happy your mother is excited about the project."

He leaned forward. "Honestly, I think it's you she's excited about."

"We need to talk about that. Ian, I like you very much."

He reached forward and took my hand. "I was kind of hoping you did."

"No, you're not getting what I'm trying to say." I pulled my hand back. "I like you very much. You're a great guy. You're witty and charming. But I'm not interested in pursuing a relationship with you."

His eyebrows hit the ceiling. "Oh."

"I've been trying to tell you since the first date. And then your parents were at the second."

He blinked several times then shook his head. "It's fine. Really. I just thought that when I found a girl I liked and that my parents approved of, that she'd just naturally . . ."

"Maybe so, but I'm afraid I'm not that girl." My phone buzzed in my purse. "I should check this."

"From someone else already?" he asked, then took a sip of his wine.

I glanced at my phone. "From my father." I took a peek at the picture he sent.

"Who's that?"

"Just a suspect." Then I took a closer look at the image and almost dropped my phone. Bob had pale blue eyes. "He couldn't have been responsible for the break in, though. Wrong color eyes." I looked up. "A witness said the person who broke in had dark, piercing Russian eyes."

"Russian eyes?"

"All he saw was the eyes. Said he'd know them if he ever saw them again."

"Your witness sounds like a character."

"Whoever it was didn't get what he came for, though." I smiled. "Apparently he didn't know his hairspray."

Ian sent me a confused look.

"Sorry." I laughed. "It's just that I think I beat my dad to a big break in the case—well, really my sister-in-law Cathy did." I explained about the change in label of the Aqua Net.

"I've heard of people putting their valuables in mattresses and in freezers, but that is a new one. I guess if you're going to hide something in a barber shop, a can of hair spray is as good a place as any."

"Ingenious, isn't it?" I said. "I hope my dad lets me know what he finds."

When a magnificent dessert cart came around, Ian waved it off. The message was clear: girls who break up with him don't get luscious French desserts. "We should be getting back."

"I hope you'll still consider our project," I said.

"Absolutely. Once you get the paperwork together, send it on and I'll definitely consider it."

I noticed the change in wording from "fast-track" to "consider." Good thing Lori promised to keep those fundraising ideas.

When Ian dropped me off, he was pleasant enough, but he didn't even get out of the car. He must have driven off before I reached the door. When I turned around to wave goodnight, he was already gone.

# # #

I put the dress on a hanger and slid it in my closet next to the other two. I wasn't sure if I'd have any occasion to wear any of them again. Once comfortable in my pajamas—this evening called for my Batgirl fleece jammies—I curled up in bed with a cup of cocoa and texted Cathy the bad news. I pictured Ian off somewhere having a good laugh that I'd thought "I'll consider it" meant that we had a chance.

I thumbed through my pictures and looked at the photo of Bob. No way those eyes could ever be called dark and piercing. So someone else had broken into the barber shop.

And since it was a man who'd overpowered Lionel Kelley, that eliminated all of Marya's clients that I'd been tracking for a few days.

I sure hoped Dad was having better luck.

Chapter 24

During that dusky mental twilight that just precedes sleep, my idle brain tossed the details of the investigation together with snippets from my personal life into a very unusual salad of thoughts.

Of course, the whole idea of a thought-salad is unusual, too, but that's how my brain works when I'm half asleep.

If I assumed that the person who broke into the barber shop was the same person who killed Marya, then the killer had to be a man based on Lionel Kelley's description of the attacker. And the only men I could think of who'd been suspect in the investigation were Ken, Bob, and Pastor Pete.

Without flicking on the light, I grabbed my phone and cropped the picture of Bob and an old picture of Ken, so that only the eyes were showing. I did the same with a JPEG of Pastor Pete that I downloaded from the church's website.

If Lionel Kelley was sure he'd recognize his attacker based on those "deep, piercing Russian eyes," why not give him a full lineup? So I also cropped pictures of Dad's eyes, Parker's, and Ian's—from the photo of the two of us that was in the paper.

"You awake?" I texted Lionel. Since I wasn't sure he'd

respond just to that, I also texted that I might have a picture of his attacker's eyes.

"I'm up," he said. "Right out back, in fact."

I considered taking my phone down there so I could see his reaction, but I didn't want to leave my warm bed.

"Six pictures," I said.

First I sent the picture of my dad's eyes, then Bob's, then Ian's, then Ken's.

"That's him!" he texted back, before I even got to Parker's. My heart sank. I never wanted to believe it was Ken. I trusted him once, shame on him. Trusted him twice, shame—

"No on the fourth pic," Lionel texted back. "But the third is definitely him."

I looked back. The third picture was Ian's eyes. I sent the picture again. "These?"

"*Yes*!"

That just didn't make sense. From all accounts Ian didn't know Marya, and the only connection I could think of was that Marya cut his mother's hair. I decided that Lionel must be mistaken.

Still . . .

I mentally replayed my conversations with Ian. He was ambitious, true. And he was also a bit detached, almost heart-less. Would he kill someone? If the stakes were high enough and if he thought he could get away with it? Quite possibly.

But why kill Marya?

Romantic involvement gone awry? Not that I knew of. Something to do with his business? I'd not heard of any connections.

Still, something didn't sit quite right, especially when I recounted our conversation over dinner. I recalled quite clearly saying that the picture of Bob was a man suspected in a break-in. And a little bit later, he'd said that hairspray was a great place to hide something in a barber shop.

I just didn't recall mentioning to him that the break-in was in the barbershop, and I didn't think the news had covered it.

My phone buzzed again.

"You got a late date tonight?" Lionel asked.

"Had one," I said. "In bed now."

"Someone just parked out back. I'm going to check it out."

As soon as I read that last bit, I shot up with a surge of adrenaline. Over dinner I told Ian that a witness could identify the attacker. I'd also let slip about the safe, and I still hadn't heard if Dad had gone there to pick it up.

"Don't!" I texted back.

But I didn't get a response.

"You OK?"

Still no response.

I pushed the covers aside. Startled, Othello went flying.

I swung Dad's door open, but his bed was made and empty. On a chance, I found him sleeping in his recliner again with Val in his lap.

I shook him. "Wake up!"

"What!?"

"Did you get to the barber shop to check out that can of hairspray?"

"No, first thing in the morning." He tried to doze off again.

"No, you don't understand. I think I know who the killer is. And Lionel Kelley might be in danger right now."

"What are you talking about?"

"Come on! Get up! And bring your gun!"

Without waiting to see if he followed me, I tore open the

apartment door and ran down the stairs, using only the ambient light to navigate. I paused at the back door and tried to peek through the window. Other than Ian's Prius parked in the alley, I saw no signs of anyone about.

I mentally kicked myself. Lionel had also said he thought his attacker might have come on foot, because he never heard him drive up. A sick feeling curdled my stomach when I recalled how I hadn't heard Ian drive away after our last date. It was remarkable how quiet a Prius can be at low speeds.

I looked back to see Dad come out of the apartment. His gun was tucked into his holster. "Hurry!" When he joined me downstairs, I pointed out Ian's Prius through the small window.

"What's he doing here?" Dad asked.

"There's no time to explain all that," I said. "Ian knows about the hairspray and he knows Lionel can identify his eyes. You have to do something!"

Dad looked more perturbed than anything. "Fine, I'll see what kind of trouble that fool PI's gotten himself into now, but maybe you should go back to bed. You're not making any sense."

With that he pushed open the door and stepped outside.

As soon as he left my frame of vision, I started to panic. Dad never quite received the whole message.

Still, he was a trained professional, and he had his gun.

Except I'd also just awakened him out of a sound sleep, and I'm not sure he quite understood what he might be walking into.

But if anyone could handle the situation, Dad could.

Stress had tied my stomach in knots, or maybe whatever I'd eaten for dinner—I never quite figured it out—didn't agree with me.

Finally, when I couldn't stand it any longer, I pushed open the door a crack to peek outside.

When I did, the whole door flung open. Ian Browning wrenched my arm and jerked me outside, holding me in front of him.

Just down the alley, Dad, who had his gun trained in our direction, lowered it, so it was pointed down into the snow. Kelley stumbled after him, alive, but apparently injured again.

"You don't want to do this, son," Dad said.

"Son." Ian snorted. "That might have happened if Mother had her way."

"Let's talk this out," Dad said. He'd stopped advancing and just held his place in the alley, his eyes never off Ian. "Right now you haven't done anything we can't work out."

"He attacked me!" Lionel said, stepping forward. "*Twice*!"

That's when I first saw that Ian also had a gun in his right hand. Dad could name the model and tell you the range and all relative stats. I just knew they shot bullets and were dangerous. And right now I was at point-blank range.

Dad put his hands up to quiet Lionel, but he'd already gotten the message and shrank behind Dad.

"How's this going to work?" Dad said, his voice unnaturally calm. I expected it was from long practice.

"I want the hairspray," Ian said.

Dad inhaled. "The hairspray in the barbershop."

"It's a safe," I said. "At least I think it is."

"And what exactly is inside this . . . hairspray?" Dad asked.

"Drugs!" Lionel Kelley said. "That's where Marya must have kept the drugs!"

"Now what would you want with drugs?" Dad asked Ian.

"It's not about drugs," he said. "Look, Marya had something

she shouldn't have, something that didn't belong to her. All I wanted to do was get it back. That silly tart wouldn't give it to me."

"Something she'd taken?" I said, trying to reflect my Dad's practiced calmness in my own voice. "Stolen maybe, from your mother's purse?"

Ian's grasp on my arm grew tighter, and I knew I'd gotten it right.

"Silly woman," he said. And at this point, I wasn't sure if he was talking about Marya or his mother. Or maybe me.

"She always called herself 'the woman behind the man.' Only for her it wasn't a mere figure of speech. For thirty years, she was working behind the scenes. Dad assumed all his achievements were due to his great business sense, that he had some kind of Midas touch. And yet Mother dear was clearing the way, leaving a trail of bribed officials in her wake."

"Just because your mother may have crossed a few lines," Dad started.

Ian snorted. "It'd be bad enough if she was discreet. But no, she stuffed all the proof a jury would need to convict her into her four-hundred dollar handbag and did what? Went for a discount haircut. To the chief of police's wife! At first I thought that maybe he was in on it too. That maybe he was having her investigate for him."

"Marya was looking for oxycontin," I said. "If she found anything incriminating in your mother's purse . . . Is that how you became involved? Your mother told you?" Had the whole Browning family been complicit in Marya's death?

"No, Mother went on for months paying blackmail. Then I noticed household bills weren't being paid. Dad was too busy with his 'important work,' so he had me look into it." He rolled his eyes. "I found the cash withdrawals right away, and when I confronted her, she admitted what she had done."

"It sounds like you don't approve," Dad said. "Look, if you only found out after the fact . . ."

"They'd take it all, anyway."

"Who's that?" Dad asked.

"The government. The lawyers. As soon as hard evidence of that kind of corruption hit, they'd be on us like vultures, picking the carcass clean. We could have done with a little less money. She could have let Dad work a little harder for it. But instead, she ruined us all."

Ian Browning would be the heir apparent . . . of nothing.

"So you went to Marya to get this evidence back," I said, still trying to keep him calm and talking. I was finding this increasingly difficult with his grip on my arm cutting off circulation and the cold seeping in through my footed pajamas, feeling like a thousand hypodermic needles jabbing my toes.

"She'd promised my mother that she'd give the evidence back if she paid her blackmail. But Marya demanded more. So I went to see her."

"And Marya wouldn't give you back the evidence, either," I said.

"She said she needed more money. One more payment. So I tried to scare her. Threaten her. But she screamed and said she'd turn me in. I didn't know what to do. She just kept screaming. Sooner or later, someone would hear. So I grabbed the hair dryer." His grip tightened around me.

"Whoa, whoa, whoa," Dad said, inching forward. "Don't you think this has *snowballed* far enough?" But I swore he looked at me when he said it.

When Dad advanced, Ian pulled me back with him. Back

271

to where gigantic icicles now hung from the awning over the back door. With all the craziness, none of us had found time to clear them away.

"Put down the gun," Dad said. "Put the gun down. Let my daughter go. Then we'll sit down and talk this over." His voice was soothing, but he kept inching closer.

Ian pulled me back one more time. "I have to think—"

I used his momentary distraction to wriggle out of his grasp and then I lunged toward the icicles. A large one broke off into my hands, and I swung it like a baseball bat. It connected with Ian's arm, breaking into several large chunks and sending off a spray of glassy shards in all directions. The gun went flying into the snow bank.

Ian reached for me again, and I found myself caught between him and the dumpster. I don't know exactly where my next move came from—maybe the inspiration came from the Batgirl jammies I was still wearing, but as he continued to advance, I braced myself against the dumpster and kicked, as hard and high as I could.

In all the kerfuffle, I didn't see where my kick had landed, but it did—I only know because I felt the impact all the way up my leg and I hoped I hadn't broken any numb toes. But when Ian lay in the alley, curled up into the fetal position, I had my suspicions.

Dad was on him in an instant, pinning Ian face-down in the ice and securing his arms behind him. "Liz," he said, "get my cuffs? They're upstairs."

# # #

Hours later, I was still in my Batman pajamas, to the amusement of all the men at the police station. I had a bandage on my cheek where an ice shard had given me a nasty slice I didn't even feel until the excitement was over. I was also limping a little. Someone had put me in a chair and found, of all things, an icepack for my swelling foot.

Howard Reynolds had been in charge of taking my statement. He'd been amused at my attire from the moment I sat down and had to turn away and clear his throat when I reached the part about kicking Ian.

"It was Dad who reminded me about the icicles," I said, "when he said Ian's plan had *snowballed*. Parker and I used to go out and have 'snowball' fights, but Dad caught us more than once chucking ice balls at each other and sword-fighting with icicles. We got into so much trouble."

"So this was your father's cue?"

"At least I think so," I said, but Reynolds was looking past me to the door, where Jenkins and another uniformed officer were escorting Valerie and her husband in.

Valerie made eye contact, tried to smile, then the look grew cold. She turned as they were led to the conference/interrogation room, officially showing me the cold shoulder.

"What's going to happen to them?" I asked Reynolds.

He took a long breath. "It depends on how much they knew, and how deeply they were involved."

I considered what this meant. From what Ian had said about his father being clueless, I suspected Mr. Browning knew nothing of his wife's activities. But that didn't mean their holdings wouldn't be seized when the bribery allegations started flying. Valerie, on the other hand, was up to her eyeballs in white-collar crime, even if she wasn't an accessory to murder. But if she knew that Ian went to confront Marya on her behalf . . .

I sighed.

"Yeah," Reynolds said. "It's going to be that kind of a day."

I was still answering Reynolds's questions when Mark Baker arrived. He squeezed my shoulder as he passed but followed my father into his office. When the door opened, I could see the mayor already inside, but the door closed behind them before I could hear anything.

When Reynolds finished with me, I lingered at the coffee for a bit, snagged the last of the doughnuts—red velvet—and nonchalantly stared at the closed door to my dad's office. Reynolds had said I was free to go home, but two things kept me at the station. One, I was hoping to get an idea of what was going on behind those closed doors, and if Dad didn't tell me, Mark might. Since it looked like he'd been called in, I suspected that the contents of the Aqua Net safe did indeed point to the white-collar investigation Mark was working on.

Of course, the second reason I didn't leave is because it would mean parading down Main Street in my Batgirl jammies in broad daylight.

Lionel Kelley finished his interview and joined me at the coffee. He picked up the empty doughnut box and sighed.

"Sorry," I said, still chewing on the last bite. I washed it down with the strong, hot coffee.

"I was right, though," he said, pouring himself a cup. "About the eyes, wasn't I?"

"Have to give you credit there."

"You must have suspected him, though, to send me his picture."

"Actually, I'd suspected his mother until I realized she didn't have the physical dexterity to . . ."

"Off Marya Young." Lionel glanced at his watch. "I suppose

I need to brief my client. Let him know the investigation is officially over. Do you think it will hit the papers before tomorrow?

"I think it probably will make the evening news," I said.

"Maybe I can still charge him for half a day."

"No other clients on the horizon?" I asked.

"Not in this sleepy town."

"Give it time," I said. "One thing I learned over the past few years, East Aurora may look like a sleepy little town, but there's more going on under the surface. Something will bubble up."

"You think?" His eyes lit up. "Thanks, Liz. Something to look forward to!"

New voices entering the room drew my attention. Ken Young and his sisters walked in. He made a beeline to where I was standing. "Is it true? They caught her killer?"

"We," Lionel said, putting his arm around my shoulder and gesturing to himself and me. "*We* caught the killer."

"And my father," I said.

"Who was it?" Ken said, his eyes wide.

"Ian Browning," I said.

"That smarmy new boyfriend of yours?" Ken said. "Where's he at?" His gaze swept the room, and he looked like a bull ready to charge.

"Whoa there," Lionel said, putting up a hand.

Ken swatted his hand away and advanced toward the chief's office.

Reynolds stood up and planted himself in Ken's path. "Is this appropriate?"

That stopped Ken in his tracks, but not those two bulldogs, Nancy and Grace.

"Can he talk to you like that?" Grace asked.

"Back home, nobody would talk to the chief of police like that in his own department," Nancy said.

"Settle down," Ken told his sisters, but he cast a wild look toward his former office, then tried to duck around Reynolds.

There was never really a scuffle, but while trying to skirt his former detective, Ken upset a garbage can, which clattered to the floor, spewing its contents. Several officers at their desks jumped at the commotion and a chair tipped over.

The chief's door swung open, and my dad stepped out and whistled to quiet things down.

"I want in," Ken said. "From what I hear, I've been cleared."

The mayor stepped out of the office behind my father. "Ken, there's still a lot to wrap up. When everything has settled down, we'll talk about the possibility of reinstatement."

"The possibility?" Ken said. "You're firing me?"

"They can't do that, can they?" Nancy said. "Maybe we could get that lawyer working on it."

Ken's face grew rigid. "I'm afraid that wouldn't do much good. I serve at the pleasure of the mayor." I could see he struggled to keep the emotion from his voice. "It's him, isn't it?" He pointed to my father. "Now that you have Hank McCall back, you don't want me."

The mayor shook his head. "That's not it."

"Son," Dad started.

But Ken wasn't ready to hear anything from him. Instead he addressed the mayor. "If you're not pleased with what I did, tell me. Here and now. What did I do wrong?"

Mayor Briggs took his time to answer, but looked Ken straight in the face. "Fine. A woman in our community was stealing drugs, harboring an undocumented alien, and blackmailing at least one person. That woman lived in your house, right under your nose. If you knew about this—"

"I didn't," Ken said.

The mayor cleared his throat. "*If* you knew about it, people won't trust your character. If you didn't know about it, people won't trust your capability to do this job. This is going to be public knowledge very soon. How much confidence do you think you'll have in this community when folks learn the truth?"

Ken's face blanched. "Fine," he finally said. "You'll have my resignation on your desk today."

"But can he do that?" Nancy asked.

"He just did," Ken said. He strode up to my father, shook his hand, and said, "Good luck." Then he turned and walked out, his sisters following behind.

I watched him leave, then tapped Dad's sleeve. "What did he mean, good luck?"

Dad tilted his head toward the office, and I followed him inside. It was a bit crowded. The mayor was still there. Mark Baker sat at my father's desk wearing plastic gloves and looking over curled paperwork. The Aqua Net safe was also on the desk, now in a plastic evidence bag.

"What did he mean?" I asked again.

"Liz, Mayor Briggs just asked if I'd stay on permanently as chief of police."

"Dad—" My voice cracked, and my father grew blurry as tears started welling.

"And I was just about to tell him no." Dad turned to the mayor. "If you'd like, I'd be happy to make a recommendation. You got a good man in Howard Reynolds. He has the experience, the instinct, and the respect of the rest of the men in the department. Give him a few days so he doesn't feel like he's stealing his former boss's job, and I think he'll take it."

The mayor clapped my father on the shoulder. "He was my second choice. Thanks." He winked at me on the way out. "Nice jammies."

Mark looked up from the desk and gave me a broad smile.

I collapsed into a guest chair and self-consciously crossed my arms in front of my chest. "I was right about the safe, huh? Anything good inside?"

Mark looked at my father. Dad looked at Mark. Finally, Dad said, "Up to you. She probably deserves it, considering."

"I agree," Mark said. "Without going into specifics, Marya intercepted bids for a municipal contract."

"From Browning Construction?" I asked.

Mark shook his head. "From their competitors. These bids were supposed to be sealed, but someone on the committee leaked the bids to Mrs. Browning. The Brownings could then submit a more competitive bid. It's how they won so many contracts. It also gives us a reason to subpoena all of their financial records."

"Ian said she'd been the woman behind the man for thirty years," I said. "That's potentially a long history of corruption."

"Just keep it on the QT," Dad said. "This is going to topple more than one prominent official."

"In East Aurora?" I asked.

Mark shook his head. "In a number of communities in the area, but apparently he didn't like to . . ." Mark stopped there, but I knew the colorful expression he'd been going for.

"Pee on his own dumpster?" I offered instead.

Dad laughed. "You got it."

"There's also good news for Anechka in there. Apparently Marya did manage to acquire all her paperwork. She has a valid green card that's up to date, so she's not in the country illegally after all."

"That is good news," I said, stifling a yawn.

"Maybe you should get home and get some sleep," Dad said. "Nothing keeping you here. Is someone minding the store?"

"Cathy," I said. "Although she's going to want details when I get back. Only . . ." I pointed to my clothing. "I could use a ride, preferably to the back alley."

Dad winced. "They cordoned that off while they sweep it for evidence. It'll have to be the front door."

"I guess I can make a run for it."

Mark stood up. "I'd be happy to drive you home."

Dad looked at Mark but raised no objections.

I was failing to stifle more yawns in the car and also failed to keep up with the conversation.

Mark laughed. "You have no idea what I just said, do you?"

"Sorry."

"Look, maybe we should cancel tonight."

"No!" I said. "I just need a few hours sleep, then I'll run to the grocery store."

"Tell you what. How about we alter the plans, then? You come over to my place, and I'll cook for you."

"You cook?"

"No gourmet, but I haven't killed anyone yet," he said, echoing my words. "Besides, it'll be easier to tell you . . . that thing that I need to tell you."

I must have looked worried.

"It's not *that* bad. I think you'll be okay with it."

"What time?" I said through another yawn.

"I'll text you that and the address. Okay?"

I nodded and wiped my eyes.

He leaned over and kissed me on the cheek. "Sweet dreams."

I put my hand on the car handle, waited a minute for foot traffic in front of the shop to clear, then made a run for it.

# # #

Cathy was busy with customers in the shop. And of course they did a double-take when someone wearing Batgirl jammies entered. I went to the backroom and waited for them to leave, which took about ten minutes. I stared at the coffeepot, but my stomach was already roiling.

I started to tell her the story. I'd gotten to the part where Ian had pulled me out of the shop, then sentences stopped forming.

"You need sleep," she said. And then the shop bell rang. "And I need to get that."

"Tell you what." I looked at the clock. "Give me five hours, then come up and wake me. I have to get ready for dinner with Mark by then, and I'll tell you the rest."

Of course, the cats didn't care how tired I was. They let me know, in no uncertain terms, that they were on the brink of starvation. I poured out two full cans of something. Not even sure what kind, but I figured it would hold them for a while.

When I found my room, I quickly slipped into a fresh pair of pajamas and directly under the covers. In moments, the worries, cares, and stress of the past couple of weeks melted into a deep, dreamless sleep.

When I awoke, Cathy was pushing garments around in my closet.

I stretched out some of the stiffness and propped myself up. "What are you doing?"

"I am your personal wardrobe consultant, and you have a date tonight, right?"

"And I guess I have an upscale new wardrobe in the closet."

"Which will do us no good tonight," she said. "I rather think Mark likes you just the way you are." With that she turned back to the closet. "Something cheery and Christmassy, maybe." She pulled out my warmest red sweater.

I picked up my phone and checked the time—just a little before five. And four messages. There was one from Mark that said, "Six?" Followed by the address. I did the math, decided I should have plenty of time, and returned his text. I got a few emojis back.

I laughed. "I swear, outside that man might be some high-powered FBI accountant, but on the inside, he's a big kid."

Cathy sat down on the foot of the bed. "I think that's just your type."

"Do you need to get back downstairs?" I asked.

She shook her head. "Parker left work early, and he's covering the shop while I'm up here. Dad's actually home, too, but just. He's sleeping already."

Cathy helped me get ready, doing her best to hide the gash in my cheek under a good foundation, while I recounted the rest of the story. I even let her fix my hair with her Bibbidi Bobbidi-Goo.

"I guess we'll have to take Lori up on her fundraising ideas," Cathy said.

"It'll happen, though," I said. "I have all the faith in the world that you'll make it work."

She closed her eyes. "I'm sorry I kept pushing you back in the Browning direction. You never wanted to be involved with him."

"He was charming at times," I said. "I'd thought he wanted a nice girl his parents would approve of. Now I'm beginning to wonder if it was a way to buy more respect. Or even to keep tabs on the police investigation. It was pretty clear at the end there that he had no real feelings for me." I shivered, thinking of his cold grasp.

She gave me a tight, rocking hug. "I'm glad you and Dad are both okay."

Chapter 25

If there was such a thing as liquid courage, and if I wasn't a teetotaler, I'd be chugging the stuff as I sat in Mark's long driveway looking up at his house. At six, the sun had set already, of course, and there were no streetlamps here, just outside the village. Still the cedar shake shingles and white-shuttered house glowed in the icicle lights dripping from the eaves. A couple of illuminated reindeer stood sentry in the front yard. Huge wreaths hung on the dormer windows. I guess I'd known that Mark owned his own house, but I pictured it more of a bachelor pad of neglect. Nor did I know he had this much holiday spirit, although I found it a pleasant surprise.

When the front door opened and he poked his head outside, I could no longer linger in the car. What was I so nervous about? The date? Or whatever bombshell was about to accompany it?

"You look nice," he said, kissing me on the cheek. "Maybe a little more put together than this morning."

"It isn't every day a girl catches a killer in her pajamas."

He put his hand up to his face, fingering an imaginary

cigar, and in his best Groucho Marx impersonation said, "And how that killer got in my pajamas, I'll never know."

That broke the ice, and I found myself comfortable and relaxing. Just before a little blonde girl, maybe about four, came tearing down the hallway.

"Uncle Mark! The chicken dinged. You told me to let you know when it stopped spinning."

"That I did." He picked her up. "Hannah, I'd like you to meet someone very important. This is Miss Liz."

I held out my hand and Hannah pumped it, then we did high fives. She giggled when I reached in and tickled her belly.

Mark set her down and she tore off back into the other room.

He stowed my coat in his hall closet. "My niece will be joining us, it seems."

"Fine by me," I said. "Do you need a hand with anything?"

"Nope. Dinner is about ready, although I promised Hannah we could watch *Rudolph* and *Frosty* tonight, so I hope you don't mind eating in front of the television."

"That," I said, "is my MO."

We assembled plates from the buffet at the kitchen island, then carried them and beverages into a cozy family room, warmed from the fireplace and scented with pine from the scraggly Christmas tree decorated with glittery balls and construction paper ornaments. I slid to the floor with my plate on the coffee table, and Mark sat next to me.

Hannah, as I expect most four-year-olds are today, was a pro with the remote, and soon the reindeer games began.

"Hope you don't mind," Mark whispered softly. "This might not be the evening you had in mind."

"If you must know, I adore Rudolph. And Frosty. But be forewarned, I liked to sing along with all the songs. I've been on my best behavior so far, but I might just forget myself."

Hannah looked up. "We always sing along with the songs."

"I can sing louder," I said.

"I can sing really loud, too," Hannah said. And when the next song came on, we all sang as loudly as we could, until we were laughing too hard to keep up with the words.

Mark cleared his throat. "Maybe I should put on some coffee. Or cocoa?" He wagged finger at me. "But it would have to be the instant kind with the desiccated marshmallows. It's all I got."

"Cocoa!" Hannah said.

"Sounds good to me."

Somewhere during Frosty, Mark's arm snaked around my shoulder and I leaned into his warmth. He shifted away just before the closing credits.

"Can we play a game?" Hannah said. "I have Candy Land."

"I love Candy Land," I said.

But Mark looked at his watch. "Sorry, kiddo. It's time for bed."

"We'll play some other time," I said.

And off she went without much fuss. "Excuse me a moment," Mark said, and I could hear him step her through her evening routine.

Maybe ten minutes later he rejoined me in the family room.

"So Uncle Mark, huh?" I asked. "Your brother or sister's kid?"

Mark stared into his cocoa. "My sister's."

"She's adorable. How long is she staying with you?"

He put his cup on the coffee table. "With any luck, until she's done with college. That's what I needed to talk about, before things went any further with us. I'm not babysitting. I'm Hannah's legal guardian."

I took his hand and he told me about his sister, who'd already been a single parent when she'd received her cancer diagnosis and grim prognosis.

"That must be difficult," I said.

"I have good support. My mother comes and spends a lot of time here. I have a good daycare center I use during the day, and a woman down the street babysits if I need to go out at night." He tipped his head. "I ran her background, of course."

I drained the last of my cocoa and leaned against the sofa.

"Here's where you say that you're cool with it and it doesn't make a difference."

"But it does make a difference," I said, then smiled. "I think it's wonderful."

The next two hours were spent talking about everything and about nothing, those meaningless but all-important conversations couples have as they're learning more about each other. There may have been a few cocoa-flavored kisses interwoven with the conversation.

"Another confession," Mark said, "I have a terrible sweet tooth."

"So do I," I admitted.

"I should have made dessert. Let me see if I have any cookies left." He went and rummaged in the kitchen but came back empty handed. "I also have a little cookie monster in the house."

"That's okay. Hey, you know what?" I opened my purse

and pulled out the handful of fortune cookies I'd stuck in there after Joan's book signing. "I came prepared."

I pushed one of them toward him. "Let's see what your fortune is going to be."

He removed the cookie from the clear wrapper then cracked it open and read the paper inside. Even in the dim light, I could see his ears turn red.

"What is it?"

"Liz." He paused and scratched the back of his head. "I like you very much, but I just don't think we're quite *there* yet. Maybe someday, but—"

I ripped the small fortune from his hand. Now it was my turn to flush, and I couldn't blame the heat of the fire, which had been reduced to glowing embers.

"I'm so sorry," I said. "I got these from an author. I guess she had them made up and used quotes from her book as the fortunes." I buried my face in my hands. "I didn't realize. I'm so embarrassed."

"So this is from a book?" he said.

I nodded, still unable to meet his eyes. "*Won Ton Desire*. Page ninety-seven."

# # #

"Have you seen my suspenders?" Dad exited his room holding up his Santa pants. "They won't stay up."

"It's all that weight you lost working nonstop," I said. "You're the only person I know who could lose weight on the doughnut, coffee, and fast food diet."

He tugged at the waistband. "They are a bit looser than they were last year."

"Try the hall closet," I said. "I think I might have seen them in there."

"Thanks."

When he shuffled off, I shook my head at Cathy. "Why is it so much easier for men to lose weight?"

"I wish I knew. I'm still trying to work off that pregnancy weight."

I tweaked her cheek. "But you make an adorable elf."

"I don't understand why Dad made me dress up but you don't have to," she said.

I shrugged. "Seniority? Or maybe it's because you will be retrieving presents for Santa." I gestured to the fruits of her labor. "Those dolls are gorgeous—and that means a lot coming from me. And I'm sure they'll get everyone excited about the program for next year."

Cathy crossed her fingers. "I hope so. You don't think giving the first of the dolls to the children of police officers is a bit self-serving, considering that one of Lori's fundraising ideas is—"

"Shh!" I put my finger to my lips as Dad came back with his suspenders.

"What?" Dad said.

"We were just talking about giving the dolls to the children," I said. "I think it's a great idea. Not many people realize how stressful growing up in a cop's home can be."

Dad kissed me on the cheek. "The kids do make a sacrifice. Liz, I'm sorry if . . . I'm sorry that I wasn't always . . ."

I stopped him with a hug and Cathy joined in.

When we arrived downstairs, Amanda was already arranging napkins on the food tables. Kohl sat in a nearby chair, drawing in his notebook.

I looked at the spread. "Everything looks lovely."

"We're still short cookies," she said.

"They should be on their way," I said. "We had plenty of volunteers."

"Great!" Then she cast a worried look in Kohl's direction. "Liz, Kohl really wanted to come to the party tonight, but he can sometimes get a little over stimulated with all the noise."

"Do you need to leave? I'm sure we can cover."

"No, at least not yet. In fact, Jack is coming and he could help keep an eye on him, but if we need to get him away from the party for a bit . . ."

"He's great with Kohl," I said. "It's fun to watch them together."

"They adore each other," Amanda said. "It's going to make the next year a lot easier." She reached up to a chain around her neck and pulled out what I first thought was a necklace, but a moment later realized was an engagement ring on a chain. She put a finger quickly to her lips. "We want to let the families know over the holiday, so we're keeping it a secret. But you're family, at least as far as I'm concerned."

I reached in to hug her. "Congratulations," I whispered. "And the apartment's unlocked if you need a quiet place for Kohl," I said. "Maybe a bit of a mess because we were all getting ready up there, and I think Cathy's wearing enough glitter to keep Martha Stewart busy for a month." I pointed to the trail on the floor.

Amanda winced. "We're going to be finding that years from now."

As she turned away to her work, I found a tear growing in the corner of my eye. Not that I was weeping over the prospect of persistent glitter, but there was something hopeful and comforting about thinking about being in the same place, doing the same thing, with these same people years from now.

I was home. And there was truly no place like it.

When I looked up, Irene and Lenora were tapping on the front door and I went to unlock it. I had to push past Dad's inflatable toy soldier. He was still sporting a patch on his leg from a violent encounter a couple of years earlier. At first, we'd considered throwing him away, that maybe he was too much of a reminder of a tragedy that occurred in our shop, but I'm glad we hadn't. Now, every year at Christmas, he stands sentry, his smile just as bright and undimmed. He's become a testimony to resilience.

"I know we're a little early," Irene said. "But we thought you'd want the cookies ahead of time."

I took the package from her arms. "Come on in and warm up," I said. "The coffee's hot and we have cocoa. Or punch if you'd rather."

"Children's punch or big-people's punch?" Lenora asked.

"It's yummy," I said. "But suitable for children—and let's keep it that way, okay?"

As they made their way to the beverage table, I handed over the cookies to Amanda, who was ready to arrange them on a waiting platter.

Lori Briggs came rushing in with Glenda trailing behind her.

"You're both here early," I said.

"I need to get set up," Lori said, pulling out a camera. "I want to get lots of pictures of happy little girls. I think it would be a great way to drum up support for the program, especially if we launch into *phase two* of the fundraising."

"Phase two?" Glenda asked.

I looked around to make sure my father wasn't in earshot. I nodded to give Lori the go-ahead.

She leaned in close to Glenda. "We want to do a police calendar."

"The police department already does a calendar," Glenda said. "A little magnet thing. I have one on my fridge."

"No," Lori said. "This would be a *different kind* of calendar."

Glenda grabbed her arm. "With naughty pictures?"

"Not naughty exactly," Lori said, taking her arm. "But definitely casting the boys and girls in blue in the best possible light." She winked. "Drool-worthy. And the more pleased they are with tonight, the greater chance we get the green light for the project."

"And the more likely we are to get volunteers," I said, "when we show them pictures of their own kids having fun."

"Too bad we couldn't get Ken Young to pose," Lori said. "Say what you want about him, he was quite a looker. I, uh, saw that his house is up for sale."

"Maybe it's for the best. There's not much left here for him," I said, then looked again in Dad's direction. With any luck, he'd need help. I wasn't sure I wanted to get in a long conversation about Ken Young with anybody. Not quite yet.

Glenda followed my gaze to where my father was setting up the Santa throne. "And you don't want Hank to know about the calendar because, what? Think he'll disapprove?"

"No," I said, "but it's . . ." I looked to Lori to finish.

She leaned closer to Glenda. "We kind of wanted him to be in it. He'd be very popular among some of our senior ladies. Liz thought he'd be more likely to participate if we didn't spring it on him until he knew other people were already involved."

"Hank McCall, centerfold," Glenda said. "I'd buy that."

I excused myself—another awkward subject for me—and turned on some cheerful holiday music.

Jack arrived, and not empty-handed, either. He carried in several boxes of munchies from the restaurant. Amanda had to scramble to find room for them on the overloaded table.

Parker carried Drew in, all bundled up in his snowsuit. He even cracked a drooly smile when he saw his mother. How he could recognize her with the elf ears and the face glitter, I didn't know. Smart boy.

A few of the officers and their families wandered in next. Those who had never been in the store meandered the aisles before letting their sons and daughters find a space on the rug by the tree.

Reynolds walked in with the mayor, and Dad rushed up to greet them. He pulled down his Santa beard. "Congratulations," he said to Howard, shaking his hand. "I heard it became official."

"Thanks," Reynolds said. "Your confidence means a lot to me."

Behind them was Mark Baker, hand-in-hand with Hannah who was all decked out in a little red coat with a white fur collar.

"Uh-oh, better behave," Reynolds said. "The Feds are here."

"Well, one Fed accountant, and I'm off duty," Mark said, shaking Reynolds's hand. Then he made a beeline for me and kissed me on the cheek. "Thanks for including us. Hannah's been talking about nothing else all day."

That's all he got to say before she grabbed him by the arm and tried to drag him toward the dolls displayed on the front table, along with a small collection of games and other toys, for children who might not be into dolls. Or who, like me, found them a little bit creepy, even when they *didn't* seemingly move on their own.

"I'll catch up with you later," I called after him.

"You can count on it," he said.

With a flicker of the lights and a brief ching-a-ling, Santa stood up to give a brief speech.

"Thank you all for coming, and a special thanks to my main elves here. Cathy had half of a great idea when she decided she wanted to rehab old dolls and get them in the hands of children. And Liz—who's out of her elf costume, but she is a Claus, a subordinate Claus."

A couple of groans ensued.

"Although I should call her 'Iz,' today. You know why?"

"Why?" one of the kids asked.

"Because no L. Noel?"

The kids, who hadn't heard it before, laughed. The adults just shook their heads.

"Anyway," Dad continued, "she thought that the children of our bravest and finest deserve a little something special, so we have a gift for each child here today. And a picture with Santa, of course."

Lori waved her camera.

"I see Mrs. Briggs brought her *North Polaroid.*"

After a few more groans, the children started lining up. Except for one little girl, who started crying immediately after being placed on Santa's lap. Dad took it well, teasing that she must be *Claus-trophobic.*

When Hannah's turn came, she marched right up and took her spot, turning to the camera with a cheesy smile, dimples and all.

Mark stole up next to me. "Your dad is great at this."

I shushed him, trying to hear what Hannah was saying.

"I know who you are," she said.

Dad leaned closer to her, the twinkle in his eye never brighter than as he cradled the little girl on his lap. "I'm Santa. Santa Claus."

Hannah nodded. "And you know who else you are?"

"No, tell me."

"Uncle Mark said that if he plays his cards right, you could be my new grandpa!" she said in a loud whisper.

Mark studied the floor, and his ears turned that signature red.

I pulled him aside. "Uncle Mark said that, did he?"

"Uncle Mark *might* have said that," he said, backing away from me.

"Well, I'm not quite sure we're ready for that discussion, but . . ." I waited until he realized he had no more ground, his back up against the display case of our oldest tin toys. And then I kissed him.

Acknowledgments

Often the acknowledgments are a laundry list of names, and there are certainly many people I'd like to thank. But since the list hasn't really changed from the last few books, I'd like to say "ditto."

Instead, a heartfelt thank you to all those people who encouraged me. Thanks to those who told me I could write when I didn't believe it myself, to those who nudged me to finish when I was more ready to give up, and to those who took on tasks that let me follow my dream, when maybe I should have been doing something else . . . like cooking dinner. You've made all this possible.

But a special thanks to readers who've told me they enjoyed spending time with my characters. To see a book that I've written, bound and with a pretty cover, is a joy. But to know that it's been opened and read and enjoyed is truly priceless. Thank you!

10/18